Praise for

A QUIET LIFE

"Ethan Joella's *A Quiet Life* explores the depths of grief through a widower, the daughter of a murder victim, and the mother of a kidnapping victim. . . . As their lives begin to converge, Chuck, Ella, and Kirsten walk unique roads to find their way to healing."

—*PopSugar*

"Once again, Joella's characters are as real as they come. With an observant eye and poetic sensitivity, Joella captures poignant moments and intense feelings, leaving the reader with a sense of recognition and comfort. . . . One of the most meaningful things a person can say is simply 'I'm here,' and this is the level of profound connection that Joella evokes without ever straying into cliché."

—*BookPage*

"Community and grief are at the center of this tender novel in which three residents of a tightly knit Pennsylvania suburb are each grappling with losing loved ones when their lives begin to converge in unexpected ways."

—*The New York Times Book Review*

"Joella develops his characters with enormous empathy. . . . The pleasure of discovering connections is one of the most basic joys of reading and is key to Joella's storytelling. . . . The soothing tone and warm worldview of this grown-up bedtime story will be good for what ails you."

—*Kirkus Reviews*

"Heartwarming, character-driven charm. Empathetic without becoming saccharine, *A Quiet Life* highlights the power of closure and the importance of a connected, compassionate community."

—*Booklist*

"*A Quiet Life* is filled with people I'd like to meet. Ethan Joella's latest novel reminds us that life is made of journeys, not only destinations. Read this one slowly; you'll want to savor the details."

—Charmaine Wilkerson,
author of *Black Cake*

"*A Quiet Life* shines with the courage and heart of its characters. Through elegant prose, this powerful book reminds us that in grief and loss we stand united in the love, resilience, and connection that define our humanity. Readers will emerge from these intersecting stories transformed, hopeful, and inspired."

—Qian Julie Wang,
author of *Beautiful Country*

"I adored *A Quiet Life*. Soft as silk, powerful as a punch, Ethan Joella doesn't shirk from the trauma of grief but delivers real hope in our capacity to survive. A beautifully written page-turner like this one is hard to find."

—Nikki May, author of *Wahala*

"*A Quiet Life* is about the transformative power of connection if we are willing to risk opening our hearts. Joella's characters help each other shoulder the burden of grief and unearth the shards of beauty to be found in the wreckage of loss. There is magic at the intersection of these stories, a rare and addicting alchemy of ordinary moments and choices that add up to whole, brave, flawed, joyful lives. This novel insists on our essential strength, resilience, and empathy in an age of isolation."

—Katie Runde,
author of *The Shore*

ALSO BY ETHAN JOELLA

A Little Hope

A
QUIET
LIFE

— *A Novel* —

ETHAN JOELLA

SCRIBNER

New York   London   Toronto   Sydney   New Delhi

Scribner
An Imprint of Simon & Schuster, Inc.
1230 Avenue of the Americas
New York, NY 10020

This book is a work of fiction. Any references to historical events, real people, or real places are used fictitiously. Other names, characters, places, and events are products of the author's imagination, and any resemblance to actual events or places or persons, living or dead, is entirely coincidental.

First Scribner trade paperback edition November 2023

SCRIBNER and design are registered trademarks of The Gale Group, Inc., used under license by Simon & Schuster, Inc., the publisher of this work.

For information about special discounts for bulk purchases, please contact Simon & Schuster Special Sales at 1-866-506-1949 or business@simonandschuster.com.

The Simon & Schuster Speakers Bureau can bring authors to your live event. For more information or to book an event, contact the Simon & Schuster Speakers Bureau at 1-866-248-3049 or visit our website at www.simonspeakers.com.

Interior design by Jennifer Chung

Manufactured in the United States of America

1   3   5   7   9   10   8   6   4   2

Library of Congress Cataloging-in-Publication Data has been applied for.

ISBN 978-1-9821-9097-2
ISBN 978-1-9821-9098-9 (pbk)
ISBN 978-1-9821-9099-6 (ebook)

For my mom, Gerry,
who read to me and sketched pictures
I will never forget

———

I am living. I remember you.

—Marie Howe, *What the Living Do*

———

Remember, no man is a failure who has friends.

—*It's a Wonderful Life*

CHAPTER ONE

When Chuck Ayers thinks about Cat, he thinks about the faded yellow-and-white-striped towel that lately he has been wearing around his neck like a wrestler on his way to a match.

That damn towel.

She used it for every bath, the towel hanging over the linen closet door to dry afterward, the smell of her pink soap as he walked by. And when they drove those hundreds of miles to Hilton Head every winter, she took the towel along, and it became her beach towel. Even as she got older, there was something alluring about the way she draped that towel around her body, or shook it out over one of the lounge chairs at the pool in South Carolina.

What can he do with this towel now, this towel he should have buried with her, this towel that he sleeps with some nights, this towel that hangs there, that stays wherever he leaves it?

He should fold it and put it into a box on a high shelf in the closet with the word *towel* written on it so he never forgets. So he never opens it again. So he never remembers her holding the towel over her arm, so naive, unaware that the towel would outlast her, that she'd never have a chance to donate it, to tear it into cleaning rags, to use it to protect something in the attic: an antique lamp, an old mirror.

He is glad for a second it didn't come to that. That she got to use the towel fully and without stop.

And that is the first thing in forever he has been glad for.

—

December 29, late in the afternoon, and the sun is going down. The quiet street is shadowed and darker outside the windows. Instinctively, Chuck lights the small ceramic Christmas tree and switches on the front porch light. He looks out the window and notices all the other houses. He imagines good smells of dinners, random sounds of family: someone calling up the steps, the surge of a dishwasher running, dice from a board game, wineglasses clinking.

He looks around his living room. Cat's painting of a river and trees hangs over the blue sofa. The dim floor lamp stands next to the chair in the corner, her basket beside it with word searches and Sudoku, and he remembers how alive the holidays used to feel. Even well into their sixties, Cat insisted on cutting down a tree every year. He pretended to object, but he didn't really mind because he liked walking through a field with her, didn't care what tree they finally decided on as long as he was physically able to saw it, drag it, as long as neither of them twisted their ankles in all those groundhog holes that seemed to be everywhere at the tree farm.

He liked watching Cat's eyes when the children were younger, holding Ben's and Leela's hands, looking so proper in her wool coat and leather gloves. "Ooh, I think we found our candidate," she'd say, and the kids would clap because she made everything fun.

Cat was the glue; she was the ringleader of every occasion. When they'd get home, she would be the one with Christmas music on the record player, a plate of cookies for the kids. She cherished each ornament as she removed it from the box, finding just the right tree branch for its weight.

He crosses his arms. Looks at the spot in the corner where the tree used to stand. He used to have so many feelings about the year ending, the winter ahead, the hope of the new year.

Now he just feels guilt, and his guilt spreads everywhere. He feels guilty that the woman who delivers his newspaper in her noisy car waved to him through the window this morning, and he didn't wave back in time. He feels guilty because he saw lumber at Ace Hardware the other day, and remembered Leela and Ben used to beg him to build a treehouse, and he meant to, he meant to, but they grew up before he ever did. He feels guilty for all the guys who didn't make it back from Vietnam. Why did Chuck survive? And so much guilt about Cat. As if he's in a supermarket of guilt, and his cart's overflowing.

—

What should he do about the rental in Hilton Head?

He stands in the kitchen the next morning. On the table he sees the listing agreement, prepaid, and check-in information on a small blue card. They included the parking pass for the condo association, too, but all that anticipation he used to feel, that tease of warm weather and long days and the pool and the ocean, is gone.

Christmas came and went, and it was such a quiet, uneventful day. Now, instead of that excitement of going south in mid-January, instead of his and Cat's fifteen-year tradition of driving the twelve or so hours with the car packed with luggage and groceries and cleaning supplies and that faded beach blanket, he doesn't know what to do.

He thought the holidays would be the hardest. He didn't know the ultimate challenge, *the boss battle*, his granddaughter, Gabby, would call it, is Hilton Head, the island where he and Cat felt most alive. How can he need to be there so much right now and never want to see the place again, both at the same time? Can he go there without her? Does he want to be there without her? Can he stay here for the endless Pennsylvania winter that's just beginning?

He wants to rip up the agreement. He wants Hilton Head to be gone, too, because Cat's gone and he assumed they had at least ten more years to keep doing this. They had argued over what the other one would do when one of them died, but they never discussed Hilton Head.

I want to go first.

No, I want it to be me.

I just don't want to live without you, one of them always said.

—

Now Sal's at the door. Chuck can tell from the fast, single-knuckled rap. Ever since Cat died, Sal comes over more often, brings his dog with him. He has never asked, just lets Cocoa's leash drop when Chuck opens the door, and the dog walks right past him and settles in the living room.

Chuck says nothing, but the whole act frustrates him. Why didn't Sal ever bring Cocoa before? Why does he make it seem as if Cat prevented the dog from visiting? As if Cat wouldn't have stooped down to rub the dog's belly, and used a squeaky voice when she talked to Cocoa. Chuck was lucky if he saw Sal once a month in the past. Either at the barber's, or Sal would drop by for car wax or to borrow the drill. Now he's here several times a week.

"How goes it?" Sal asks, his once-dark hair messy and grayed, Cocoa looking up at Chuck.

"Wait," Chuck says. He pops into the kitchen and returns with a small box of biscuits. He was at the market yesterday and

4

bought them, the way someone might buy lollipops for grandkids. He shakes them. "Here, girl."

"Hang on," Sal says. "I should see the ingredients."

"They're dog biscuits."

"Yeah, but the vet said she has to watch."

"They're standard goddamned dog biscuits." Chuck half glares at Sal, and Sal just shakes his head and makes the *go-ahead* motion as he pulls out a dining room chair and plops down. *What are you even doing here?* Chuck wants to ask.

Know-it-all Sal, who lives five houses down. A retired mailman, a guy whose kids ran in the same circles as Chuck's kids—in band together, on the swim team together. Cat and Sal's wife, Marguerite, were close, and maybe Marguerite urges Sal to come over and keep an eye on him.

"Want coffee?" Chuck says as Cocoa takes two biscuits and goes back to her usual spot. He sits on the chair by her and rubs her head. He always wanted a Labrador like this, but he hated the puppy stage, which led them to usually adopt older rescues.

Sal looks around. "Got decaf?"

"Yeah."

"Then sure." He looks over. "She likes her chin rubbed." Sal pulls out a handkerchief and blows his nose. "When are you heading south?"

"Good question," Chuck says, and shrugs.

Chuck looks into Cocoa's small dark eyes. He wonders if he should get another dog. He saw a commercial for a nice local shelter called Rescue Ranch, but the prospect feels like throwing a small stone in a lake.

Then his mind circles back to Hilton Head: the people walking dogs, their pace slow and welcoming, all the folks riding bikes, the pine trees, the golf carts. The pancake house where he and Cat would have breakfast once a week. The alligators sunning themselves everywhere that Cat used to sketch in her book. He pauses for a moment and thinks about how they worried about alligator attacks. They were always careful and kept their eyes open. But now he would almost welcome being dragged into the water, wouldn't he? No, he thinks. He wouldn't.

"I don't hear the coffee," Sal says after a minute.

—

Chuck turns out all the lights as he walks to his bedroom. He sighs and looks at their long dresser. The bedroom is dim, so he turns on a lamp. Leela has been planning to come home so they can start going through Cat's things, and the thought of this crushes him. It hasn't been that long, has it? Just since May.

He thinks he should go through her things first. Leela can be reckless, bagging up a whole drawer at a time without feeling, and he wants to have a moment with Cat's stuff before it's in a bin somewhere. Lately he has worried that if he goes to Hilton Head, Leela would come into the house while he's away and remove every single item of Cat's, thinking he would be better off with a fresh start. He can't imagine coming home to a place with her shoes gone, with her nightgown not hanging on the back of their bedroom door. The thought makes his heart race, and he has an image of himself patrolling the house like a soldier to protect Cat's things.

Of course Leela would only be doing it in the name of efficiency and moving forward, but he still hates the idea. Is there any rush?

He pulls open the small center drawer of their dresser, and he sees her bras and underwear folded neatly. There is a matching set, pink lace, that he remembers her wearing. He remembers her hold-ing her hair as she let him zip up her white dress before a spring concert. That pink lace just tickled him.

Cat was full of surprises, full of different layers. He shakes his head.

After Ben finished college and Leela was in the graduate pro-gram for physical therapy in Georgia, Cat used to go to Lloyd's Cafe a couple of mornings a week to work on her sketches. Lloyd's always looked like someone dropped it out of a set from a 1950s movie with its stainless steel siding and neon sign and its row of spotless windows.

Cat used to draw in college, and even though she was an art teacher for twenty-five years, her own art had gotten away from her. So Chuck liked the idea of her going somewhere alone and ex-ploring this part of herself, sitting at the Formica table with a cup of coffee and sketching whatever she saw—the leaves of a plant in the corner or the hostess behind the cash register. When she got tired of Lloyd's, especially in the warmer months, she would walk around Freeland Park and sketch a dog standing with its owner by the evergreen trees, or pigeons waiting for the woman at the bandstand who brought bags of old bread.

There was something simple and elegant and almost Parisian about Cat, her hair up in a loose bun, her satchel with charcoal pencils and sketchbooks over her shoulder. He imagined her qui-etly wandering, keeping her eyes open for the best subject.

Often, however, she found herself going back to draw some-thing at Lloyd's, and that's where she met Natasha.

As he scoops Cat's small rolled-up pantyhose out of the back of this drawer, he sees the keychain Cat had once wanted to give to Natasha, and he feels something sink inside him.

Natasha was a young woman, just eighteen years old and

working at Lloyd's as much as she could. She took a liking to Cat, grinning at her and asking if she could see what she was working on. "She liked my drawing of a milk shake," Cat said. "So I autographed it and tore it out of the book."

"Nice to have a fan," Chuck said.

He doesn't know how it started, but Cat started giving Natasha money every so often. *I slipped her a ten*, she'd say. Or a five, or one day a twenty. Cat said she hated how tired Natasha's eyes always looked.

Once, Cat gave Natasha their phone number because Natasha needed help making cupcakes for her friend's birthday, and Cat said she could walk her through the recipe. After that, Natasha would call the house every so often, and Cat would sit with her legs crossed on the big wicker chair in the sunroom and nod for over an hour while Natasha went on and on about some problem.

"Doesn't she have parents?" Chuck had asked when they spoke about Natasha.

"Her mother died when she was eight, and her father sounds like a horrible man. He basically only lets her leave the house to work."

Chuck remembers leaning against the doorway, watching Cat transplant the aloe plant into a wider pot. "She's eighteen, isn't she?"

"She is." Cat shrugged.

He had a feeling the friendship with Natasha was a small flicker that had the potential to become a forest fire. Whenever he tried to dismiss his reservations, another doubt presented itself. "Maybe you should keep your distance," he finally said. "What did your mom used to say about feeding strays?"

She looked over at him, incredulous. "Are you serious?"

He felt the words still burning his mouth. He knew he had gone too far. "I don't know."

"Well, I hope not." She pressed the dirt down in the plant, held the pot out and squinted at it. "She's not a stray. She's in pain. She barely gets by, her boyfriend just broke up with her. I'm just trying to be a good ear for the poor thing. She needs me."

"Oh, I know," he said. But he felt a pang of something he couldn't explain. When she said Natasha needed her, he felt betrayal, envy. Was this fair to their kids? To him?

That key chain. He can't erase the look of hurt on Cat's face that day a few months later when he finally put his foot down. *Chuck, can we at least talk about this?* Those moments of regret seem to stay with him, and the words they exchanged were fierce and terrible. He can't do anything to brush away the memory. Cat's hand so limp, her eyes looking down at the key chain like it was a wounded bird she found in the garden.

He lets the key chain, no key, a Monet scene on it, rest in his palm. It is heavier than he expected. There are lily pads and blue water and green grass, all defined, but in swirls. He holds it, and his shoulders sink as he plods toward the bathroom for a long shower.

CHAPTER TWO

Ella Burke leaves her apartment on Carlton Drive at three forty-five in the morning and slips on the bottom step, almost catching herself before wiping out. She wears a padded down coat and thick mittens, and she will gradually shed these as she delivers her newspapers.

Her ankle feels a little twisted, but she'll be okay. No time for any type of injury.

The morning is so still, and there is fog and a freezing drizzle. She takes slow steps as she creeps toward her car. She is in her early forties but feels so much older these past few months. The wind starts now, the ice stings her face, and her big puffy coat blows behind her like a cape.

Her knit hat sags. "Shit shit shit," she says when she gets to the car. A coating of ice glazes her old Jeep, and even when she hits the unlock button and pulls, the door remains where it is. She touches the windshield, and the coating is a quarter inch thick.

"Barnacles," she says. She remembers when her daughter, Riley, used to watch *SpongeBob* nonstop on the living room floor. She remembers how Riley relished expressions like this. How she used to say in her little voice with her R's not fully formed: "Tartar sauce, Mommy!"

Ella yanks the door as hard as she can, and finally it makes a cracking sound as it pulls open. She sits inside and turns the key in the ignition. Her husband, Kyle, used to say, "Just let it get warm, or you're doing all that scraping without any help from the car."

She shrugs and hits both defrost buttons. She makes sure it's on full heat, climbs out, and crosses her arms. *Kyle*. She only can see his angry, terrible eyes. *How could you?*

She looks up at the dark gray sky and at the building that houses her two-bedroom unit and the two other apartments. The rest of the houses on the block in Bethlehem are single-family homes, and each place is set back a good distance from the road, with a sizable yard in the front. Most have sprawling, mature rhododendron shrubs, sagging today with ice. Her building has a fenced-in yard in the back that none of the other tenants use, and the landlady faithfully mows the grass in the warmer months. There is a picnic table back there and a tulip poplar that must look like a storybook tree when it holds out all its yellow-orange flowers in spring. Since she moved here three months ago, the picnic table seemed like a perfect place to sit and relax, but she refuses to go back there until she has Riley.

She imagines showing Riley the yard in bloom.

She imagines going to the market and making a French picnic for Riley: a baguette, some cheese, strawberries, grilled vegetables, and some pastel macarons. She'd buy sparkling apple cider and they could toast.

Ella can picture the scene perfectly. When she tries to fall asleep at night, she sees it in her head. Riley. Riley a little taller. Riley's eyes, hopefully, hopefully, not losing that spark. The two of them just talking about nothing. "So what will we do with this long, long day?" she'll say to her daughter.

Little details jump out at her before she can chase them away: Riley's cluster of three freckles on her temple, her long, thick eyelashes, the smell of maraschino cherries on her breath. "Did you sneak something from the fridge?" Ella would say, smiling and scrunching her eyebrows.

"Maybe," Riley would reply, giggling.

Now the car surges and hums, the muffler so loud, and Ella's coat is wet. She reaches into the back seat and grabs the long ice scraper.

What has her daughter become in these months without her?

She needs to get moving. She has to be at the distribution center before four thirty, she has to get that pile of newspapers folded and bagged, and then it will take forever to get all her deliveries in, driving and sliding on the terrible roads with these damn bologna-skin tires. She is so tired, and this newspaper route is seven days a week with an eight-hour shift at Today's Bride afterward. This week begins the god-awful bridesmaid dress sale, which will have all the crazies lined up around the block—*saints preserve us*, her mother says.

Ella's days are long. She stays awake too late, gets up too early. At night, her legs cramp, her feet ache. She keeps her cell phone ringer on loud all the time in case there is any news. She jumps every time it rings. She answers every single call. She wants to scream when it's a robocall or the cable company with a message about upgrading her Wi-Fi.

She cannot sleep because she is not programmed to sleep like this. For the last eight years, she only slept when she knew Riley was safe and sound. Now she feels like a bird that has come back to her nest and found her egg gone. She doesn't know where to settle herself in the new apartment. She paces around, sits on the step stool in the laundry room and listens to the tumble of the dryer.

She wonders what her girl is eating, what she watches on TV. Is she safe? Is she scared? Has she forgotten her mother? It's too much to consider. She scrapes the thick ice on her window, and her arm hurts after a while, but she plows the scraper back and forth because it feels like she has found Riley and she is breaking through the ice to get to her.

I will find you. I will find you.
I will not stop until I find you.

CHAPTER THREE .

Chuck sits at the kitchen table with the striped towel across his lap as though it's a large dinner napkin, and he thinks about the rental in Hilton Head. The palm trees and blue skies and lush golf greens they could see from their screened porch. He thinks of Cat's name still on the rental agreement.

He should go, shouldn't he?

The escape would be a relief. He thinks he's going crazy here. He needs sunlight. He imagines how making the journey would feel. Getting there an accomplishment. Something he could whisper to her about. *I made it. I made it for us.*

He looks at the rental agreement again. He remembers how, each year, they'd get the letter from the real estate agency to re-up for next year with an incentive of 10 percent off or something like that. He remembers how they'd say, "yes, and yes," and smile as they checked the box.

"Count me in," Cat would say.

"See you there," he'd say.

Didn't it seem it would always be this way?

The promise of one year to the next. He and Cat were just in their sixties, and then just in their early seventies. They still seemed to have time. Death or a retirement home seemed like a whole chapter away, and they would cross that bridge when the moment came. Later.

What could happen in just months? How couldn't they be back in whatever car they'd had, the cat left with Ben and his husband (when they used to have a cat), the electric and water bills prepaid, the rest of the mail forwarded from Pennsylvania. The houseplants brought to Marguerite to tend to, the heat turned to fifty-five degrees, the water shut off.

There were always a hundred little details, and the car ended up being more packed than they'd planned, but it felt decadent to winter somewhere else. They had dreamed about it when Chuck's job as a shift supervisor at Ludwig Iron used to make his left eye twitch, when Cat spent her long days teaching middle school children, when Ben and Leela had those hours and hours of homework at night. It had seemed like a goal they would never realize, being free and limitless.

But then that time in their life finally arrived, and they'd drive as if they had escaped everything. As if this was the only version of themselves they would now tolerate.

They had places they loved to stop in every state. The fruit stands, the hot dog joints, the drive-in with the chocolate milk shakes they'd share. He thinks of the music they'd listen to: Elvis, Billy Joel, Broadway show tunes. They'd turn the volume up and sing-shout together and start laughing.

"What would the kids say?" Cat laughed, wiping a happy tear.

"They'd throw us right into a damn home," Chuck said. He remembers feeling young and unstoppable. He remembers looking over at her and thinking, *Do we really get to do this?*

Now his Shredded Wheat has gone mushy, and he looks at the rental agreement. He doesn't care if he can't get his money back. He can't go to Hilton Head without her.

—

Upstairs, the Monet key chain rests on their dresser.

He remembers the night, all those years ago, that Cat looked at him, the wind and rain outside. She had such a disappointed expression on her face as she set down the key chain. She shook her head. "You're absolutely horrible," she said at the end of their fight, and that word had echoed in the room when she walked away. *Horrible.*

They didn't speak for days afterward. Even now, he thinks of that time, and he gets a cold, hollow feeling. Guilt. Shame. Pain. Why couldn't he have fixed any of that?

He walks to the upstairs study and takes some of her sketchbooks out of the desk drawer. He smiles as he looks at a drawing of a pelican from Sanibel Island, a picture of himself that he never saw, resting his chin on his fist while he looked out the window of their breakfast nook. God, she captured her subjects in such a noble way. He thinks he looks like a better person in this sketch: thoughtful, maybe even wise. Did she know he wished he looked this way? What does he look like now? Sad probably. Failing.

There is also a sketch of their old cat Felix and one of a photograph of Ben and Leela in matching Christmas sweaters. He flips through more pages. Sometimes something was abandoned, and she put a line through it like a voided check.

He turns the page and comes across one of Natasha in the café. Her collared uniform, her socks and sneakers. A cluster of straws peeking out of her apron. She was doing a *ta-da* pose by the kitchen.

Natasha. He takes in the scenery around her—the pies in the glass case, the small cereal boxes at the breakfast station, the coffeepots, the juice dispenser. Cat got all the details right. It *is* the scene. She was like the old man who painted the last leaf in O. Henry's story—the leaf looked so real that it kept the sick woman from dying because she thought if the leaf could hold on, she could, too. Cat was that good.

He thinks about Natasha and wonders how old she must be now, where she ended up.

The sketch had to be about fifteen years old. The kids were just out of the house, and he retired at fifty-seven, taking a penalty off his pension because he couldn't stand one more year. Cat retired at the same time because her school district offered an incentive for teachers with twenty-five years. So if Natasha was eighteen then, she'd be in her early thirties now, five or six years younger than Ben. He stops and counts the years and realizes Leela will be forty this year. Holy cow. Leela, Ben. Even Natasha. How did all these teenagers grow and change so much?

But Natasha being in her thirties stuns him.

She was just a young thing. What is she up to? Where in the world did she go?

—

He met her at the café when Cat took him for lunch one day, and he was alarmed—no, not alarmed—but it was noticeable that they were close. It surprised him because Cat was sweet to everyone but avoided getting as close to people as she and Natasha seemed to be. For example, Natasha seemed to already know that Chuck didn't like mayonnaise, and she seemed to know the cat's name, Maple, that they had at the time, and she referred to Cat as *Catty*, something only he'd ever done.

"Catty, you didn't get that manicure," Natasha said right away when they walked in.

Cat smiled, and Natasha motioned for them to sit in a booth, sliding two menus over to them. "Unfortunately not," Cat said. "The day got away."

Natasha smiled politely at Chuck. "Hi, there," he said, and

she made him feel old—her bright sneakers, her smooth skin, the effortless way she turned on her heels and grabbed napkins, ketchup, whatever anyone needed.

"What are you two up to today?" she asked. She had dark eyes and long eyelashes. Her fingernails were painted, and her wavy hair was back in a loose ponytail. She was the kind of young woman who would look gorgeous in a gown or in exercise clothes or even in men's pajamas. He liked her, he thought. He saw what Cat saw. She brought Cat a water without asking, one with very little ice. When he asked for coffee, she poured it expertly, and smiled as she set it in front of him.

"Our plans? We are going to do some planting, some mulching, and some weeding," Cat said to her.

"Lucky us," Chuck said, and Natasha laughed.

"The only thing I plant is my butt in the lawn chair," Natasha said. "I love feeling the sun. It's like we haven't felt it forever, and now here we are, full-on spring."

She brought them their BLTs. When Natasha asked if they wanted dessert, she sat down next to Cat and gestured toward Chuck. "Why didn't you bring your sketchbook? You have the perfect picture right here in front of you."

"I have that picture memorized," Cat said, and they laughed. Awhile later, he paid the bill and tipped her well, and Natasha waved as they were leaving. Something caught Chuck's eye that made him glance back.

Later, after the bags of mulch were loaded in the trunk of the station wagon, after they had picked out some hosta and sedum to add to certain drab areas of the yard, he looked over at Cat while they were driving. "That necklace," he said.

Cat was staring at the road. He wonders now if the stuff had started to gather in her body already at that point, if the cancer cells had begun to do their evil work that early—were they always waiting to pounce? But she seemed fine. She had always seemed fine. "What, sweetheart?" she said.

"That necklace she wore . . ." He looked over at her, and her eyes shifted.

"I gave it to her," she said hesitantly.

"It was *yours*."

"Yes."

The magnolia trees on their street were starting to bloom. He looked at the forsythia bursting to life. "Did I buy it for you?"

He couldn't remember. He had given her many things over the years: emerald rings, gold and silver bracelets, earrings that looked like tiny chandeliers.

"No." She sighed. "Of course not."

"But it was yours."

"We said that already."

"Why the hell are you giving her your jewelry?"

She didn't look at him. He signaled for their driveway, and the plants bounced in the back as he put the car in park. She said nothing. A blue jay sat on the ledge of the empty birdbath in the front island of the yard where he had put down river rocks a few years ago. The windows of their small Cape Cod reflected the sun, and the house looked pleasing, nicely tended to with its painted blue shutters and manicured boxwood in the window boxes. A framed piece of stained glass sparkled in the window above the garage. Cat unclicked her seat belt and went to open her door.

Chuck held the car keys in his hand and didn't know how to feel. Something made him sick about this situation. He felt like she was a stranger all of a sudden. "You're not going to answer me?"

She shrugged. "I like helping her." She stepped out of the car and slung her purse over her shoulder. "She needs someone to care."

She didn't look at him and headed straight for the house, closing the door behind her.

Birds sang in the trees. A truck pulling a trailer rumbled by, and he was left to haul out each bag of mulch on his own. He planned in his head what he'd say next: *What is this about? Don't feed strays.*

CHAPTER FOUR

Kirsten Bonato drums her fingers on the stack of files at Rescue Ranch and feels like she is waiting for something.

Some days, the barking gets to her. Once, for a week, they had an alpaca outside, and it let out a dinosaur yowl every so often and ran around in agony. *Acquaaaa*, it seemed to be calling, and her father loved hearing her imitation. "Ah, he's speaking Italian," he said.

She had rolled her eyes. "Not everything has to be about Italy," she said.

She is startled by how she can hear her father's voice without even trying, as if he is still around. She loved his soulful green eyes, his light hair that always spiked in certain parts, how young and modern he seemed. She loved the little traces of his accent that would return every so often, even though he had lived in the States longer than he was ever in Milan. She relished hearing about the food his parents and grandparents would cook (osso buco, polenta, cassoeula). He'd tell her so honestly how many cigarettes he'd smoke a day when he was in the military for two years out of high school, and then the story of how he met her mother at the University of Delaware. "I was still taking ESL classes, and I felt like such a baby with my folder of worksheets. I was trying to read these simple short stories, and she came by, long red hair, holding an organic chemistry textbook that was bigger than she was."

Her mother always laughed. "It was *in*-organic, Alberto."

Kirsten loved seeing her parents next to one another: her mother's freckled skin and blue eyes, the way her father smiled shyly when they shared a story.

She can see him sitting at their kitchen table, the evening sun in the window over the sink behind him, his favorite mug that he sipped tea from all day. "See. I didn't even know organic chemistry had two sides to it. It looked so, so . . . uninteresting."

Her mother would throw a dish towel at him. "You were scared to even speak to me."

"Damn right I was."

His eyes. And his voice. It was like he was one person in English and another in Italian. She loved the cadence when he phoned a family member or when they hosted her aunt or another relative. They would sit at the table and speak furiously and passionately. She loved his expressions: *Dio ride*. God laughs. Anytime they had plans that went badly, he would shake his head and say, "Ah, *Dio ride*." Or, *La goccia che ha fatto traboccare il vaso*, which meant something like the straw that broke the camel's back except it was a vase overflowing with water.

It had taken him graduating from the English program in his early twenties, and a few more months after that, before he felt comfortable approaching her mother. Kirsten thinks back on that time and wants to know both of them then. Her mother with a laser focus and long lab sessions, her father trying to memorize idioms and watching sitcoms like *Family Ties* and *Mr. Belvedere*, writing down expressions to practice later:

You're pulling my leg.

You can't be serious.

She answers the phone now at Rescue Ranch, the first call of the day, and tells a man their hours. She smiles and nods and says, "Sure, no problem." Marmalade, the old cat that weighs eighteen pounds, walks by her and settles in the patch of sun by the long window, and the bichon, Gloria, who has permanent streaks of reddish tears by her eyes and came in last week, sleeps in a bed by Kirsten's feet. She looks down. "How's it going, cutie?" and Gloria opens one eye and gives Kirsten a calm stare.

She has been out of college three years. Her mother said this job was made for her when she was hired two years ago. "You found work—a *career*—doing something you love." Kirsten is an animal person in and out, often stopping to feed apples to the Clydesdale that lives on the farm next to theirs, his sleek body trotting across the grass when she stands at the fence.

Last year at this time, she was applying to vet schools and had every intention of commuting to Philadelphia or moving to another city, wherever she got in.

But God laughs.

Animals are the only things that make her smile lately: videos her friends send on Instagram of newborn zoo animals, and pictures of old dogs in bow ties. As a child, she adored petting zoos, pet stores at the mall where her father would give every dog and kitten, even birds, a voice. "You must leave," he'd say in a parakeet voice. "The workers are meeeeeaaaaan."

"Oh, stop," her mother would say. "All the animals look fine."

"That's because they're drugged," he'd whisper, and she'd laugh.

Kirsten has no idea what is next. She feels like she's waiting for a sign. She feels like her dad would be just the person who could bring her one. What would he tell her? What would save her, open her up, make her smile again?

In some ways, she could see herself at Rescue Ranch forever. She doesn't feel as though it's a career the way her mother refers to it, but they trust her with a lot: handling adoptions and surrenders, managing the office, overseeing marketing and social media.

She has even earned awards (employee of the year, customer service certificate), which she has framed behind her desk.

Her boss, David, supported her when vet school was on the horizon, and after last year, he is polite enough to not mention it.

At five o'clock, she makes her rounds, shutting down her computer, making sure the evening crew has shown up: the woman who cleans the cages and litter and keeps the animals' food fresh, and the guy who is half security guard and half custodian. She confirms the vet appointments for the next day, the list of scheduled surrenders, the weather for the outdoor animals.

A day goes by, and then another and another.

But she hates to go home. Her mother is so absent lately, putting time into a new research study she's working on, or on endless phone calls with her grad students at Lehigh, and the evenings at the farmhouse are long and dark. Maybe they used to tough out the quiet because they knew her dad would eventually come home to fill it. Kirsten feels as though they're still waiting for him to walk through the door.

"The traveling salesman has returned," he used to say triumphantly, his voice like a church bell, and even when she was a teenager, as silly as it felt, she would stop what she was doing and run to him, down the steps from her room or up the stairs from the finished basement.

The light in the foyer would put a glow on him and he'd hold out his hands, the way she pictures him doing at the gas station that night.

The gas station. That gas station outside Philadelphia—she imagines it brightly lit, she imagines it busy inside. Sometimes she has to work hard to *not* see it.

"Everything's going to be okay," he probably said. "Don't shoot. Please don't shoot."

And even to this day, she's surprised the gunman didn't listen.

—

Today is an easy day so far. Good old early January. She likes days without surprises. She likes having her coffee and talking with David, who is in his thirties and balding, serious but thoughtful, recently divorced. He has solid opinions on everything: politics, shows on Netflix, constellations, and weather patterns. He wears blue or green oxford shirts, slightly wrinkled, and striped ties. "Well, here's the thing," he'll often say; or, "How you managing, Kirsten? What can I do to help?" And his eyes. Those caring eyes just melt her.

David pushes back against the higher-ups if something they want isn't in the animals' best interests, and she admires that. He makes sure they are all paid fairly, too, and given overtime when necessary. Once on a slow Friday, he stood on his chair and said, "Oops, I think the clock is malfunctioning," and he wiggled the minute hand back and forth and finally said, "I can't be sure of the time. You all better just leave."

David's assistant is Grayson, a guy about her age who is finishing his master's in counseling at Villanova. Grayson has a buzz cut and bright hazel eyes. He calls her Kiki, which makes her smile, and he wears khakis and polo shirts. He has a tattoo on his bicep that sticks out of his sleeve, flames and some type of writing. Her mother once visited her at the office and said, "How do you get any work done? I would follow that Grayson everywhere." Peggy, the part-time accountant who is almost ready to retire, has said to Kirsten more than once, "What in Hades are you waiting for?"

But Kirsten is more drawn to David, who is older and calm.

With his kind, steady voice and well-rounded opinions. David with his two kids on the weekend and various weeknights. She knows it could never work. He's her boss, for God's sake, but still, she smiles when he talks to her, she gets nervous when he approaches her desk. In her head, she has imagined both David and Grayson hanging off a cliff, something she used to do when picking out who was really her best friend in elementary school, and although she admires Grayson's playful spirit and strong arms, she has never once in her fantasy not offered David her hand.

Now she makes her coffee in the kitchen, and is about to wander toward David and Grayson's area down the hall when her phone buzzes. "Please call when you are able," her Aunt Bria texts.

Kirsten's stomach clenches. She does the calculation. It is about three in the afternoon in Milan. She writes back, "I will try."

She knows what Bria wants, and she doesn't know what to tell her.

Bria, her father's younger sister, has left a couple of messages. She was supposed to get married in June to Nikolas, a man she met while working in Switzerland, but she canceled the wedding when Kirsten's dad was killed at the end of May. Bria flew over here to stay for a few weeks, since Kirsten's grandmother was too ill to travel. She sat by Kirsten and her mother at the funeral. She cooked for them and pet the dogs and ran Kirsten hot baths. She poured wine for them and they all sat in the living room and played the records he liked and cried.

Every day Bria got up early with Kirsten's mother, and they took long walks. When Bria left in June, Kirsten didn't want to see her go. It was as if she brought a hint of the same energy to the table that her father had, and she always had the right words to say. "How about we see New Jersey beach today?" she asked one day, and the three of them stopped crying, drove the two or so hours to Spring Lake, and walked around and bought fudge and a flag for outside and tried to forget.

Now Bria has rescheduled her wedding.

She is getting married in Zurich in early February at an old hotel with a spa that overlooks the city, with mountains and a lake in the distance. It will be gorgeous with snow-covered trees and winter-themed things to do: sleigh rides, ice fishing, thermal baths. The invitation has sat on the sideboard in their dining room, and neither Kirsten nor her mother has responded. Maybe Bria wants her to have a role in the wedding.

Her father had been so excited at the thought of seeing everyone in Europe at the wedding in June. He had bought a fedora that he planned to wear on the plane, knowing his family would laugh when they met them at the airport. He bought a new blue suit for the rehearsal dinner and had it tailored.

Kirsten looks at her phone now and pauses.

"You should go," her mother had said when the invitation came. "You could go to Milan first and see Nonnina." Her mother's eyes looked somber. "Get lost in Milan and buy yourself nice things, help Bria with last-minute wedding errands." She smiled. She and her father had gone back there together right after they were married for a big family reception, and they had taken Kirsten there when she was five, but Kirsten only remembers what she sees in pictures.

"I'll go if you go with me," she told her mother.

Her mother shook her head. "I can't."

Her mother offered up reasonable excuses: department chair duties, teaching duties (she has two doctoral students in analytical chemistry who need close supervision in their final year), farm duties (who will feed the chickens, the goat, the dogs?), but Kirsten knows these are just pretexts.

Italy was the place her young, charming husband had brought her, had shown her off like a prize. How his family had fawned all over the young, successful couple: the Italian dream, the American dream. And then they had gone back a few years later with young Kirsten as a small family, and had stayed for two weeks and taken trips to Venice, Verona, Lake Garda. Her mother didn't want to revise what Italy had meant to her and the symbolic future ahead of them. She didn't want to see an apricot tree that the Bonatos planted in his memory. She wanted Italy to be the way she left it.

Kirsten holds her phone. Could a trip to Europe help her forget him, or keep remembering him, but in a happy way? Now she only imagines the sound of the gun, pictures his terrified face.

She can't decide. She wants to figure her life out, but the thought of going alone scares her.

She sips her coffee and walks toward Grayson and David, Grayson's horseshoe-shaped desk in the area outside David's office, the fiddle-leaf fig tree in a pot on the floor with the fish tank of black mollies and orange goldfish by the copy machine.

Her work is a happy place, and she's grateful to have a happy place.

"It's Kiki!" Grayson says, and stops typing. David peeks his head out of his door. He waves to her, crosses his arms, and leans against his doorway. Her heart flutters seeing him. A phone rings in Peggy's office, and some dogs bark in the background.

"Did you get caught in that accident on 309?" David asks, and she shakes her head. "Phew. Thank goodness for Waze."

She thinks she will just talk about how cold it was this morning, how the new Mod Pizza shop is pretty decent, how she didn't even watch the ball drop this year on New Year's, but instead she surprises herself and looks at David. "Would you hold my job if I took a month off?"

CHAPTER FIVE

He has gotten through three of her dresser drawers, and he is okay with letting go of a nice-sized pile of items so far. But each drawer gets harder, like one of the kids' Nintendo games they used to play where it would shift to a bigger challenge with each level.

The underwear was level one, effortless, and then below it, he found T-shirts she wore around the house, blue and white and nothing remarkable, nothing he really even remembered except maybe peeking out from beneath a cardigan. But one shirt she had gotten on vacation stopped him, an iron-on with just the word *Newport* on it, and he put it in his *keep* pile, a collection of clothes that he will store in a plastic crate with her towel folded on top.

But now another shirt jumps out: the striped one she wore when they took that river cruise in Germany, and then another from a walk they did that benefited multiple sclerosis, and suddenly his keep pile is swelling. When he opens the next drawer, he is almost knocked over by a wave of surprise, because all her nightgowns are there, at least five that he loved her in: one soft pink paisley that felt so good against him when he pulled her close, one with small roses that have faded. Even a flannel one she took out every year in late fall. He feels greedy when he sees these, and he gathers them up and puts them to the side. Then even a couple of pairs of socks jump out at him, and they are now *keep*, too, and he feels angry, betrayed, that Leela would show up here and start tossing all of this into trash bags—as though her mother hadn't lived so fully in these clothes.

He holds one of the nightgowns against him, and he wants to quarantine the whole dresser now because he can smell her on the clothing, the smell like a friend he has forgotten. This won't ever get easier. He is always just moments from falling into the abyss her death has created.

He pretends now she is in the living room or kitchen, a stair's length away, and in minutes he'll hear her slow-walk up the steps, saying something like, "Whatcha up to?" as she comes into the room. Her "ahh" when she lifts back the covers and sinks her back against her heating pad.

Now he looks at that Monet key chain, like a tiny fool without a key, and he wishes he could call Natasha and explain. That she could help him make sense of all this.

—

For Sale. Low Miles.

He uses black permanent marker to make the sign for her car. Or his car. Whichever one he decides to sell, the sign still applies. He doesn't need two cars, and neither of the kids are interested in taking them. Which annoys him to a certain extent because there was never a time in all his years when he would have refused a perfectly good free car, with decent tires and the oil changed without fail. He has even offered the car to Gabby, who will be driving soon, but Leela said Isaac was going to upgrade his car then, and Gabby would take his.

In the last few years, they went most places together, so neither car was really Cat's or his. They had the car they used most days, the Subaru kind of wagon/kind of SUV, and the smaller Honda hatchback that they used if they both had appointments at the same time. He finally decides to sell the Honda because it reminds him less of her and them as a couple. They got it three years ago, and it barely has twelve thousand miles on it. The trunk space is way too small if he does make the trip to Hilton Head, which he won't.

Now the front door swings open and he jumps. Cocoa walks in, dragging her leash, and Chuck says, "Oh."

"Hang on," he hears Sal yell. "I'm coming."

Chuck rolls his eyes. "Hey, girl," he says to Cocoa, and quickly finds a biscuit and tosses it to her. She catches it, nods, and goes into the living room, her leash trailing behind her. He thinks about Rescue Ranch again and wonders if he should take a drive over there. Maybe a kind, easy dog like Cocoa is waiting for him.

"Your paper was in the bushes." Sal comes in, shaking it off and peeling it from the plastic to look at the headlines. "You should tell them."

"Yeah, sometimes she is in a rush."

"Who?"

"The girl. The girl who brings the paper." She's not a girl—he shouldn't say that. She's a woman, probably in her thirties or forties. Sometimes when he's up early, when he can't sleep anymore, when he sits in the dark living room with the ceramic Christmas tree turned on, he sees her at 5 a.m. in her car with the loud muffler, even in the snow and rain, while he sits and watches the overnight news or an infomercial for luggage or a fitness program.

He sees the lights of her car so early, and he feels comforted for some reason, knowing someone is out there, knowing her car is probably warm.

His house is set so far back because of the wide front lawn and long driveway that usually she gets out of her car so the paper at least reaches the porch. Whenever he sees her, she is dressed helter-skelter: a long, shabby coat, messy hair, sometimes a hat or big snow boots. He has never really seen her eyes—just this blur of her. The way she walks makes her seem older—she walks slowly, as if careful not to fall. He notices teenagers and people in their twenties never walk this way. But she is still young—much younger than he is. When she waved at him the other day, he was startled because he wasn't entirely sure she could see him in the window, as if he's become a ghost or something. He thinks again about not waving back and feels awful.

He looks at Sal, who is turning the paper every which way to see all the headlines. Chuck would never call the paper to complain about her. He only reads it some days anyway.

"Looks like they got the go-ahead to build that new baseball stadium," Sal says, sitting down, flipping through the A section.

He can't stand the thought of being trapped here with Sal for the next hour. "I'm going to Lloyd's to get some breakfast," Chuck says. He stands, pats his side pocket to make sure his wallet is there, and Cocoa walks over to him when she hears the jingle of the car keys.

Sal smiles at Cocoa, puts the paper down, and stands. "Are you buying?" he asks.

—

From the table at Lloyd's, Chuck continues to look at his Subaru parked out front. "You sure the dog's all right there?"

Sal doesn't look up from the menu. "We cracked the window. We won't be here long." He holds the menu out in front of him then brings it closer to his face. "Here, gimme those a second." He reaches for Chuck's reading glasses, and Chuck sighs. "What are you getting?"

"Eggs. Toast. Juice maybe."

"I'm not that hungry."

"Then just get coffee," Chuck says.

"I haven't had French toast in years."

"Then get that." He glances around, and the place looks the same. The hostess at the cash register with the box of Peppermint Patties and donate-to-cancer bucket next to her. The cooks in white undershirts back in the kitchen. He has been here a few times over the years since that day he met Natasha, and unreasonably, every time a waitress comes out today, he expects it to be her. Still the same age, still balancing a tray on her right shoulder, still with those smart, wide-awake eyes and shiny dark hair. An older woman comes over to their table, wearing scrubs that remind him of what a nurse would wear.

"Good morning, boys," she says, and the thought of being called a boy seems ludicrous and lovely at once. He imagines himself and Sal in varsity jackets. He imagines his first car waiting out in the parking lot, a 1958 Oldsmobile coupe, cream colored. Sal doesn't seem to notice the compliment, and he gives her his French toast order using hand gestures and clear instructions about the bacon being on a side plate. He wants coffee now and juice later, not until the meal comes. He delivers the instructions as though he's walking her through how to deactivate a bomb.

When they have finished breakfast, Chuck goes up to the hostess station to pay. The woman smiles at him, and she punches the information from the check into the cash register. He drops the quarters into the cancer donation bucket, and he thinks of Cat and how those last months took everything from her. He tries not to remember her so thin and pale, and he turns toward the cashier. "You've been here awhile, haven't you?"

"It'll be thirty-five years in July." She smiles proudly and writes something on his check before she stabs it onto the metal spike. On her blouse is a pin that looks like a poppy.

"Holy cow. That's terrific."

"I like what I do. I like meeting all the nice people."

Chuck puts his hands on the counter, and lowers his voice. "Do you happen to remember a young lady who worked here? Her name was Natasha . . . It was a number of years ago."

She looks up. He can see her thoughts working. "Natasha." She smiles and points at him. "Natasha Vargas. Young. Pretty. I used to tell her I wanted to steal her curly hair." Her whole face lights up. "She was so dear. What's she up to?" She folds her hands in front of her as though she's ready to hear a long story.

"I don't know," he says. "She was a friend of my wife's."

She shrugs. "I can't really remember what happened. Max never got along well with her."

"So you don't see her around here anymore?"

"No, no. Not for ages." He notices a woman standing behind him, and the cashier reaches for her check. "You know, though." She points at him again. "I do remember her coming in for her last paycheck one day." She whispers. "Poor thing was crying. I never saw her after that." She shrugs.

The woman behind him hands the hostess her credit card, and on Chuck's other side, Sal pokes him lightly in the ribs. "Done flirting?" he asks. "Our dog's waiting."

—

When Chuck was drafted during the Vietnam War, he hadn't met Cat yet. Every so often he imagines how much that would have helped him—to have known her before. To have had her to write letters to. To have her waiting there at the airport when he was discharged, and he came back so thin and haggard, his mother touching his cheek and saying he looked like he didn't know them.

He remembers how his mother wore a flag pin on her sweater when they met him in New York that day, how his father just kept reaching over and squeezing his shoulder at the restaurant. He remembers how surprised they were when he said he didn't want to come home that night. He was twenty-one, and he asked quietly if they would pay for a hotel room in Bethlehem.

"What's wrong with your bed?" his dad said.

"I freshened the sheets and everything," his mother said.

"I know. I just need one night."

And when they agreed, when his dad let him drop them off with the car and handed him some money and they watched him incredulously, he remembers how the tears streamed down his face as he drove the dark roads, not stopping in Bethlehem or Allentown, where there were plenty of hotels, but instead to an exit outside Philadelphia, and he was surprised how driving came back to him after so much time away from a car. He let the radio play low, and it felt so free to be in the car alone on the road, knowing how cold it was outside, knowing if he wanted to, he'd never have to think about that world over there again.

Chuck checked into a hotel that night, and he just breathed and breathed. It felt good to shower, to lie in the white sheets with no clothes on, and stare at the blank ceiling, adjusting the thermostat in the room to blast the coldest air, even though it was cold outside.

In that hotel bed, he shivered and breathed, and it would have been nice if he knew Cat then because she would have let him say everything he wanted to say. She would have rubbed his back and nodded and kissed his head and told him it wasn't his fault, none of it was his fault, and he shouldn't have been there, they were all wrong.

Tonight, he holds her towel and he puts the ceramic tree away, carefully, wrapping it with packing paper. Happy New Year, he thinks, because he is lost, and he hopes he finds something this year that will stop the hurting.

—

That night, he sits in bed and reads the news on his iPad. Then he tries that game Gabby told him about, the one where the icicles are melting, and the polar bear has to place the buckets out in time, but his old fingers feel slow and stubby and the game frustrates him terribly. He texts Gabby and says, *Honey, new high score. Love, Pap*, and she texts him back an emoji with hearts around its face, and then she sends a picture of the kitten she just got that has sweet blue eyes.

I can't wait to meet him, Chuck writes.

He wonders if she thinks of her grandmother. He wonders how Leela and Ben have been doing. He feels lonely, and selfish. He goes back on the iPad and searches Natasha Vargas. There are a lot of hits, but one Facebook page catches his eye. It looks like Natasha with sunglasses on, but it's hard to tell, and the account is private.

By her name it says, Norfolk, Virginia, so he types in her name again with this city and state, and she comes up on White Pages. It has her age listed as thirty-three, which seems right, unbelievable but right, and it has her listed in a few different places in Pennsylvania, but also Norfolk. And Las Vegas. And Orlando.

So young to have lived so many places. He sees a profile on LinkedIn come up, and he can't read much because he doesn't have an account, but her job in Norfolk looks like it's a banquet manager at a Hilton, and he feels something—like pride usually reserved for his kids. *Good for her* type of thing. He doesn't know what he would say to her—maybe he'd try to explain, but without thinking, he reaches over for the phone and dials the main number for the Hilton in Virginia, and a woman with a cheerful almost-southern accent answers.

"Hello, may I have Natasha Vargas's extension please? Banquet manager." He pauses. "I know it's late—I was going to leave her a voice mail."

"I'm sorry, sir, but I don't have that name in my directory."

"Oh, um, not the banquet manager?"

"No, sir."

"Natasha with a different last name?"

She types something. "Nope, I'm sorry."

After he hangs up, he tries to search for her some more, but he doesn't get anywhere.

He's not good at the Internet. *Where did you get to?* he thinks, and then he says this out loud, in his quiet house, as if she can hear his voice and the echo it makes.

CHAPTER SIX

Ella's phone rings while she's working on the floor at Today's Bride, a giant store with fluorescent lights and too many mirrors and walls of plastic-wrapped gowns that sits inside a shopping center about ten minutes from her apartment. She jumps and grabs the phone, doesn't recognize the number and feels a hopefulness in her chest as she answers.

She remembers teaching Riley her letters and numbers, their address, and her cell phone number. The phone number they practiced again and again. During a school field trip to the aquarium last spring, Riley had one of the chaperone mothers call Ella.

Ella was at the grocery store at the time, and when she picked up, the woman said, "Hi, this is Casey's mother. I'm at the Camden Aquarium and I'm leading Riley's group . . ." Ella's heart had dropped—*what happened? Did she get hurt? Did they lose her?* "Everything's fine," she went on. "Riley just wanted to talk to you."

Ella felt air return to her body. She breathed slowly and her little girl's voice came on the line. "Hey, Mommy. They have sea horses here."

"They do?" She wanted to scold her for bothering the woman and making her call, but that disintegrated. Her marriage was awful and dead, and she was always fighting with Kyle, who had moved back to his parents' house. During that time even Kyle's parents were calling her and shouting at her and blaming her for everything. It felt terrific to talk about sea horses.

"Yes! They're tiny, and they bounce when they swim. I'm going to ask Casey's mom to take a picture for you."

Ella stood in the produce aisle, holding the green plastic bag for broccoli. That kid. That kid. She was the antidote to the harshness of the world. Her *sincerity*. That is what always struck Ella the most. Her damn downright lovely sincerity. "Oh, I wish I were there, Bitsy-Boo."

"Me, too. That's why I wanted to call you. Okay, bye."

Now she'd give anything for a simple call like that. Three and a half months since she's heard her child's voice. No leads, the officers say. No sign of Kyle, of Riley. Now, standing there amid the racks of white gowns and wild colors of bridesmaid and flower girl dresses, she says hello quickly and prays it's Riley.

"Ella, it's Mason."

She heaves a sigh. Her boss from the *Lehigh Valley Ledger*.

"Hello, Mason."

She hears him typing in the background. She hears phones ringing and people answering. She has never seen him in person, and his calls are always deflating. She imagines a big warehouse of desks and phones. She doesn't even know if they print the newspapers there or where that happens. She just gets the stack of them, with ads and inserts sometimes, and delivers them to her seventy-five customers. "Well, we've gotten some complaints about papers not being on porches, or papers getting there a little later than usual."

She shakes her head. This accusation is mostly untrue. She tries to be careful. Her aim is bad, and sometimes she's so late that she leaves a paper where it's fallen, just for the greater good of getting everyone their paper by the expected time.

Delivering papers is a row of dominoes. While she listens to him talk and lecture her, she holds the steamer up to a mother-of-the-bride dress, blue with a rhinestone brooch in the center. She thinks about being a mother of a bride, imagines Riley older, in a wedding gown. Imagines kissing her on the cheek on the big day, pulling her grown daughter against her before she walks down the aisle.

Not only does she want to be reunited soon with her, she wants this time apart to not matter, to not have been anything in the whole scheme of things. She imagines Kyle being led away in handcuffs, and she can't even envision that scene or what she'd say to Riley. She just wants her safe. That is the only horse in the race. Once in a while, a voice in her head surprises her and asks, *How do you even know she's still alive?* It turns her blood cold. But she chases it away. She knows Riley is somewhere, and she's okay.

"You there?" Mason says.

She tries to focus. It's hard not to get lost in her winding trail of thoughts. "I'm sorry, Mason. The weather's been—"

"We know the weather. We all live in Northeastern PA, Ella, right?" He clears his throat. "So we have to plan accordingly, knowing what we know."

"Yes, you're right." She wishes she could hang up on him, or call him something like *pissant* or *jackass.*

"So you'll take care of this going forward?"

Her shoulders sag. Her eyes are tired. The lights overhead are too bright. Gentle music plays over the loudspeaker—she thinks it's The Beatles.

She could just say *I quit* to Mason, she could forget about this horrible paper route, and while she's at it, she'd love to stop being in bridal sales. The brides are horrible. The friends and family they bring in with their Pinterest opinions are worse.

She always wanted to open her own preschool. She wanted none of what she currently has—the dismal, tiny apartment, the hours she currently keeps, the empty check-in calls from Jared

Kinney and Detective Modelo, from Kyle's parents who are meek and nonyelling now when they speak, his parents who allegedly were kept in the dark about this.

She needs to keep paying her bills, saving money, being ready for the moment when they find Riley or when she gets a better car and some more cash stocked away so she can take matters into her own hands and get Riley herself. She imagines all of a sudden knowing where to find her. She imagines being the person who *could* find her. She hears Mason huff, waiting for her response. Did she always take so long in a conversation? She pauses before she responds. She *wishes* her only problem was worrying about a damn newspaper and where it lands. She can't believe their luck. Bored old crabs. Who still gets a newspaper? "I can definitely take better care of this, Mason . . . and I'm sorry."

"That's what I needed to hear," Mason says, and hangs up.

—

Another cold morning, and her car muffler is loud. Under the hood, the car makes a rattling sound. The morning is so blank and peaceful. She wishes she didn't have to interrupt the tranquility with her noisy car.

She pulls onto Fillingham Bay Road on the rural outskirts of Bethlehem, not far from the country club, and the houses are modest but well taken care of. She comes to a stop for each newspaper box, green plastic, that sits below people's mailboxes, and she looks at the quiet houses, their dusk-to-dawn post lights and lanterns over their garages, the bare hydrangeas and flowerless shrubs. She loves how the yards are just smooth sheets dusted with frost, how occasionally she sees a deer or fox trotting by. These mornings would be almost joyful if they weren't framed in the events of now.

Pull up. A paper in the box. Done. Pull up. Another. Pull up. No box. Heave the paper so it hits the porch steps. Luckily, it doesn't fall. She hates when they fall; she feels guilty when they fall and she doesn't fix them, and now, according to Mason, she needs to be more vigilant.

Keep driving.

But one house always stops her.

It is five in the morning, and she sees the old man in the chair by the window, the light of the television illuminating his face, and there is something sweet about him, something gentle and broken.

She's only had this job for two months and wonders if there is more to the story: a wife in a nursing home, or something else. What happened to Ella in these last few months has filled her with a fresh curiosity about others. No one who sees her car passing on the road in the early morning tossing out papers would guess what happened to her daughter, no one who sees her at the minimart buying a can of soup and a quart of milk. She wonders how many women come into the bridal shop with stories she could never guess: who's taking care of a relative with dementia, who has been abused, who has a doctorate. She even wonders about Mason. It's easy to think of him as rotten, and she hates his petty, confrontational tone, but she wonders if he's been hurt, if he has worries she would never know. Maybe the world has beaten him down, too. The dark mornings are so long, and she fills them wondering about what everyone else is carrying around, and whom they can share their pain with.

She looks up at that window of the small Cape Cod with the blue shutters and sees the old man's messy hair, his glasses that don't sit right, his haggard face, and for whatever reason, she gets out of the car today and brings the newspaper right up to his porch so he won't have to walk far, so he won't slip when he comes out.

He always looks up when he hears her car coming, and there is a moment where he peers out at the darkness, and she feels comforted by his recognition even though they can't see each other's faces.

She places his paper on the edge of his porch, and she hears the sound of his television, and she vows to help him out in this way, every day, by caring about his paper.

—

She has thrown herself into all this, and it feels necessary to have these two jobs, even though her head pounds so hard after an eight-hour shift at Today's Bride, or TB as she calls it, even though getting up at three thirty in the morning is dreadful. For the rest of the day, she feels sleepy, almost delirious.

But her mother, always so levelheaded, advised her to focus on the tangible. "You cannot possibly just wait around for the phone to ring. Busy is better."

Between the loss of Riley and taking on these jobs was the move. The move that wrenched everything out of her body, the move that gave Ella nightmares about Riley returning home to a vacant house. But the money was gone, and keeping the house wasn't an option.

Her mother helped her relocate to the smaller apartment, setting up her toiletries neatly in the bathroom closet and smoothing out new shelf paper in the kitchen cabinets. Her mother called Kyle's parents and told them to please pick up his boxes in the garage of the old house, and her mother helped her make the second small bedroom in the new apartment a careful re-creation of Riley's old room, using a paint roller to color the room a similar soft pink, and hanging her framed Mickey Mouse poster over her bed. "She'll feel right at home when she's back," her mother said, and kissed Ella's head. She patted Ella's shoulder, advised her to work as much as possible—for income, for people to talk to, for the distraction.

Ella thought it would be easy to find a job she liked. She called the local schools to get put on the sub list again, but no one responded. (Better anyway, she decided. She didn't know if she could handle being around children.) She looked for clerical work in doctors' offices and law offices and accounting firms, but she didn't make it past phone interviews. Maybe they could sense how distracted she was, what a fog she was in. When she saw the ad for newspaper delivery, even though the salary was barely anything, something about being forced out of bed first thing in the morning, the time where she wallowed, the time when all the doubts crushed her to the point she could almost not breathe or move—she liked the sound of that. "Is the job still available?" she had said to Mason when he answered the company phone.

"Sure is," he replied, and she began two days later.

She wasn't planning on selling dresses at TB. One of the doctors' offices she had applied to had shared applications with the general manager at TB, and they sent Ella an email asking if she was interested in bridal sales. She realized she had a large day to fill after the paper route and figured, what the hell?

—

She owes so much to her mother. Her mother stayed with her for two weeks after Riley went missing. Her mother slept in the same bed with her at the old house on Hickory Lane, and rubbed her back and let her cry. When they realized Kyle had drained the bank accounts and stopped paying the mortgage a month before, and the property taxes awhile before that, it was her mother who found the apartment for her, paid the deposit, and made all the arrangements.

Ella sobbed leaving their house. Not because she loved it. She had grown to hate it when her marriage soured. It had stopped feeling like home for at least the last year. But what if Riley managed to escape? What if she could tell someone her address? What if she got free and ran to the door of the old house and pounded on it, calling, "Mommy, Mommy"? Ella couldn't stand the thought of it. She wrote a letter to the bank begging them for an extension on the loan payments. But they declined.

Finally, her mother convinced the new owners to let her leave the small ceramic frog on the doorstep with a ziplock bag around its neck. A sealed envelope was inside with Riley's name on it in large letters—the first thing she'd see.

Her mother had the owners promise that they'd help Riley if she showed up. "Of course," the retired woman said, and she had tears in her eyes. "I will keep her extra safe if she shows up, and I'll call the police in a jiff." This made Ella feel a tad better, and every so often she drives by the old house to make sure the frog and the note are still visible.

Eventually, Ella's mother had to get back to Massachusetts. She needed to be at the restaurant she owned in the college town that was busy night and day, needed to assist Ella's father, who is in a wheelchair and cooks and bartends. "I'll sell the café and move here if it helps," her mother had said. Ella's brother, Wyatt, was traveling in South America as a photographer for *National Geographic* and offered to come back, too.

Ella stared out the window of the new apartment on the opposite side of Bethlehem from their old house, seeing the poplar tree losing its then-reddish leaves. She imagined having her parents and

Wyatt here and how pleasant that sounded. How they'd welcome Riley home, all of them. The thought seemed ideal. Better than facing this alone.

But she couldn't ask that of them. Her brother was restless, always on a new assignment, and he told her in the past he worried they would find someone else if he said no to any job. And her mother and father barely got by from the café income and Social Security. "I'll be fine," she said.

"I'll keep carving out times to be here," her mother said. And she did. She has returned three times since Riley disappeared in September, and Ella's father came over Thanksgiving.

Ella stands now in her apartment, eating cereal for dinner over her kitchen sink, the heat crackling in the baseboards the only sound, and music from the neighbor below her. He's a younger guy, probably in his thirties, and he always waves to her if they happen to be out at the same time. His name is David, and he has a tired, handsome face, and a son and daughter who sleep there some nights. Ella sees the mother drop them off or pick them up in her Land Rover, and sometimes Ella watches from the window and sees how David interacts with his ex. He always keeps his arms crossed as though he's protecting himself, squinting at her as she shouts something from the car window. He usually nods in a resigned way and walks back toward the apartment.

She wonders what she and Kyle used to look like when they handed off Riley. She wonders if that caused Riley stress. She wonders what the hell happened that they went from married to handling custody drop-off to all of a sudden being in this position that no one she knows can ever understand.

She hears David's music, and feels incredibly lonely. She hates this apartment. She hates its stale smell, the depressing linoleum

floor, the too-large space between the refrigerator and the cupboard above it. It has been almost four months, and she doesn't
know if she can take one more day of this.

The night is so black, frozen, and windy outside her window,
and her neighbor's music radiates through her floorboards. She
rinses her bowl and places it in the dishwasher. She closes her eyes,
but she can't tell what song he is playing. Maybe it's not anything,
she thinks. Maybe it's just music without words.

CHAPTER SEVEN

Kirsten is walking to her car after a long day at Rescue Ranch. She sees a cardinal fly overhead and she thinks for a second of her favorite teacher in middle school, Mrs. A., who used to say cardinals were the most special birds because they kept us company in winter when the other birds leave. She watches the red bird disappear. Behind her she hears, "Hooray for quitting time, Kiki."

She turns around and smiles at Grayson in his gray polo shirt, no coat, his briefcase strap slung across his chest. She looks past him for David, as they usually walk out together. He raises his eyebrows. "He's on the phone, fighting with Baby Mama." She can see Grayson's breath in the air.

Kirsten frowns. "That's probably hard."

"Probably." He shrugs. "Poor guy." Grayson hops into his car, an old Saab. He rubs his hands together. "Damn, it's freezing," he says, and waves to her as he drives away.

"Have a good night," she says, even though he can't hear her now. She stands by her car for a moment longer. She looks at the building. She pictures David at his desk, his tired eyes and five o'clock shadow.

It is still light, but the sun has faded, and the air feels heavy with precipitation about to come. Kirsten takes her time, knowing there's nothing to rush home to except the dogs greeting her in the quiet farmhouse. She's about to slip her coat off because she hates driving with her coat on—it feels like a straitjacket. She looks at the Rescue Ranch entrance once more, and now David is walking out, his old camel wool coat slung over one arm. He looks defeated, and she feels protective of him.

"Having a hard time leaving?" he asks.

"Funny," she says.

"Don't worry—it'll still be here in the morning." He winks, gives her his crooked grin that makes her head buzz for a second.

"I'd be lost if it wasn't." She laughs. She hears those words, and realizes her job is one of the only things keeping her going.

What does she want? What is she waiting for? She wants peace. She wants to be settled. She wants to know the things she needs to do to get over this.

She wants to find her exact place, doesn't she? People lose parents. People figure out how to be adults. She doesn't want to just go from work to that lonely house every night and have nothing else. She wants more happiness—like a Sunday lying in a hammock with someone she loves; or a Friday night out sipping a cold beer. She wants luck. She wants a sign from her dad—a big, huge sign that shows her the way.

David puts his hands into his pockets. "What are you doing tonight?"

She thinks of her home, her mom always busy, every room boring without her dad's infectious laugh. She imagines putting on her sweats, pulling her hair up, and scrolling through social media while lying on the sofa in the quiet living room, the fire crackling, until her eyes get tired. She still has to connect with Bria about her visit and finalize dates. If she gets home soon, she can probably catch her tonight, as Bria stays up until midnight her time. Kirsten feels grateful that David agreed to the time off from Rescue Ranch, without any hesitation. "Not too much," she finally says. "How about you?"

David leans against his salt-stained car. "I'm toying with a stupid idea even though I'm tired and I have the kids for the next three days, and it's already late." He looks into her eyes, and then up at the darkening sky. "Do you ski?"

She smiles. "I snowboard." She took lessons when she was young. She had excelled, signing up for ski club in high school with her friends, and there was a group of five of them who never missed a week. They called themselves the Snowflake Five, and she thinks of them now going down the different slopes, some of them more daring, some of them slower and careful like her, and all the fun they had singing along to the music that played over the speakers, sitting in the lodge with their feet propped up, eating chicken tenders and drinking hot chocolate. She hasn't been snowboarding in years, since college, and she wonders if the skills have left her.

His eyes light up. "How about night skiing at Bear Creek? I haven't been out on the slopes yet this year. I took the kids for lessons two weeks ago, but I just watched and cheered them on. Coop's not doing bad, and Stella is a whiz. But I haven't gone and had fun like an adult in, um, years. Want to keep me company?" He looks unsure and nervous.

She can't decide how she feels. Her instinct is to say no, to just be alone, to let her loneliness wash over her the way she's used to, but it's David. David. "I could do that."

"Really? You'll meet me there?" He looks around, as though he wants to tell someone about the good news. "Awesome, Kirsten. Awesome."

—

Two hours later, and the skills have come back. It is all muscle memory, and her body remembers the way it needs to arch, the direction she needs to look, the way her hips and knees need to point, and her old board, the one her parents got her for her seventeenth birthday, aqua and green, feels like a broken-in baseball mitt. She loves her warm coat and the green fleece headband and matching ski gloves. She watches David ski in front of her.

He wears a yellow jacket, a black and gray helmet, and he moves in his skis like they are soldered to his feet. She is surprised at how youthful he looks—younger with the helmet on. Leaner, taller. He wears iridescent goggles, and for some reason his mouth is highlighted this way: his smile, the stubble on his jaw and chin, and she is drawn to his excitement.

She loves being out at night like this, so many stars above them, the cold air hitting her face, and she remembers: this is why she loved ski club those years ago with the Snowflake Five. When else can you be out in the open for so long like this in winter, high up and soaring, nothing between you and the giant moon and sky?

She closes her eyes and thinks of her dad, always thinks of her dad when she feels grateful for small seconds to be alive. She remembers how her dad would go for long walks by himself after his father died. Once, she saw him standing by the apple trees, and looking at the sky, and he smiled. Kirsten was young, only seven or so, and when he came into the house, she asked him why he was smiling. "Because we have to smile through pain," he said to her, and kissed her head.

Wouldn't he love to see her having fun? To be smiling through this?

She watches David zigzag, catching up with him and nodding as they go around the next bend.

"Look at you shredding the slopes!" he yells.

"I'm dying," she says, and laughs, but in her head, she keeps hearing that word, *dying*, echoing over and over.

In a moment, they have reached the bottom, and something is released in her, something so pure and perfect she's forgotten, and she catches her breath and they stand at the bottom and look back at where they were: this place of all white. This land of rocks and mountains and trees, and an enormous sky. The people who are high up on the hill look miniature, as though they are pieces from a Christmas village.

Overhead, the ski lift moves lazily along its long cables, and a group of children ski by them with an instructor. David takes his helmet off and looks around. His cheeks are red, and his eyes water. "Let's go to the top," he says, and she follows him into the lift queue.

—

The lift creeps and rocks occasionally, and he claps his skis together and sprawls out. She loves the cold. She loves the faint music playing in the background on the speakers, the calls of the other skiers and snowboarders. His leg touches hers.

"You have to admit," he says. "On the whole, snowboarders are more obnoxious." He puts his hand up. "Present company excluded, of course."

She likes this jokey side of him. Why does he seem so much more her age tonight? Maybe because he's her boss, maybe because he was already married and had kids—she always felt like he was a generation older. But tonight he feels like someone she could meet at a party, someone she could be set up with on a date. He's only eight years older. But he's a decent guy. She can't imagine him dating someone who works for him.

"I do not condone snowboarder hate." She smiles and looks out at the pine trees dusted with snow and the occasional fallen ski pole and mitten below them.

"Exhibit A," he says, and points toward a bunch of high school kids with their snowboards who have camped out on the side of the slope they just went down, all of them sitting in a huddle.

"They're *talking*!" she says.

"They're *sitting* in the middle of a run. You have to admit, that's a dick move. Someone could crash into them." She never heard him swear before. His voice is light. He holds both his gloves in one hand and scratches his cheek. He smells clean, like citrus and cedarwood.

"Okay, it's kind of dicky."

"You wouldn't do that."

"In my old days, I might have." She smiles.

"Oh god, Kirsten!"

She sighs. "Snowboarders are just more expressive."

He rolls his eyes in a playful way. "I'm going to pretend you're a skier, whose skis somehow fused together."

"Fine," she says. She looks over at him, and she thinks of being in high school ski club—how she envied the cool kids who would smoke on the lift, the girls who would lean into their boyfriends and make out on the long lift ride. She always felt lonely, so invisible as she shared her lift with a stranger in the singles line or sat by herself for the ride up the hill. It feels good to have him this close, and it doesn't even matter what this is: friendship or just a pleasant work thing or something else.

But he is magnetic. That's what she keeps thinking. She looks at him and feels awful that anyone would ever overlook him. His genuineness almost makes her want to cry. She hopes her face doesn't look goofy as she stares at him in the dark.

"Are we going to try the Widow Maker?" he says then.

"Hell no."

"Aw, come on. It's not too bad."

"You're a dad!"

"True." He rocks his head back and forth and shrugs. "But sometimes I'm also just a guy who wants to ski fast."

"I went down one like that years ago, and it was all ice. I practically slid down on my face."

"That builds character . . . Frostbite and character." He puts his hand out as though he's showing her the whole frozen white world.

She laughs. "I'll do Mama's Drama with you, but that's as challenging as I get."

"Not Devil's Dance?" He sets his lips in a tight line, but she can see the smile in his eyes.

"I have my limits," she says.

He looks straight ahead. A sign says to raise the bar. The little booth where they disembark is near. She imagines what it would feel like if he leaned over and kissed her, but she pushes that thought away.

His life is complicated; hers is, too.

The lift squeaks on the cable as they go higher and higher to where they will have to disembark, and she wants to thank him for inviting her along.

She wants to tell him how unmoored she has felt this last year. She wonders if he would listen if she said how afraid public places make her, how she imagines when she's alone some nights at the farm that someone with a gun will storm inside and do to her and her mother what that guy did to her father. She has a whole catalog of thoughts that no one has heard, and she feels for a minute that David could help her. If she'd let him.

He reaches for the bar and lets it glide up and then winks as if he can read her mind. They both sit up straighter and press their feet forward, and when her snowboard hits the ground and they take off down the small hill, she can tell the air is different up here.

—

Later, at the lodge, David waits at a table for her because her veggie burger took longer to cook. She isn't a complete vegetarian, but lately she finds herself preferring nonmeat options. He sips a beer, and his coat is on the chair behind him. He has gotten a beer for her, too. His chicken sandwich is still in the foil, and the fact that he waited to eat pleases her. The big fieldstone fireplace is behind him, and there is a flat-screen television with a basketball game on.

"Thanks for the beer," she says, and sits down.

He nods. "My legs are aching. I'm getting old."

"You look like a boy . . . especially in that sweater." His sweater is green with small reindeer on it, and seeing it makes her feel something. He is tender, and he's not afraid to be tender. She can see the dad in him as he smiles.

"Why, thank you." He points his beer in her direction. "Cheers."

She clinks her glass to his. "Cheers."

He takes a bite of his sandwich and looks at her. "Thanks for hanging out with me. This is the most fun I've had in . . . how old am I?" He looks down at the place mat as he chews.

She removes the bun and cuts her veggie burger with a plastic knife and wonders for a second if she looks weird. "Me, too." She stabs a piece of black bean and eats it. Being this close to him makes her nervous, but she also feels incredibly relaxed. It's David. It's easy to be with David. "I'm glad you asked me along."

"Things are just tough lately," he says out of nowhere. He stops himself and looks at her as though he wants to apologize. She wonders if he's thinking he shouldn't complain, knowing what happened to her dad, or if he thinks it's unprofessional to talk with his employee about his personal life. He shakes his head. Is he referring to his divorce or something else? "It's fun to be with someone who gets it," he says. He sips his beer. "You just get it." She wants to ask what he means, but he looks thoughtful as he holds his sandwich. "So, uh, how have you been . . . with everything?"

She feels herself blush. She shrugs. "I get by, I guess."

"Yeah."

"But it sucks," she says.

He nods. "I kind of know." He pauses, swishes his beer around in the glass. "My best friend in college was killed. He was just standing outside a theater buying a movie ticket."

She tilts her head to the side, drinks more of her beer. Something in this confession makes her feel grateful. As though she's been on a planet alone for months and has finally encountered another person. "Oh no, David. How awful."

"Shawn. Shawny Brawny we called him." The easiness in his eyes disappears.

"It makes you not trust anything," she says.

He nods. "I had nightmares for months."

She leans closer. She feels her jaw relax, her tight shoulders loosen. "Me, too."

"Oh, Kirsten. You always seem to be handling it so well. I look at you and think, she's solid. She's remarkably put together." He takes a breath. "My mom wanted me to go to a therapist, and I was like, *screw that*. But I probably should have. I was messed up from it. When I told, my, uh, ex, she never really wanted to hear about Shawn." He frowns. He looks around and drums his hand on the table. "Sorry, didn't mean to make this about me."

She smiles. "You're fine. I didn't go to therapy either." She thinks about what that would look like, and the thought of talking about her dad so much, the thought of opening up every detail of how she feels, just seems overwhelming. She thinks she would break in half if she had to do that every week.

"Way to ruin our fun night, eh?" He holds a fry out to her and lifts his eyebrows. She takes it, touching his fingers for a second. "How often do you think about him?" he says.

"My dad? Um, pretty often." She pauses. "At least once every couple hours—sometimes every few minutes, if I'm being honest."

"I would guess."

"Yeah." She knows her answers are short. She thinks of her mom always telling her that she keeps her cards too close to her chest. "I just can't make sense of it." She glances down at the place mat on her brown tray. She realizes she's barely touched her bean burger. "I think that's what I want: to make some sense of it all."

When she looks up, he stares into her eyes and holds her gaze for a second. "Don't you hate when people say stupid shit—like they're in a better place. That drove me nuts. How is *that* better?"

She nods. She has heard nothing but that from well-meaning family members, neighbors, and even her own friends. Or people will ask how old he was, as if they're looking to discount the loss of his life. "I just wish I could talk to him. One out of every hundred days even. That's all." She realizes she has tears in her eyes, but she doesn't think they're blatant enough for him to notice. And she trusts him.

"There'd be nothing like it, would there?"

"No," she says. "I'd take small talk, big talk, whatever. Even just joking around. I miss joking around." She feels the big thought come to the surface, and she doesn't want to push it away. "I keep hoping my dad will save me. That he'll send me a sign about what I should do next, so I can . . . you know, make it through this."

David watches her, and she feels something in his stare. He

pauses, and as she waits, she wonders if he's going to tell her that there are no signs, that death is death, and she just has to live. "That makes perfect sense," he finally says, and she melts.

A band has set up near the bar, and they are tuning their guitars. "We're about to get started," a singer with a white beard says into the microphone, and a woman beside him with long dark hair, gray at the temples, smiles at the crowd.

The band starts. The keyboards and guitar play, and she recognizes the song right away: "Faithfully" by Journey. The man and woman lean their heads together, and his voice is gravelly and hers is higher and smooth: *Highway run into the midnight sun.*

The music hits Kirsten, and she feels lucky for the fire so close to them, lucky for the night with David, lucky for the loveliness of this music, these voices. Two couples proudly march out to the small wooden square of a dance floor, and she and David watch it all happen.

"This is a good way to end the night," David says, and the woman in the band shakes her head gently as she sings, making her long hair sway behind her. The two couples dancing hold on to each other way too tightly.

"I don't want the song to end," Kirsten says, and now they are both staring at the dancers. He keeps looking back and forth between her and the musicians and the couples swaying as they dance, but he doesn't say anything.

She feels her face flush. He is her boss. She shouldn't. She has learned, all these years, to be reserved, quiet. She has not one outrageous, overzealous bone in her body. She hates looking foolish. But there is another part of her, too, a part that wants to escape tonight. Her insides feel hollow when she speaks. "We could dance," she says. "I mean, if you want."

After she says it, she feels like she accidentally sent out an email that she can't recall. She hears her words echo in her head and blushes.

He surprises her by taking her hand, his palm and fingers smooth, and they join the others. Before long, he is leaning closer, and she is leaning in, and it feels odd and lovely to be against him. Their ski pants swish as their legs touch. His body is solid, and the singers are singing and the music is just right, and once in a while, the other dancers bump into them, but they don't seem to notice or care.

She rests her head on his shoulder, on the line of his collar bone, and outside, she can see skiers still on the slopes and the white spray of the snowmaker. She always loved snow's ability to create new beauty over winter's faded grass.

She feels like she's not even in her body. Like the camera has pulled back and she's watching herself with this man she knows but barely knows. Is it really happening? *David*. She keeps letting the two syllables of his name bounce around her head.

She pays attention to the way it all feels, his hands near her hips, her hands on his shoulders. The way she can feel him slowly inhale, the beer on his breath. If he let her, she feels like she could stay here all night, just swaying. Just watching all this new snow and seeing where it lands.

—

When she gets home, her mother sits on the sofa in the living room, staring at the small fire. Only one lamp is on, and Kirsten sees some of their framed photographs reflecting the light and flames. "Hello, angel. Did you have a nice time?" Her mom pats the sofa next to her.

"Yeah. It was really fun." Kirsten can feel the smile on her face.

Maybe it's the beer, but probably it's David. That song seemed to go on and on, as if the singers held every note for them.

After the song finished, he had high-fived her in his professional way and said he was going to call it a night. He had walked her to her car, and they stood there, his skis on his shoulder, her snowboard at her side, and she just smiled. It would have been weird if he kissed her, she reasoned, but she hoped for it anyway. "I guess I'll see you bright and early tomorrow," he said and grinned. "I'll be the guy limping."

She laughed. "Thanks, David."

He opened his car door, started to say something, and then he didn't. She waved as he drove away.

She realizes how tired she is when she sinks into the sofa. Their dogs, Hildie, an old German shepherd, and Sandra Dee, a mixed breed, snore in front of the fire. Her mom's red hair, gray at the temples, is pulled back in a bun, and she holds a glass of chardonnay. "Want some?" she says, and offers Kirsten her glass.

"No, I'm okay." She looks at her mother, the lines by her eyes, her half smile, and she feels something loosen. "It was good to get out. It was a nice night."

"I'm so glad," she says, and places a leather bookmark into the novel she was reading. "Who else came besides David?"

Kirsten blushes. "It was just the two of us."

Her mother raises her eyebrows. "Oh."

"No, not like that. I mean, he's so . . . professional." She has the image of his hands on her hips, the way her head felt against him for those minutes.

Her mom finishes the wine and stands up. "Well, it's good to see my twentysomething girl not home when I get home. More of that, please." She looks around and claps for the dogs to wake up so she can let them out before bed. "And if he stops being so professional, I think he's a very nice catch."

Kirsten doesn't answer. She rests her head against the back of the sofa, and when she hears her mom open the back door for the dogs, she lets out a silly grin. She is surprised her mom would approve. She knows her mother thinks David is a nice guy, but she would guess a divorced thirtysomething man with two kids would not be something her mother would wish for her.

She stays there for a while, feet stretched in front of her, the warmth of the dwindling fire, the sound of the back door closing with a small draft. She might fall asleep right here.

If her dad were alive, she would be careful about telling him anything David-related. He would never be able to resist bringing him up. She knows he'd do something like hang a printed picture of David on the bathroom mirror or he'd find a reason to show up at work to tease her. He was the biggest teasing dork she ever knew. She closes her eyes then and lets his voice fill her head. She can hear it so clearly, that small trace of an accent. "Kirsten and David, sitting in a tree . . . K-I-S-S-I-N-G."

When she climbs the stairs, each footstep feels hopeful, as though she finally has a map in her hand. Her legs already feel sore, but the pain doesn't feel real, or near her at all.

CHAPTER EIGHT

If Ella is still for a moment, before she catches herself, she can relive that day in September. She sits at the kitchen table, and since the rent has just been paid, she writes out the checks for the electric and her cell phone. She stares at the swirls of her cursive, and before she realizes, she is transported back to the beginning of the school year, when Kyle took Riley.

That sunny, warm day, the doors of the yellow bus opened and only Annabelle Rousseau, a kindergartener, stepped off. Ella had shrugged at the bus driver politely and walked up to the door when no one else came out.

The bus driver scrunched his eyebrows and looked to the back of the bus. Ella wondered for a second if Riley had dozed off. She was often worn out from the long day; second grade was much more tiring—more homework, more hours in her seat than before, more rigorous playing on the playground during recess. Plus, maybe she wasn't sleeping well from the trouble between her parents, which broke Ella's heart. Ella imagined her slumped against the window in one of the back seats, her light snore, her mouth open, her wavy hair sweaty. She imagined Riley's backpack beside her.

"She's not here, ma'am," the bus driver said. He was good about knowing which days to drop Riley off at Kyle's parents'.

Her heart. Her heart. It felt like someone grabbed it and wouldn't stop squeezing. She felt dizzy. Her pulse quickened, her feet tingled. "Did she get off at the wrong stop?"

"Riley left early," a boy who sat near the front called out. She couldn't see his face.

Ella climbed on to the bus and crouched down beside the boy. She'd known him since preschool. She saw his parents at school concerts and parents' nights, and she thought his name was something like Liam or Nolan. "What, honey? When?"

"They told Riley to go to the office while we were doing math." The boy had messy hair with a cowlick and wide eyes that made him look like a little owl. *Math.* Math was early in the day. Riley's favorite subject. Riley had left school early in the day and no one had told her.

She watched as the bus pulled away, some of the kids kneeling on their seats to look at her as they passed.

Annabelle's aunt, who had gotten her off the bus, stayed with Ella for a minute or so to see if she could help, but Ella ignored her as she dialed Kyle's number over and over. The street was getting busier with the afternoon traffic, and Ella stayed at the bus stop area on Hickory Lane, their modest house in the background looking plain with its basketball hoop in the driveway and garage door open.

Minutes earlier, Ella had poured a glass of lemonade for Riley and peeled her a kiwi, which sat waiting on the kitchen table. She had gotten her a pack of unicorn erasers at the store that day, and she was planning to take her to Shoe Zoo that afternoon for new sneakers. She was growing so quickly.

Ella went from being worried to just being irritated.

Maybe Riley was sent home sick, and the nurse had called Kyle, and Kyle had forgotten to let her know. Riley was probably at his parents' house, just five minutes away, propped up with a pillow on the sofa watching cartoons. She imagined Kyle's mother, Cindy, constantly checking her forehead for a fever, bringing her some chicken broth and saltines on a tray. She started to feel furious. She should be told these types of things—it often felt as though Kyle and his parents wanted her out of the picture.

He didn't answer, so she sent a text. *Do you have Riley? She wasn't on the bus.* She waited a minute for him to respond (even at their worst, he usually responded). She slowly walked up the driveway, the sound of birds chirping and a neighborhood kid jingling his bike bell down the street. The September sun was high in the sky. The leaves on the trees had started to turn.

A terrible voice deep inside her started with something dreadful (*an accident—they were both dead*) but she dismissed it. She worried too much. They'd be pulling into the driveway soon, Kyle with a sheepish expression on his face. Or he'd text her back with something quick and direct, and she'd be able to stop worrying. She could still be angry with him, and maybe she'd tell her lawyer about it, but Riley would be home and that would be that.

He wouldn't just *take* her, she kept telling herself. Was that really what her inner voice was saying? Not a terrible accident, but him ripping Riley away? No. She knew him better than that. They were going through something bitter, and she was surprised at the general ugliness of their separation, the stuff his lawyer was throwing out, how intent he seemed on getting full custody, but it wouldn't make any sense. His parents lived nearby, he'd had a job for the last ten years at the community college doing alumni relations work. He was angry and frustrated, but taking their girl would not be an option.

She called his parents' house. "Yes?" Cindy said in her usual curt voice when she realized it was Ella.

"I'm looking for Kyle. And Riley. She wasn't on the bus."

"Was it even your *day*?" his mother asked.

"Of course. Mondays and Tuesdays. Fridays and Saturdays. Did you talk to him today?"

"Not since breakfast," she said.

"A classmate said Riley left early."

"I don't know anything. I'll see if I can get him. But maybe you should call the school and find out," his mother said, and Ella hung up, annoyed that she hadn't thought of that herself.

"Mrs. Burke, your husband signed her out at nine forty-five," the assistant principal said.

"For what reason?"

"It appears there was a family emergency. That's what he told us." Then her stomach really started to flip. What family? Kyle was an only child, and Ella had just spoken with his only other family, who didn't mention an emergency. Why would he lie? What was happening? She started to feel panicky, but somehow knowing Cindy was home and answering the phone calmed her. Maybe he was surprising Riley with a trip to a museum or a show—maybe in Philadelphia or New York. Maybe he thought he'd be back in time, but he'd hit traffic.

Maybe his cell battery died. He never remembered to charge his phone. She used to do it for him. She breathed. Yes, he was being an ass, but he wasn't a criminal. She would hear from him soon.

—

Today, on the Feast of the Epiphany, or Three Kings' Day, or whatever anyone calls it, Ella takes down the few decorations she had out and puts them into a bin. She hates this apartment, and she really hates the small attic above her laundry room that she has to access on a stepladder to store things like this.

Her mom, always the optimist, told her she shouldn't be in an undecorated house during the holiday season, and it occurred to Ella that maybe the decorations, maybe some wrapped presents for Riley, would somehow return her. Her brother, Wyatt, once dated a woman who believed in the law of attraction, and she would buy a dress for a job she didn't have or sketch pictures of a mansion in the Hamptons that she said would come to her if she believed in its possibility.

So much for that.

Ella turns the heat up in this drafty place, and gathers their stockings from the spot she hung them in the hallway. When she had found Kyle's stocking with the holiday items, his name written in gold glitter, she dropped it into the garbage and poured coffee grounds on it.

Now she takes apart the small artificial tree that they used to have on a stand in their family room. She stuffs it into the bin, grabs the Christmas towels she had in the bathroom, the JOY sign that she hung above Riley's door, and the porcelain angels that stood hopefully on the bookcase. She is about to put the lid on the box when she sees Riley's few wrapped presents: a necklace with her name on it, a new pair of sneakers in a bigger size, and a pink sweater, still waiting on the end table. She picks up the presents and stuffs them into the plastic crate with everything else. It is too full, so she presses the lid down hard, crushing everything, and snaps it into place.

So much for positive thinking. So much for a holiday miracle. The Magi aren't coming. She texts Sgt. Jared Kinney. *Any new developments?* But she knows what his answer will be.

She opens up her ladder and grabs the heavy bin, her body swaying as she climbs each step. She braces the bin against her hip and pops the ceiling cover with one hand. The stale dust from the attic gets stuck in her throat, and the ladder rocks as she thrusts the bin over her head. "Fuck it," she says. "Fuck you, Kyle." She looks at the bin once more, sitting there among her other boxes in the darkness, and wonders if she'll ever see this box again, and if things will be different.

The ladder feels unsteady, wobbling as she climbs down. She can see Riley's face so clearly. Sometimes she feels like Riley watches her do these things. She imagines her fascination with the ladder, the attic, the packed-away decorations.

"Are you ever coming back to me?" Ella asks.

CHAPTER NINE

It is January 7, and Chuck forgot about an appointment at Dr. Francis's office. Nothing big, just a routine visit to check his blood pressure medication. The woman from the office is nice about the missed appointment and tells him he can come in tomorrow at ten. Chuck doesn't have a piece of paper, so he writes it on his hand the way he used to do in high school. The pen tickles his palm, and he feels like an eccentric old man.

He shuffles to the window and swears he sees an owl sitting in the tall oak tree. He squints and it just stays on its branch, so high up, staring into the house. "Hey, there," he says.

He remembers when Ben once climbed that tree, getting so far up that it made Chuck's palms sweat. "Hang on, bud. Let me get a ladder, and I'll help you down." He knew he himself couldn't climb it. Ben's blond hair was matted and sweaty, his long thin limbs relaxed as he took in the view.

"Okay, Dad," Ben said, but when Chuck returned, the long ladder from the garage dragging at his side, Ben was sitting at the picnic table. "Hi," he said, his glasses back on his face, his eyes victorious.

Chuck gasped. "How?"

"I climbed down. I want to be a mountain climber one day," his boy said proudly, and Chuck can see a clear snapshot of his smile, his teeth before braces, the satisfied expression on his small, flushed face. His boy now in his thirties, a chief information officer, working long days in that tall shiny building in

Wharton, Connecticut, and his cell phone and email constantly buzzing.

Chuck wishes Ben had time to climb trees and mountains and do whatever he wants to do. Same for Leela, who used to love setting up small scenes out of homemade objects—a fairy garden in the backyard, a tiny library on the bookshelf. He mourns that their children had to leave their childhood selves. He thinks of all his years working at Ludwig Iron and how often he felt the shift supervisor job robbed something of him—the early mornings, the mental drain on a Sunday, knowing the long week that lay ahead, the disgruntled crew that seemed to barely tolerate him, the feeling that years and years were going by and he wasn't enjoying his days.

Did he and Cat not teach the children better? Do they love what they do? He hopes so. They both excel in their fields, but he wants them to live well, to enjoy themselves. Why are things like this so hard to say when he's with them? Did he and Cat at least show their kids that maybe work is worth it? Without all those years that he hated at Ludwig Iron, they would never have had those winters in South Carolina. Is life just one big negotiation? He isn't sure. He isn't sure what it has meant, and this feeling haunts him.

He looks at the owl, and the owl holds its wings out in the air as if stretching and then puts its head down and rests.

—

He is awake the next morning listening to the news, the world outside dark and icy, only 5 a.m. and he can't go back to sleep. The minute he opens his eyes, that's it. No matter if he goes to the bathroom. No matter if he turns on his side or situates himself perfectly. He is a terrible sleeper without her.

She used to have to wake him up. She used to nudge him and call him sleepyhead or papa bear. Now he is cranky all day because he doesn't sleep enough. He holds his coffee, and all of a sudden there is a knock at the door that makes him jump. He walks slowly over to it, and sees headlights in the driveway.

"Sir," he hears, and he doesn't recognize the woman's voice. "Sir, I saw the light on. I deliver your paper," she calls through the door.

"Oh." He opens the door and his expression must be one of annoyance, but he tries to change it.

"I'm so sorry to bother you this early," she says.

"It's okay." He looks down at his slippers that have holes in them.

She wears a hat that droops at the top, and a long coat. She has bangs and fine brown hair. Her eyes glisten. "The weather is terrible, and I was worried your paper would get covered in sleet, and I was just going to tuck it inside your screen door, but I saw your light, and I know you're usually awake at this hour, and I didn't want you to hear the screen door and think someone was trying to break in. So here you go."

"Thanks. That was kind." He nods at her.

"Hope I didn't scare you."

"You didn't." She waves and starts to turn around. "Um, be safe out there," he calls.

"Thanks."

"It's awful getting up so early," he says.

"Yes. It really is." She smiles at him as if she knows him, and her face is somewhat troubled, very tired.

"Wait a second," he says, and he takes five dollars from the drawer of the hall stand. Cat always kept money there—ones and fives in a thick paper clip for pizza delivery and things like that.

He holds the bill for a second and feels a connection to his wife. "Here, buy yourself a coffee or something."

She looks down at the money. Her face seems lost, hurt or confused. "How nice," she says finally. "Thank you, sir, but really . . ."

He puts his hand up and smiles. She smiles back, but looks like she could cry afterward. She stares at the money and slips it into her coat pocket. He nods and watches through the screen door as she gets into her car, the light from her headlights shining out to him before she drives away.

—

When Leela comes over the next day, she doesn't knock, and he sees the January sun bright behind her, reflecting off the snow from the day before. She carries what looks like a cake from a bakery. Her glasses are on the top of her head, and her chunky necklace makes a jingling noise.

"There you are," he says, and her light brown ponytail bobs as she walks. When she hugs him, she whispers, "Hi, Daddy." He kisses her head, and she smells like good face cream. She has tears in her eyes as she looks around.

"For a second, when I walked up, I thought she was going to open the door and be standing there smiling." She puts her hand over her mouth. "Why does your brain trick you like that?"

For a minute, he wants to tell her everything: his longing for her mother. His inability to decide about Hilton Head. His awful fear that she'll strip this house away of all its lovely clutter and meaning. He wants to tell her that maybe he's starting to forget—he forgot that doctor's appointment the other day. He looks at her and opens his mouth, but he can't talk. "I just don't know, honey."

—

"So how are we going to do this?" she says.

"What?" He looks straight ahead as he walks toward her so the coffee won't spill. He goes back to the refrigerator for the creamer. "Sort through her stuff?" His stomach feels strange.

She nods.

He cuts one of the carrot cake muffins she brought in half and pops some into his mouth. "Actually, I've already done a few things."

"Oh, that's good."

"And there's really no rush." He feels nervous when he says this because he knows she doesn't agree. He knows she wants to bag up everything like a tornado. Her husband Isaac's parents died a couple of years ago, and Leela was instrumental in clearing out the house as though she was up against the clock. She emptied it, got it painted, and it was on the market in a week. "She doesn't fool around, that girl," Cat had said.

He wonders now if Leela will tell him to sell the house and move into some assisted-living apartment. He imagines her tossing important papers into the garbage and bringing in one of those junk removal crews to empty out his attic and basement. He takes a deep breath. He can go through it all. He just needs time.

He thinks of Cat for a second—they should have done this together. He feels abandoned.

"Nate says it's not good to let the dead keep walking the halls."

Chuck shakes his head. Nate is her friend from college. A grief counselor. Cat loved him. "Well, tell Nate I just want to have a few of her things. She's not Jacob Marley dragging chains." He imagines Cat for a second in ghost form and realizes he'd welcome that. He'd welcome her any way. He hasn't had one hint of her, and she promised him on one of their drives to Hilton Head that she would greet him often, with cardinals at the window and knocks at the door. He said he'd do the same, but now that he thinks of it, her expression seemed resigned, as if she somehow knew she'd be first.

She said she'd make the electricity surge, but the lights haven't blinked once. He hasn't even dreamed of her. Eight months and nothing.

Leela brings their coffee cups to the sink. She wipes her hands on her pants. "Well . . . shall we?"

"Let's get to it." He feels shaky. His hands feel like they're not attached to his body; his throat is all of a sudden dry. What is the rush? he wonders again.

He follows Leela up the stairs the way he used to when it was time to read her bedtime stories. He closes his eyes and wishes he could be transported back to those days—when the house was noisy and lovely, when the days seemed to stretch and sparkle. When any clothes they had in their closet, any rake or umbrella or work boots in their basement, was a by-product of their life, something they might use later, and not something that needed to be tossed away. In some ways, he never thought his children would be gone one day, or that he and Cat would fade away. Is life all about those sweet denials, the ability to trick oneself in order to be happy?

He doesn't want to bag up Cat's clothing. Any of it. He doesn't want this house to be sold one day—all this furniture, too.

He watches his daughter in front of him, and he holds on to the railing, and he doesn't want time to happen anymore—or for Cat to be forgotten.

—

If he were to go to Hilton Head, he would have to leave in a week. Well, he wouldn't *have* to. He could check in whenever he wanted.

They have the place until April, but he would have to go because Cat never wasted a day like that. She would check in to a hotel or any type of rental the second she could, even early if they let her. So if he were to go to Hilton Head, he would have to leave next week and check in the second he could, because if he goes, he wants to do it Cat's way.

But his house. *Their* house. How can he leave it so defenseless? She died in their house. Maybe by staying, he's guarding her.

He thinks of having the night watch in Vietnam, and how he would stare out into the darkness and try not to blink, because blinking was weakness, blinking led to sleep, and he had to see if anything was coming.

—

Leela stuffs four garbage bags so full that they strain and break.

"You still buy cheap garbage bags," she says. "You've learned nothing in all these years."

He laughs. "When you put two kids through college, you get thrifty."

She rolls her eyes and pulls the last two bags down the steps. The bags are big and misshapen, and he imagines them not even fitting into one of those donation bins. He wants to offer to take out anything excessive like they make you do in the airport if your bag is overweight. He imagines hoarding these things somewhere, and he wonders what Nate the grief counselor would say about that.

"So what about South Carolina?" she says now, dragging the bags to her car.

He shrugs. "I don't know, honey." He presses his lips together. "I never canceled."

She pushes the bags into her car quickly, turns to look at him. "You should go," she says. She nods as if she's agreeing with herself. "You should, Daddy."

He barely blinks. "Huh."

"I would if I were you. You probably need to in some way, no?" She gets tears in her eyes, and she smiles at him. "And I'd tell her to do the same."

"Yeah," he says quietly. "I'm thinking about it." He looks down at his feet.

She nods and looks away, wiping her eyes.

He wishes they could say more. He wishes he could pour it all out, but he keeps his guard up. Leela looks so smart and competent and beautiful. Their girl. Their beautiful girl. Is he trying to protect Leela by not saying how badly he's falling apart? That he feels himself going crazy in this house and how he forgot about that doctor's appointment the other day? He trusts Leela. Of course he does. She doesn't look like she'd throw their stuff away; she doesn't look like she'd force him into assisted living. She's a wonderful person with her own sweet family. *We did well.*

"I know it's hard," she says, and she hugs him and stays there for a minute.

"Tough stuff," he whispers, and she nods. He kisses her head. He can't think about how strange it will be to pick out something from his closet now and not see so many of Cat's coats and dresses beside his things. "I hope it'll get better."

"It has to," she says, and smiles at him, a beaming, sad smile that makes his heart leap and fall.

He taps her car window twice and watches Leela pull away. She creeps slowly down the driveway, and he makes his way up to the porch and waves.

He thinks of Cat standing beside him and waving, too. She

and Leela always got along well. They rarely fought the way some mothers and daughters do. He should have asked Leela what she remembers about Natasha. She has the best memory in the family. He sees the garbage bags through the back windows of her shiny car. He sees her Delaware license plate. He is happy she took that small bag of things for herself and Gabby: a cardigan, a few silk scarves, a clutch, and a lot of the jewelry. She has also put books of Cat's aside as well as a wood and glass valet box that she thought Ben and his husband, Asher, might want.

He feels a void as he keeps waving. He wants to call her back. He wants to break down and tell her to take him to her house, or come with him to Hilton Head.

He stands there on the porch now, lost and looking at nothing. He hears a car, but he can't snap out of this. He just stares and stares and the day seems too long.

This is no way to live, he thinks for a second.

"You're going to catch a cold," he hears someone say, and a car door slams, and it's Sal and Cocoa.

"Cocoa," he says, and she trots up to him. She pushes herself against him lightly, as if she's protecting him.

"Hey, Sal," he says, and his throat pulses. He can barely swallow. He can't help it. He's glad to see them.

CHAPTER TEN

D uring her lunch break, Ella strolls the shopping center parking lot. A big plane takes off overhead from the Lehigh Valley International Airport, just a few minutes away. Rescue Ranch, the place her neighbor David runs, is holding an adoption day.

"You came," David says, and waves. The sky is overcast, but there are bright blue and white balloons and a trailer parked in the lot with hot chocolate and pet adoption appointments inside. David wears a blue Rescue Ranch T-shirt over his usual Oxford button-down and holds the leash of a small bichon. A handful of his crew are answering questions about some cats and smaller dogs in crates.

Ella rubs the bichon's curly white head and strokes her ears. "Find any good homes?"

He shrugs. "Well, we're getting some applications filled out, so that's promising." A pretty young woman in a Rescue Ranch shirt comes over to them, smiles politely at Ella, and whispers something in David's ear. She notices that David's posture stiffens as the woman gets close to him. His ears get red. He swallows before he speaks. "We'd have to talk with their vet," he says, and she nods and walks back to the couple she was talking to. David watches her leave and then looks back at Ella. "Um, how's the bridal world?"

She puts her hands into her pockets because she worries they might start trembling, as they sometimes do. Why does she feel so uneasy everywhere now? Why doesn't she remember how to act around people? "Um, it's exactly as you'd expect. But at least things are on the quiet side today, which is much better than bridal mayhem."

She hardly ever has much interaction with David besides a polite hello, so she was surprised this morning when she was heading out the door and he was loading up his car that he said she should stop by.

She never discussed Riley with him, but she wonders if the landlady told him about her situation. She feels like he must know. He always looks at her with a concerned face, and now she thinks inviting her to the adoption event was a way for him to reach out. Or maybe he just knew he'd be near her store and wanted to tell her. Who knows? Regardless, it felt good to have something to do during her lunch break. Usually she just gets something from the vending machine and watches *Days of Our Lives* with whoever's on break at the same time.

She walks with him to the cat cages, and suddenly feels almost normal. Just talking to a friend or an acquaintance and being outside. It's cold but sunny. She notices small rips in her jacket where pieces of goose feathers stick out. David tells her how hard it is to adopt out old cats. She reaches her hand in the cage of a white cat, and the cat, Felicity, rubs her face against Ella's finger. "Hi, girl," she whispers.

The cat looks into her eyes, and it warms her. Reminds her of something. She is about to ask if he needs volunteers at Rescue Ranch. She imagines walking a dog or scooping litter or doing whatever else needs doing, especially just sitting and petting these animals, even just one Saturday a week, when a little girl walks up beside her in a way that feels so familiar, and peers in at Felicity. The presence of the child jolts her brain, and in a second, she places her hand on the girl's shoulder without thinking. She quickly pulls her hand away. "I'm so sorry," she says, but the girl isn't paying attention.

David clears his throat.

The girl, who is Riley's exact height and breathes in the same loud way Riley always did, stands there and baby-talks to the cat. Ella's heart thumps and she backs away.

"You okay?" David says.

"No," she mumbles. "My daughter."

He looks at her and shakes his head. "I heard," he says quietly.

"Oh."

He looks down at the leash, and she wonders if he's going to hand her the bichon or something, but she doesn't want a dog or cat; she doesn't want any of this. She wants the easiness of having the child she loves be that close to her again. She squeezes her eyes shut for a second. "I'm sorry, David. I need to get back to work."

—

That day in September, when Riley wasn't on the bus, Ella went to the police station. She asked for Jared Kinney, a sergeant now. He had gone to high school with her brother, Wyatt. Jared had been a constant at family dinners and sometimes even family vacations. He always teased her the same way Wyatt would, but they were friendly. Ever since Wyatt moved away and her parents bought the café in New England, she saw Jared less and less.

She had gone to the police station not because she was worried it was a full-on crime, but because she trusted Jared's ability to find out information quickly. Also, she didn't know where else to go, or whom to turn to. Jared was the only person in town who resembled family.

When Jared confirmed for her there were no accidents or incidents, he advised waiting, telling her this was more of a custody issue.

"Maybe he just needed to clear his head. Maybe he surprised her and took her to the movies," Jared said. He had been recently promoted, and Ella had occasionally seen him interviewed on the local news about a robbery or shooting. She always felt like there were two Jareds: the one in the pressed uniform with his chest stuck out, and the plainclothes one who still looked like the boy who went to the Jersey Shore with her family, who used to always ask for seconds of her mother's apple-raisin crisp.

"I think Kyle took her," Ella finally said. She realized at that moment she was biting her thumb nail, a habit she had broken as a teenager more than twenty-five years ago.

She looked at him, and was hoping he would say of course Kyle didn't. She wanted Jared to tell her he'd seen things like this hundreds of times, and they were usually misunderstandings.

But his expression gave nothing away. He kept his mouth flat, his eyes looking straight at her. He leaned against the table of the conference room they were in and crossed his arms while he listened to her. She wrongly assumed he would start making calls to track Kyle down, but instead he just nodded and said, "Yeah, I don't know."

He made it clear that he was only listening because he knew her well, that they would send anyone else to family court in a situation like this. "Since there is a shared agreement in place, we want to make sure we explore all the options before we do anything else. Right now, this is just a parent seeing his kid who basically has a right to see his kid."

"But it's not his *day*!" She paced back and forth across the conference room. "Why would he take her from school so early? Why wouldn't he be answering his phone?"

He shrugged. "I'm not trying to add to your stress, El, but sometimes there are mix-ups."

She pulled her phone out of her sweatshirt pocket again and dialed his number. Right to voice mail. Again. She wanted so badly for this to be a mistake. She would have forgiven Kyle right away if it was a mistake. Their marriage had turned so stressful and bad, but she would just be glad to see Riley, smell the strawberry shampoo in her wavy hair. She was willing to forgive Kyle whatever terrible idea he'd had if he came back. She was surprised to feel this grace for him, but all she wanted was the right pieces in place, like one of those simple-shape puzzles Riley used to do as a toddler.

Jared was looking at her, and she realized she had nowhere to go. Her garage door was still open, the kiwi and lemonade still waiting on the kitchen table with the unicorn erasers.

She had taken a pack of frozen hot dogs out to thaw, and they were on the counter. Not the most glamorous meal, but Riley loved hot dogs with Ella's homemade macaroni and cheese. They were going to eat dinner and watch that SpongeBob movie for the fortieth time after they got her new shoes. She imagined Riley racing across the back patio in them. "Did you see how fast they make me?" she would say.

Ella wanted to call her parents, or Wyatt, but she couldn't imagine what to tell them. Who did this ever happen to—except in a movie, a Lifetime movie or some thriller with Julianne Moore? How bad had it gotten that this could possibly happen?

She couldn't tell her family. She still hoped it was a mistake, and she could say to Jared, or Kyle could say, "We're sorry for the misunderstanding; we're sorry to have bothered you."

She didn't even think she would have pressed charges at that point. "I'm just grateful to have her back," she'd say. It seemed outlandish not to want justice, but all she cared about was Riley; Riley with her.

And she imagined the three of them walking out of the station then like a family, but a broken family, and Riley would be by her side, and she'd glance to see Kyle walking in the dark parking lot to his lonely car, and even though it was ridiculous and terrible to think, if he had brought Riley back that night, she might have felt sorry for him. She might have thought, "This has taken a toll on all of us."

But it didn't work out that way. For another hour, she waited at the police station. Jared had work to do, but he let her stay in the conference room, periodically peeking in to check on her. She kept dialing Kyle's phone over and over because that was the only thing she could do.

She bit her other thumb nail, and finally Jared came in, pulled out a chair, and said, "Listen, I think you should go home." In his eyes she didn't see the reckless, fun teenager she'd always known. This was a new, grown-up expression. A matter-of-fact stare.

She swallowed hard. Maybe when she got there, Kyle's car would be in the driveway. If his phone battery was dead, maybe he was waiting there with Riley, and she looked like the missing parent.

"I think it'll all work out," Jared said. He squeezed her shoulder. "She'll be bouncing through the door soon." He stood up as if to direct her to do the same. "Keep calling his mom, too."

Hours went by. Ella sat at home and knew something was wrong. How could the police do nothing and let all this time get away?

All she could see was Riley. Riley in the back seat. Riley with her school bag beside her. Riley not wanting to disappoint her father, but wondering where they were going, all those long roads in front of her she didn't know, and really, they could be anywhere by now. Even Canada. They could have taken a plane to Europe or South America.

At nine o'clock, she called Cindy again.

"No news," Cindy said, her voice sounding a little kinder. "We're worried sick. I thought they'd be home by now, and I'm sure it was a misunderstanding. But I worry something happened." She let out a long sigh, and her voice was shaky. "I just called the police myself, and they're looking into it."

Ella called Jared Kinney then, and after some prodding, he agreed to go to Cindy and Matt's house for a general welfare check, as he called it, and to take down their information. None of Kyle's stuff was disturbed, he told Ella. Kyle's clothes all seemed to be there, his laptop, his important papers.

Ella had nothing to do then. She had gotten used to quiet nights when Riley stayed at her in-laws', and she would see Riley's empty bed, the pink and green quilt folded nicely in place, all her books and stuffed animals settled, and it broke her heart, but she always knew she'd see her the next day, and she could wait. Ella could eat ice cream out of the container and watch something on Bravo.

She even liked spreading out her plans on the kitchen table for when she'd start her preschool. She had all the necessary hours in now, Pennsylvania teacher certification, a master's in early childhood education. She had finished her graduate degree part-time over the last couple of years, often subbing at local schools, and in her head, she was just waiting to find the right space to rent: something vintage and bright and dreamy. She imagined antique spring riding toys (a dolphin, a zebra) like they used to have at playgrounds, and a small picket fence with marigolds in bunches. She imagined a big welcoming sign that said Miss Ella's Learning Center.

But the preschool felt far off that night as she scraped the kiwi into the garbage disposal, dumped the lemonade, put the unicorn erasers into the utility drawer (she would see them again weeks later when she had to pack everything and move out). That night, she ate candy from the cupboard—Hershey miniatures—and drank a glass of milk and paced her lonely house, wondering where her girl was. Every option was unthinkable. Either he'd just meant to take her out for a visit somewhere as a surprise and they'd run into trouble, or he had taken her away. She couldn't comprehend either option.

She went to bed with her phone next to her head, thinking it would ring soon and Riley would be found. She imagined how her little girl would run to her even though it hadn't been very long, even though she had been camping overnight with Girl Scouts or had stayed with her grandparents and Kyle for longer stretches. But when Riley would run to her, it would seem like it had been an eternity.

She awoke early the next morning, no missed calls, and for a minute, she'd forgotten the hell she was in. In her head Riley was at Cindy and Matt's, just getting up, probably eating scrambled eggs and toast before school, and Ella was here alone, and it was the same as the routine they had gotten used to. As soon as she opened her eyes and looked around, she felt that terrible weight around her whole body again.

She hoped morning would make everything all right. She tried Kyle's phone right away. No answer.

She stood up and rushed to the front window to see if there was any activity outside. She had fully expected a call in the middle of the night to jar her, had even woken up several times to check her phone.

She tried to stay calm and positive, but a hollow sensation

pulsed through her body. She crossed her arms, wearing an old T-shirt and pajama pants, and walked down the hall to Riley's room where the sun came in, hitting the bookshelf, lighting up the snow globes Riley collected over the years: from Florida, New York City, Ocean City. Ella looked at her small desk where Riley had sat two days ago and worked on a picture book about a squirrel family. She hadn't finished it yet.

Her dollhouse sat in the corner, and Riley loved nothing more than when Ella sat with her and they set up the furniture and put the dolls at the table with the tiny fake food. The curtains rustled from the slight breeze outside, and Ella stayed there and absorbed her little girl's things and had so many terrible thoughts: what if she never came back, what if something had happened to her?

She tried to steer the whole thing back on course. He had taken her, but Riley was okay. It was the lesser of two evils. They had probably stayed at some hotel last night. She imagined Riley in a lonely bed with scratchy sheets. She imagined Kyle pacing and looking out the window every so often. She thought of how awful it must be for Riley to sleep without Mulligan, the floppy moose she had since she was two. Mulligan who came on every vacation, whom Riley used to bring in her backpack to preschool so she could peek inside and feel better about being away from home. She never went to bed without wrapping Mulligan in her arms.

On the night before Riley disappeared, she came out into the kitchen after dinner, where Ella was doing the dishes, and she asked Ella to tie a bow around Mulligan's neck.

Ella had looked up and smiled. "Is he in the mood to be fancy?"

"I want him to look like a toy someone got in an old book," Riley told Ella excitedly, and handed her a red ribbon.

"He's all set." Ella pretended to shake Mulligan's hand.

"Please come back to Mommy's Bow Service Shop again if you run into any trouble."

"I will," Riley said in Mulligan's deep voice. She walked back toward her bedroom, and the next thing Ella remembers, it was brush your teeth and good night time, and then it was the morning where Riley said she was excited for the science experiment they were going to do that day in school with a balloon. She ate oatmeal and drank two glasses of orange juice. She wore her white polo shirt and her purple cotton jumper and tights. She asked Ella for a French braid that morning, but the bus would be there any minute, so Ella just slipped her hair into a simple ponytail.

She said goodbye to Ella ("Monster hug!" Ella said as she squeezed her), and then Ella remembers Riley saying "monster hug" again and squeezing Mulligan. She remembers Mulligan still being on the kitchen table after Riley left, remembers going into her room and folding her pajamas, making her bed, and putting Mulligan right there in the center, him looking so proud in his new red bow.

With her daughter now missing, Ella stood in Riley's room and remembered the day before so clearly.

Only when Ella looked toward the bed for the comfort of at least seeing Mulligan, she noticed something awful: Mulligan was gone, too.

CHAPTER ELEVEN

Tonight, Kirsten is meeting her high school friends Amber and Saks. Saks's real name is Sarah, but everyone called her Saks because she was such a good dresser. Amber and Saks have been sending her messages through Instagram, saying they have to get together. It feels good to finally socialize. Kirsten has been out more this week than she has in months. Usually it's just work and home, but something about the air of possibility, of getting home and showering and changing outfits, feels encouraging.

When she texted her mom that she had plans with the girls, her mom sent the clapping hands emoji.

David was sweet and reserved at work today when they returned to Rescue Ranch after the adoption event. "Thanks for doing so much, Freestyle," he said, and winked.

She smiled at him and asked if he recovered from last night.

He shook his head, and his eyes twinkled. "Oh, man, I feel like I rode a horse for three thousand miles." She watched him walk away slowly. God, he made her feel nervous now. Or giddy. Or something in between. She wanted to hold his hand, to hug him. She sipped her iced coffee and imagined kissing him.

She felt like a sixth grader, so awkward in his presence, and was he being shy? What had happened last night? Did it warrant a discussion, or is that something you just do—slow dance with your boss—every now and then with no implications? She never had an office romance. Her relationships in college and postcollege were simple and clear. Her longest relationship was with Evan, whom she met her senior year in college, and they kept up a long-distance relationship for a year when he moved to Boston.

Today she wanted to go into David's office and close the door. She wanted to ask, did last night mean anything?

She doesn't know. A part of her imagines by the time she goes to Europe that maybe this will have become something. She imagines calling him from Bria's apartment, sitting on the terrace she's seen pictures of, with ivy on the wall. She imagines saying, "You'd love it here."

She meets Amber and Saks at The Gritty Goat, a bar in downtown Bethlehem. "Kirsten, how are you so beautiful?" Amber shouts, and the woman at the hostess station and a few of the busboys turn to look. The Gritty Goat has an industrial feel to it with exposed brick walls and mission-style tables. Acoustic music plays, and it's fairly crowded for a weeknight.

Kirsten spent twenty minutes doing her hair tonight, and she has a little more eye makeup on than usual. She wears heels she would never wear to work and a tight red sweater. "I almost wore leopard pants, but I thought that would be too much."

"That would have looked *hot*," Saks says. They order martinis, even though Kirsten prefers beer, and they find a free high top toward the back of the bar.

They talk about work. About the holidays. Kirsten tells them that she is heading to Milan at the end of this month (they cheer), that she has her plane ticket now, and that David was so nice about giving her a lot of time off. She wonders if she says his name with any hints of her crush, but they don't seem to notice.

Amber looks around and sips her drink. "Don't turn around, Kir, but there's a table of cute guys behind you."

"Oh." She half turns out of politeness and sees some broad

shoulders and typical college-bro button-down shirts. She turns back to her friends and shrugs.

"Kir and I can hook up," Amber says, and points to Saks. "But not you, my friend."

Saks laughs. "I swear to God, Beau wants to start trying for a baby next year." She puts up her hand in a halt sign and pulls the olive out of her drink. "I said no . . . way. Not yet, buddy."

"I can't even imagine," Kirsten says. For a second, she thinks about David's nice kids and how his face changes when he talks about them. She is about to tell them about her night out with David, but she resists. It doesn't feel right. Maybe she wants to protect what's there, like a small match flame you keep your hand over. She can tell them another time, if it ever becomes anything.

They drink and talk more about their jobs and about trips they want to take. They say they should get a place at the shore for a week this summer. They want to hear about Bria's wedding in Switzerland, and they touch their hearts when Kirsten tells them what she knows. When Kirsten says Bria asked her to be maid of honor, they sigh. On their second round of drinks, Saks goes outside to call Beau, and one of the guys says something to Amber, so Amber starts up a conversation and realizes they share mutual friends from NYU.

Kirsten sits there politely, looking at the people coming and going. A woman asks if she can take Amber's stool and Kirsten shakes her head. She thinks of her dad when he was younger and imagines he would like this place. It feels good to be out again, but a part of her just wants to retreat to her comfy clothes and quiet house. She sees Saks pacing back and forth as she talks on the phone outside, her head tilting back in laughter every so often. Amber is talking more loudly now (the martini effect), and has the idea to push their two tables together. Kirsten stands dutifully, and now Amber is laughing, and the five or so guys have descended upon them, signaling for drinks all around.

Kirsten pushes her stool next to Amber and smiles at the men. She is not interested. She feels way too old, even though they all seem to be the same age, and she decides she'll finish this drink and head home. Someone brushes against her shoulder then, and the scent of cologne is familiar.

"If it isn't Kiki!"

She turns and sees Grayson's face. His mouth pulls into a wide grin. She just saw him at work today, but now she is so near his hazel eyes and strong nose. She notices his hair has grown in and is thicker than his usual buzz cut, and she sees his Adam's apple and tanned neck. "What are you doing here?" she says, and they hug.

Does he seem a little drunk? She can't tell. He's always jolly. She might be tipsy, too. She has been taking the second martini slowly.

He shakes his head and gives her a giddy smile. "Did we interrupt your girls' night? I think Trey has a thing for your friend here." He gestures his thumb toward Amber and a guy with a cropped beard.

"She seems to be fine with that," Kirsten says.

"And look at Kiki with a martini."

She shrugs. "Want to trade?"

"Here," he says, and hands her the new beer the server just gave him. She sips it, and it's cold and perfect. He leans in when he talks, and she studies his face. She never noticed how long his eyelashes were. She is about to give the server what's left of her martini, but Grayson puts up his hand and says, "Whoa. There's still some perfectly good beverage left." Her eyes widen and she laughs when he drinks it.

"Grayson Bond," she says, and touches his shoulder. She's not drunk, and she's glad she's not because the night feels fun now and full of possibility.

He does a Sean Connery accent and then finishes the whole drink. "Waste not, want not," he says.

"What about germs, Grayson?"

"Like you have any." He folds his arm on the table and looks at her. It feels nice to be with him. She always liked him, but now he fills her with a lightness, a hopeful energy she wants more of. When he first started at Rescue Ranch a year or so ago, he used to ask her and David if they wanted to have drinks after work. David was always busy, and she didn't want to go alone, but now she wishes she had taken him up on that offer. "We can stay in the kingdom of beers for the rest of the evening."

"Let it forever be ale," she says.

"Are you really going to leave me for a month to go to Europe?" he says, and arches one eyebrow. "David will make me do all your stuff, and you know the custodian—Bryce or Bruce or whatever his name is—hates my ass and won't do anything I ask." He orders another beer, and turns to her. "Plus, we'll all be in a deep depression without you around."

She shakes her head. "I think you'll be fine."

"Wow, new friends!" Saks says now, pulling up a stool next to Amber, and Amber claps her hands and orders a vodka cranberry.

An hour goes by, and they're all talking loudly. Amber says Kirsten and Grayson look cute together, and Saks has to go home to see her husband. A group of younger girls are talking to some of the other guys, and Amber and Trey are having a serious conversation. Amber keeps reaching up and touching his cheek, and Trey nods thoughtfully and listens. "I'm done with dating apps," Kirsten hears Trey say, and Grayson brings her another beer.

"Or did you hit your limit, Kiki?" he says.

She takes stock and doesn't feel too bad. Driving is out of the question, but that's why she got an Uber in the first place tonight. "One more beer, and I'll be perfect," she says, and they clink bottles.

He drums his hands on the table. "I was about to leave before I saw you," he says, and smiles. His teeth are white and straight. She likes the perfect line of his jaw.

She looks over at Amber, who is resting her head on Trey's shoulder now and singing along to a song. "Well, if you hadn't found me, I'd be their third wheel."

"Yeah, right," he says, looking at the other guys. "You think these hyenas wouldn't be circling you?" He pauses. "I mean, look at you . . . sorry, that's probably unprofessional."

She looks down. She doesn't blush this time. She lets the compliment wash over her, and she believes him. God, he is handsome. Tall, fit. And he's kind. She can tell he was the kid in high school who talked to everyone, and no one disliked him. "I was gonna leave before I saw you, too."

She wonders now why she always lets Grayson fall in her imaginary game of him and David hanging off cliffs. Why does she always choose David? With Grayson right near her, young and kind of in the same place of life she is, he seems like a fine choice. He at least seems worth saving half, or even a third of the time. Now she realizes she's touching his arm as they talk, and he doesn't pull away.

"How come we don't do this at work?" he says, and laughs.

She shrugs. "Because we're saving animals . . . and not drinking."

He looks over at Amber and Trey. He looks back at her. "We could take a walk." He clears his throat. "My apartment's on

Market Street," he says, and the words hang there for a few moments. She feels a nervous excitement. "I mean, I have records we could listen to." He raises his eyebrow again and gives her a cheesy smile, and she feels heat through her whole body.

She says bye to Amber, and Amber stands to give her a hug and sloppy kiss. "Want me to call you a car?" Kirsten asks her.

"No, thanks," Amber says. "Trey is a good guy."

"He actually is," Grayson whispers. "He and his parents volunteer for Meals on Wheels. She'll be safe. I've known him since junior high."

"Ah, well I trust the Grayson endorsement." Kirsten waves as she slips into her coat.

The sidewalks are shoveled clean, but a light snow covers the parked cars and the small front yards of the historic district's townhouses. They walk by shops that are still lit inside and old houses with electric candles in the windows. An occasional Moravian star hangs on some porches, which she loves. Grayson's apartment is on the second floor in an old house above a dentist's office. When they start to walk up the somewhat crooked steps, she holds his hand. What is she doing here with him? She doesn't know. But she likes the feeling.

He twists the key into the lock, and there is a lamp on inside. There is a small table near the kitchen with just two chairs and a lot of paperwork, probably from the graduate program he's finishing up. On the couch is a pillow with a faded pillowcase of polar bears and a worn blanket folded neatly. "Sorry, I'm a messy bastard." The kitchen counter has a dish rack with two white plates drying.

"You're not too messy," she says, and takes off her coat. "I think it's charming." His place feels cozy, and she imagines how good it would feel to have your own apartment like this. Maybe that should be her next step.

"Charming," he repeats.

She nods. They wait there for a second, and she looks around. He smiles at her.

"Want a drink or something?" he says. "I think I have some beer. Or a seltzer?"

She shakes her head. She feels her stomach tighten. Her knees are trembling. His apartment feels so far away, and safe.

"Kiki, we don't . . ." he says. "I mean, we can just hang out, and then I can call an Uber."

That is probably a good idea. She doesn't know why she agreed to come over. Being next to him tonight felt so good that she wanted it to continue. His smile, his buoyant conversation made her not want the night to end. But when she thinks about walking back down those stairs, leaving this cheerful place, she feels a stubbornness overtake her. *No.* She feels fearless tonight. "Grayson," she says, and his name just hangs there.

She steps out of her heels, kicking them to the side. She stands on her tiptoes and he bends down to kiss her. She knows this is why she's here, and why she doesn't want to leave. She could feel his magic in the bar, and she wanted to chase it. She wants his vitality, his goodness. Now as she kisses him, his lips taste cool.

She rests her hands on his shoulders. He keeps kissing her, and she thinks about David, in a white T-shirt and pajama pants, turning out the lights in his apartment or looking in on his sleeping children.

She should tell Grayson she danced with David and she didn't know what it meant. She should say she would have let David kiss her, and that she has been thinking about him so often. She should pull away now before her job becomes the most complicated place ever.

But she doesn't care if it's right or wrong, thoughtless or selfish. His hands on her, his mouth—it feels safe. She loves his whispers. His quiet, calm apartment. She's happy. She feels the warmth from his skin, and she doesn't want to pull away.

He pulls the red shirt over her head, and she unbuttons his shirt, and he looks as good as she imagined he would. He walks her into his bedroom, and peels back the comforter and places her gently into the bed. She watches him look down at her, and he slides under the covers beside her.

She wants this. She does. She reaches for him and pulls him against her as tightly as she can.

—

Her mother is asleep, and the dogs are quiet when she gets home after midnight. She still smells hints of Grayson's cologne on her body, and she holds her shoes and tiptoes around the house with just the glow of the light over the stove. He asked her to stay, but the Uber she'd already called was only two minutes away. He walked her to the door, shirt off, wearing sweatpants, waving to her from the top of his steps.

When she left, she thought about seeing him at work tomorrow and what he would say, and started to feel guilty about David. Would he notice if she and Grayson acted strangely? Would he be able to tell from their body language that something had happened? She tried to shrug it off. She wants to be a person who views the world lightly now, more like her father, who didn't get ruffled about anything.

She gets herself a glass of water and finds herself slipping into her dad's office that her mother sometimes uses. She turns on the green banker's lamp on his desk and looks around. So many books on the built-in shelves. He loved Lucille Clifton and Seamus Heaney, W. S. Merwin and Sylvia Plath. He loved to read the same books over and over, *The Bell Jar* with the cover frayed and so many pages dog-eared.

His big dracaena plant has stayed alive in its pot by the window, and she looks out at their wide, smooth yard, a covering of snow and ice, and tries to see what he always saw.

She looks at his small bulletin board and sees a poem he pinned there: "The Telephone Repairman," by Joseph Millar. She reads it and two lines near the end jump out at her:

> *We live so much of our lives*
> *without telling anyone.*

She thinks of dancing with David. She thinks of being with Grayson and not wanting it to end. She thinks of all her private thoughts, and she puts her hands on the big wooden desk and breathes in the silence.

She is the only person who can solve this. No one knows what's right for her except her.

It is liberating and terrifying. She is living her life with hardly any witnesses. She thinks about Europe. About vet school. About the men she likes at work. She imagines her grandmother's hugs and kisses in Milan, the streets that her young father walked before all this happened, before he took a risk and went to the country that rewarded him and then swallowed him whole.

It's time, she thinks, and she looks out the window at the stars and the patient winter sky.

CHAPTER TWELVE

I t is dark when Ella makes her way home from the bridal shop. She parks her car and sees someone on the porch of David's place below her. She grabs her bag with the soup and half a sandwich and makes her way up the sidewalk.

She thinks about how she almost fell apart at the Rescue Ranch adoption event, and she means to apologize to David, but she feels it's best to just let it drop. She doesn't know him that well, and maybe he didn't think too much of it. Maybe as a parent it made sense to him.

"Wait, Blair," David says now, and he rushes outside and closes the door behind him, probably so the kids don't hear. Ella holds her bag and walks past them, a polite half smile on her face, not making eye contact. "You're just going to do that? No talking it over?"

The guy is always calm and polite, and Ella has never heard him so animated. Ella puts her hand on the railing, and sees Blair, the mother, walking toward her running Range Rover, dismissing him with her hand. "I'm not doing this now."

He rushes after her, his sneakers crunching on the bed of snow. "Coop's crying in there. Stella's comforting him. We can't keep doing this."

She turns around, and Ella stands in the shadows of her steps and can't stop watching. She feels so many familiar feelings: that awful sense of impasse, that feeling that you can shout as loud as you want and the other person won't hear you. "Stop, David.

You're always the saint. I'm always the villain. You can go right back in there and make yourself the hero."

He shakes his head. "I don't want to be the hero," he yells. "I want to see them for Easter. It's almost three months away. I wasn't even thinking that damn far." His face looks red under the glow of the streetlight, and she hears his voice crack. "That's all I want. To see them."

Blair clicks her tongue, and then she looks in Ella's direction, so Ella hurries up the steps. "Since when do you care?" Ella hears her say, and then they are whispering and Ella goes into her apartment.

For a few minutes, she keeps the lights off. She pulls out her kitchen chair and sits down and puts her head in her hands. She hates the unhappiness. She hates what this is probably doing to those two kids who love their parents. She hears his door open downstairs and his voice has changed. She recognizes the "everything's okay" voice parents force for kids. She can't make out his words, but she's happy he's trying for them.

She imagines Riley's face. What made Kyle do it? She takes off her coat and reaches inside her bag and eats a piece of the baguette that came with her soup. She thinks for a second that her neighbor and his ex are lucky—that they are still talking, as bad as it seems. She wants to go down to his apartment and say, "It could be worse, buddy. It could be much worse."

—

The day Kyle took Mulligan off Riley's bed, he also took three pairs of her pants, at least five shirts, and two of her favorite games (Hi-Ho! Cherry-O and Uno) from her closet. Ella figured things out after a couple of hours, and over and over again, she kept kicking herself for not being home at the time and wondering if he brought Riley to the house while he packed those things.

She has this image now in her head of Riley sitting in the car in the driveway while it idled—it must have been about ten in the morning, maybe right after he signed her out of school. Of course he could have gone to the house before he picked Riley up, but in her gut, she sees Riley sitting in the car outside.

Maybe Riley thought a good surprise was about to come. Ella wonders if Kyle coming into their house seemed so normal that Riley thought Ella was inside, and thought maybe Ella was okay with the idea of him taking Riley away, which makes Ella feel ill and blood-drained. *I had no idea, Bitsy-Boo. I didn't know.*

Why was Ella out of the house that day, of all times? How many mornings was she mopping the floor at that exact moment, or putting together a small grant proposal for the preschool program right at the kitchen table?

But that day, she drove by the ugly cement building up for sale in nearby Hellertown that once was a used car place and then just a mechanic's. She tried to imagine Miss Ella's school there, but the broken windows and kicked-in door were discouraging. She parked the car and stood for a moment and squinted, and she could imagine painting the building a cheerful color: light blue, maybe a pale yellow. She could, for a second, imagine potted plants, the white picket fence, the sign. She imagined parents parking in the wide lot, where all the used cars once were, and dropping their children off at the front door.

She started to like the idea, and she decided to kick it around in her head for a bit. She then headed to Wegmans for the kiwis, the lemonade, a new jar of relish for the hot dogs they would have that evening.

Everything that day felt like a mistake, a misuse of time. Some horrible cosmic arrangement of events that prevented her from seeing Kyle's car in the driveway, Kyle coming out of the house with the bag of stuff, or Riley in the car. *Mommy's here. Mommy's here.*

She had spent at least twenty minutes vacuuming her Jeep at the gas station, but when she went to take it through the automatic car wash, it just made a buzzing sound, and the teenage girl who worked there came strolling out. "Sorry, it's out of order," she told Ella. So then Ella had to wait until she processed the nine-dollar refund, and her car stayed dirty from that day on.

The worst thing she did that day, the thing she regrets most, was going to the lake by Freeland Park. She had driven by, and the sun was exquisite on the water, and a family of geese huddled around the edge, and it just looked so picturesque that she had to park the car and stand there and stare at the beauty of early fall. She held her coffee and took in the scene. She keeps imagining the juxtaposition of her at the lake and Riley in the car being driven away, and it stabs her heart.

She never seemed to have free time, and that day, she saw the water and the geese, and she thought, why not? The housework can wait. The next grant proposal can wait. Another application for a teaching job can be done tomorrow. She never stopped and smelled the roses, and she told herself, *this is okay. You need this. You're going through a terrible time.*

At the lake she had breathed in and out and wished she and Kyle could have peace. Whether they divorced or not, she just wanted the fighting to end.

Where had this started? she wondered that day. They had turned so bitter toward one another. They seemed to have outgrown each other. He was intolerant of her desire to get the preschool going, and she was intolerant of his parents, of his late hours at work, of his compulsion to always look at his phone. He wanted Riley to play softball. Ella wanted their daughter to be a free spirit: art classes, hours at the library.

They had started to disgust each other. She hated the grunts he made when he chewed a bagel. When she laughed on the phone with her mother, she saw him stare at her like he wanted to choke her. In the beginning, she thought they were tired, and this was just a phase. A fighting phase. She had asked Cindy to watch Riley one Friday night, and they went to an Italian restaurant. The silence was terrible. When she looked at his face, she had a feeling she couldn't explain. He was finished with her. She wanted to cry. It was unfixable.

Unfixable because they had gone in different directions. Or maybe they had never really loved the real people they were, just the idea of who they each thought the other was. Maybe because they had stopped going to bed at the same time, stopped sleeping together, they had disconnected. They used to shower together, grocery shop together, split up the pile of bills and Christmas cards and write them out together. At some point, all of those things had fractured one by one, and their marriage was the sum of all those tiny broken parts.

So one day Kyle had picked their daughter up at school, had put the garage code in, come into the house, grabbed Mulligan and the other things, and Ella knew nothing about it. Looking back, she wonders now, when she came home that day, had anything seemed off? Did she sense his bad energy? Were his footprints in the carpet?

She had come home and put her groceries away and not suspected a thing. *You're just a bored housewife*. Kyle told her this once, and she has thought of that statement every day. She taught full-time before Riley, and then after Riley, she had gone to graduate school and subbed and put together plans for her preschool. But if she hadn't been bored, would she have been out staring at the lake, trying to let the hours go by? In fights, he had said other awful things: that she smothered Riley, that one day Riley would grow up and be happy to get away from her. He told her she was frigid, passive, and once, in a cruel moment, he said she was dull.

She looks back on that day he took Riley and hates her utter cluelessness. She could have come home and seen him driving away. Maybe the expression on his face would have alerted her. Maybe she could have recognized the wrongness and stopped him. Maybe she would have seen Riley in the back seat and followed them. She would have run every red light to keep up.

When Jared Kinney came to the house after she called him about Mulligan, he had his usual poker face and nodded as she told him what was missing. "And you're sure he entered the property?" he said.

"Completely." She stood by her kitchen table, holding on to the back of a chair, and the whole house no longer felt like hers. It felt like something she'd already lost.

—

Ella hears a tap at her door. She doesn't make a sound. Should she even answer it? She imagines David's wife telling her to mind her own business. She imagines David saying that he's sorry. She knows it isn't good news—it's never good news anymore, but she opens the door, and Cindy is standing there.

"Ella," she says.

Ella covers her mouth with her hand. Does Cindy have something to tell her? Is it bad? She feels her stomach drop, her ears ring.

As if she can hear her thoughts, Cindy shakes her head. "No news," she says.

"Oh." Ella takes a breath. "Okay." She focuses on her mother-in-law's face to calm herself down. Cindy's short blond hair, her brown eyes that look tired, her skin with too much makeup. She doesn't look good. Why is she here? "Want to come in?" Ella asks without thinking.

Cindy stays in the doorway, her big coat specked with snow-flakes. "I just wanted to check on you," she says.

"You did?"

Cindy nods. "And say sorry."

"Sorry? For what?" They are in the dark with just the glow of the light over Ella's front door. Ella's hands start to shake, and Cindy takes them and holds them.

"I'm sorry for raising someone who would do something like this," she says. "You deserved so much better."

Ella shakes her head. "I don't care about him." She feels Cindy's fingers on her hands, and they lock eyes. "I just want *her*."

"Of course you do." She touches Ella's shoulder. "They'll find her."

Ella starts crying. "She's gone."

"They'll find her. They will, and she'll come back here." Cindy's tears streak her face. "And he won't be our son anymore." She cries harder.

Ella hugs Cindy, not because she feels pure love for her but because it feels good to be in someone's arms, and the way Cindy looks matches how awful she's been feeling. Ella whispers, "Why? Why did he?"

"I wish I knew," Cindy says. Her tears are wet on Ella's sweater, and outside Ella sees the poplar tree's skeleton shift in the wind.

CHAPTER THIRTEEN

W hat's all this?" Sal asks.

Chuck makes Cocoa shake hands with him before he gives her a treat, and her teeth snap gently when she catches it in the air. Then he looks over in Sal's direction and sees Sal studying the pile of summer clothes and set of sheets and other supplies in the corner of the living room. "I'm just sorting things out."

"You're packing up?"

"No, not really."

"I didn't think you were going this year."

Chuck pauses. Since when the hell does he have to run his decisions by Sal? "I'm not planning on it." He's just *considering* it. And that's exactly what the items are for—an open suitcase, a couple of shopping bags with groceries and cleaning supplies. In case he decides to go, he's going to need to have his stuff ready.

Hilton Head still seems like the shining destination it always was. But he doesn't look forward to it the way he once did, and he gets more and more wary of leaving his house. What if it catches fire and no one's around to put it out? What if someone breaks in?

On the other hand, he feels like he's letting Cat down if he doesn't go. He knows she would hate to see him limping around this quiet house. *Is this all you intend to do, handsome?*

He has been making lists, he puts things in piles. It feels strangely similar to when they used to prepare to leave. He always liked how their house just seemed to hibernate and wait for them while they were gone. Over the years, hardly anything ever went wrong with it when they left. Once, the roof leaked over the den because there was too much snow on top, and once a squirrel had gotten into the eaves of the attic.

He wishes someone would guarantee him the house would be okay. Then he could leave.

Sal walks over to the living room and plops beside him on the couch. "Mind if I turn on the news?" he says.

"Okay."

Sal fumbles with the remote, and the four o'clock news comes on. Sal stares straight ahead at the screen. "You know, I'd go with you if you wanted. I mean, I'd drive down with you and fly back or something . . . so you wouldn't have to be alone."

Chuck looks over at him. Sal keeps watching the TV. His glasses have slipped down on his nose. His sweater has lint on it. There are cracks and lines on his face, and for one second, Chuck wants to smile.

"More snow coming." Sal crosses his arms and shakes his head at the forecast.

—

Ben calls the next day. "Hey, Dad."

"My boy." He cradles the phone between his shoulder and ear and counts out twenty Tylenol, twenty Advil, and twenty aspirin and puts them in a ziplock bag. Cat used to wonder why they took so much stuff. "There *are* stores down there, you know," she'd say, but he hated to waste money. He liked to be prepared. "What've you been up to?" he says into the phone. "How's Asher?"

"He's good. He just got a paper accepted to a conference in London in April."

"Wow. Please tell him congratulations for me." He almost says for *us*, but he stops.

He is so proud of his children—they both married well, too. Isaac, Leela's husband, manages award-winning restaurants in Southern Delaware, and Asher is a college professor in sociology with a doctorate from Yale. Chuck wishes Ben could see the smile on his face. When each of the kids got married, he felt a little bereft, but Cat was beaming. "How could we be sad?" she'd said. "They're happy. Our job is done."

"I was thinking, you should meet us there. You liked England, didn't you?" Ben says.

"Oh, sure. Your mom and I stayed in London once and then went to the countryside in Devon. We loved listening to music in the pubs. We saw thatched roofs and castles. Your mom wanted to get to Scotland, but we ran out of time." He seals his bag of pills. He puts some window cleaner in another bag, along with a roll of paper towels and a handful of big and small garbage bags. He can't quite picture himself at the beach, cleaning up, taking out the garbage. But he imagines a long winter of just him in this house, and that feels unthinkable, too.

Isn't that what he and Cat were doing each year? Escaping? Avoiding the reality of winter, and aging? Cat used to say they were different people in Hilton Head: more social, and fun loving. He listens to Ben talk about where they're staying in London, and he thinks of this idea of having different selves. Cat was right. She was always right. He was a different person around her. He's a different person alone. He's different with his kids and doesn't tell them everything, and he was different with his parents, too. Was the Cat who liked being with Natasha a different self of hers? Did she enjoy being this other person?

He hears Ben pause. "Yeah, England's terrific, but don't worry about me. You two go and have good fun there. Take Asher out somewhere to celebrate. I'll give you money."

Ben laughs politely. Chuck remembers his son probably makes more than he ever did.

"By the way," Chuck says. "You know who I was thinking about?"

"Who?"

He drums his fingers on the guest room dresser. "Natasha." He says her name quietly.

"From that diner?"

"Yeah. Do you remember anything about her?"

"Not really. Just that Mom felt sorry for her."

"Yeah." He forgot how much they kept from the kids. Different selves. He always half wondered what they would have thought of Cat's plan, whose side they would have taken in the disagreement that ensued. "I was thinking of looking her up."

Ben clears his throat. "Um, why? I mean, what would be the point?"

"Just to say hi, tell her about your mom. She'd probably want to know, wouldn't she?"

"If she Googled Mom's name, an obituary would come up."

The thought stuns him. He hates that this is Cat's last record. He wonders now if Natasha does know about her death. "I guess it isn't important then."

When he hangs up, he feels heavy with disappointment. He had hoped Ben would know something about Natasha, that he would remind Chuck of something he missed or recall another thing Cat had said about her, a place she lived. Is Ben right not to think it was important? Has Chuck blown a small moment from their past into something bigger than it should be? Wouldn't it be easier to forget Natasha and the pain from that period of their lives? The night Cat didn't come home. How he lay there all night on the sofa hoping she would come back. He actually would like to forget Natasha.

He carries the supplies up to the guest room where he has started to amass all the potential Hilton Head stuff. He doesn't want Sal to comment on any of it. He imagines that if he decides to go, he'll pull out very early one morning and leave a note taped to the door.

—

Sal calls the next morning to see if he wants to come over for lunch. "Marguerite thought you might want pizza. She made the dough herself."

Chuck happily agrees, hangs up the phone, and folds a selection of spring and summer clothes, some socks and underwear, and a sweatshirt. He zips them into his suitcase. He walks into their bathroom and pulls the toiletry bag out from under the sink. It's blue and quilted with green paisley on it, the size of a purse. Cat had it forever. He starts to unzip it, and something grips him.

He sees her travel toothbrush, her bar of Dove soap in the plastic case, her small bottle of perfume she bought in London, her hand lotion, her pink razor, and he feels the floor get wobbly. He shouldn't have opened the bag.

There is barely anything of his: a small bottle of Barbasol, nail clippers, a travel-sized deodorant, some aftershave. Otherwise, she is the whole bag: her Listerine, her eye cream, a small bottle of pink nail polish, and he sobs in a loud way that echoes through the house. How can he not bring these things with him if he goes? How can he toss them aside?

She was the whole damn thing. She was 90 percent of them.

He covers his mouth, and he remembers quick flashes of being in South Carolina. He remembers the kite she bought there one year. He saw it in the back of the car wrapped in plastic, green and yellow and blue with a long tail, and he said, "What's this?"

"I was waiting for a windy day," Cat said. That smile. That generous smile.

And he feels a sinking pain now that they never took that kite out. What became of it? Did she feel foolish and donate it? Did she toss it into the trash? Why didn't he wake her one morning and say, "Hey, today's our kite day." And even if the wind was stingy and barely there, he could have tried to make it ripple in the sky, its proud colorful chest puffed out, its tail swishing as it rose in the air. For her.

He remembers another time when she wanted to feed the ducks. She had a bag of old bread, but he said his back hurt. It did. When his back hurt, when he had that tension between his shoulder blades, it almost incapacitated him. "Maybe a stroll to the lake will help?" she said, and he was crabby and said, "Not today," and now he remembers her slipping quietly out the door, holding her plastic bag of bread pieces.

God, if she had lived, if she had pulled through, he would do anything now to go feed the ducks with her. That expanse of deck and gazebo, the fountain splashing up in the middle of the water. Those majestic ducks gliding in when they saw her, their mouths open as if in line for communion. The whole world knew she was special.

Is Natasha an extension of this? Just another small regret among all the regrets he has? Why does she feel so important? Why did that fight over her dent him so badly?

He examines Cat's cosmetics and remembers last year how she started to have that pain near her hip as they were getting ready to go home. "You probably went too hard on the bike," he told her.

"Maybe," she said. "It's just so darn tender." He can see her there in the kitchen, making that pained face as she rubbed her side, the instructions for tenants on the refrigerator behind her.

And now all of a sudden he remembers the small chalkboard in that kitchen, where she always wrote messages: *Keep on trucking* (her favorite), or *Another sunny one!*

On their last day there, she wrote in her careful cursive, *So long, farewell!*

—

A few hours later, Marguerite smiles as Chuck compliments the lunch. She washes their dishes in the sink and hands them to Sal to dry. "I'm so glad you enjoyed it. Anytime," she says. She walks over to the coffee maker and puts three scoops of decaf into the basket.

"You're lucky she cooked and not me," Sal says, and he places the creamer and a bowl of sugar cubes in front of Chuck. Cocoa lies in her green bed at the bottom of the staircase and occasionally gives Chuck a one-eyed glance.

Marguerite wipes her hands on a dish towel. "I made Jell-O for dessert. Nothing special."

Chuck feels like he's been here too long. Whenever he's out, he has the feeling he should be getting home. What is that feeling, that need to guard the house? He never had it before she died, but now he is attached to that place, like it's a roped-off exhibit of their marriage. Some nights he dreams of the house being empty, and he wakes up startled, sweating. Yet when he's home, he gets tired of the quiet and the long stretches of nothing. "I love Jell-O."

"Catherine used to make it with fruit cocktail, didn't she?"

"Yes. That's right." God, how he loves hearing her full name.

He wants to stand up and hug Marguerite for bringing her into the conversation.

"Well, this is just regular. Sorry."

"That's fine. I like it either way."

She smiles at him. "My goodness, I miss that woman. I think about her at least twice a day."

Chuck nods. He looks into Marguerite's brown eyes. He wants her to know it's okay to say Cat's name. Keep going, he thinks. He feels greedy for more of this moment. He loves that it feels normal, like Cat could be right here in the house, maybe washing her hands in the powder room. "I think about her . . . nonstop." He looks over at Cocoa, and she's sound asleep.

"Do you ever talk to her?" Marguerite says, and Sal leans in to hear his response.

"What's that?"

"Do you ever talk to her? When you're alone, I mean." Her face is flushed. "Sorry if that's too personal. But I mean, I would. If I were alone, I'd talk to her just because it probably feels natural."

"It does." He pauses. "And I do." He stares at the coffee maker and listens to the slurping sound of it brewing. He waits for a moment. "I say, 'Now what, Cat? Now what?'"

It's true. He says that at least once a day. He never thought he'd tell anyone, but Marguerite asked, and she looks so sincere at her place at the table, her hands smoothing the lace of the tablecloth. He feels such relief. He also says, *Where are you, Cat? Where the hell did you go?*

The kids never ask him questions like this, and he never asks them. Once, he almost asked Leela if she had dreams about Cat, but he couldn't for some reason. Their loss is too parallel. Has he failed them by not being the dad they could talk to about this? If he had died, wouldn't Cat have been so good at letting them express their pain? Wouldn't she have shared hers with them? Her instincts were right on the money with the kids. She knew when to run in, when to pull back, whose name to say, whose name not to say.

"You're doing good," Sal says now with surprising sincerity. "I've wanted to tell you that." He gets quiet. "I don't know how you get out of bed."

Chuck has to look away. His ears ring. "Thanks, pal."

"And if or when you're not doing so good," Marguerite says, "be patient with yourself." She reaches over and puts her hand on his arm. "This is the hardest thing you'll ever go through," she says.

He takes a breath. He's about to bring up Natasha, but he doesn't want to risk it. If Marguerite doesn't know about her, about the fight that happened over her, he doesn't want them to see him and Cat differently. They eat Jell-O and have their coffee, and he feels his back loosen and his shoulders relax.

Around one o'clock, he stands and gets his coat. "This has been nice," he says. "Many, many thanks."

"We're happy to have you," Marguerite says. She hands him some slices of pizza wrapped in foil, and a sandwich bag of snicker-doodles. "For the road," she says. "I mean, for home. For later."

Sal puts a hand on his shoulder. "What about the road? You think you'll go?"

Marguerite looks back and forth between them. "To South Carolina? Oh, is that in the works?" Chuck studies her expression, and she seems genuinely surprised. He thought Sal would have told her.

"I'm thinking about it." He wipes his forehead. "I mean, we made the reservation. We paid for it."

"That might be good for you. Would the kids visit?"

Chuck shrugs. "I'm not sure if they can, but I'd be okay on my own." Why hasn't he asked Leela if she and Isaac and Gabby would come? He didn't even mention it to Ben. He smiles at Marguerite's concern. "We know some people there—I mean, I do."

"And I said I could go," Sal says.

"You?" Marguerite laughs. "That would defeat the purpose of a vacation." Cocoa barks when the mailman steps onto the porch and the mailbox makes a quick clanging sound.

Chuck looks at Cocoa and feels nervous for a second. He smiles. "Actually, I do have a favor to ask." He looks at the two of them. "If I go, could you look after the house, maybe? Check for packages and make sure snow doesn't stay on the roof?"

Sal smiles and nods. "Absolutely!" Marguerite says.

He swallows. He holds the foil-wrapped pizza, the sandwich bag of cookies. Can he make this next request? He thinks he will. He looks up at them. "And could I, uh, bring Cocoa with me?"

The question hangs there in the air. He sees Sal and Marguerite's puzzled faces. They stare at each other in a silent conversation the way couples do, the way he used to be able to do with Cat. Cocoa stretches and closes her eyes again.

"What am I saying?" Chuck finally says, his face flushed. "Forget that part."

Sal looks at him and then at Marguerite. He offers a polite smile. "How many miles per gallon does that car get anyway?"

CHAPTER FOURTEEN

The night after being with Grayson, Kirsten shows up at work as early as possible. She seemed to get out of bed more quickly, eat her breakfast more quickly, and every traffic light seemed to be on her side. She didn't know what force was pulling her there because when she woke up she mostly felt awkward and thought for a second about taking a sick day.

She enters the front door, and only one of the lights is on in the long hallway. The floor seems to be freshly waxed, and there is a note on her desk from Bryce that tells her they are almost out of alcohol wipes. She keeps her coat on and turns the heat up a few degrees. Maybe she wanted to be here early so she could position herself at her desk and not be surprised by anyone.

What will Grayson say when he sees her? What will David think if she and Grayson are too friendly with one another? She has no poker face. And shouldn't she have mentioned to Grayson that perhaps there was something happening between her and David? What a mess she's made.

She listens to her voice mail, sorts some paperwork, looks at notes left from Peggy about payroll, and goes into the small dog room to see Gloria, the bichon who is supposed to be adopted today if all goes well.

"Hey there, sweetie," she says, and Gloria wags her tail. Kirsten clips her leash on and takes her out the back door. As she walks by the offices, she sees Grayson's desk is still dark, and there is no light from David's office. The fish in the aquarium glide back and forth, and she just hears her footsteps and Gloria's small paws padding behind her.

Out back, she studies a clump of oak and pine trees, the trails that are part of Rescue Ranch's property where the volunteers walk dogs. She heads in that direction then notices a man sitting on the bench against the building with his head in his hands.

He wears a hat and gloves and his camel coat. His leather briefcase sits by his feet, and a reusable coffee mug from Sheetz is next to him. She should just leave him to himself, but the door slams behind her, and Gloria lets out a small bark when she sees him. He looks up. "Hey, David," she says.

"Oh, hey." He gives her a half smile.

"What are you sitting in the cold for?" She unclips Gloria, who sniffs around the large section of grass.

He cracks his knuckles. This man with the sunken expression in the old camel coat looks nothing like the guy who sat beside her on the ski lift. "Just reflecting."

She wants to hug him. For a second, she wonders if he knows about her and Grayson, and gets a sinking feeling in her stomach, but that's ridiculous. She snaps out of it. "You can talk to me if you want."

He reaches for his coffee cup and takes a deep breath. "It's just tough sometimes." He twists his mouth, and clears his throat. "I feel like it keeps hitting me that my kids aren't going to have a normal life, you know?"

She nods. She wants to sit next to him, but she resists.

He sips his coffee. "There are so many small reminders that things aren't great, and I hate that we've done this to them. I don't know where it went wrong, but all Blair and I do is play games now, and I hate it." He looks down. "I didn't even think I knew how to play games, but I find myself constantly on the defense now, anticipating her next move."

She nods. "That sucks." She watches Gloria sniff the ground some more and roll in the grass, getting some snow on her white back. "Kids are strong. And you two will figure this out and get in a rhythm. You're finding out how to live this new way."

He smiles sadly at her. "Thanks. I just keep thinking, it's okay, you're trying your best, but I see how affected Stella and Cooper are, and my best isn't enough."

"They know, David. They know you're trying."

He shrugs. "The whole thing has made me petty. I just want to nickel and dime her, and she does the same to me. She made plans to go with her parents to Rhode Island for Easter, and the kids want to see all their cousins, but now they feel bad about leaving me, and I feel cheated . . . Cooper said I should just come, too." He groans, but he laughs for a second. "Can you imagine?"

"It's just new. And you and your, uh, Blair . . . your feelings are still fresh, I think."

"Maybe."

"You'll develop your own routines and traditions. And one day you and Blair will be easier with each other . . . wouldn't it be nice if when Stella graduates high school, you could sit next to her, and say, 'We did that'?" She has a flash of this image, of them outside in a stadium looking at their daughter in a cap and gown, smiling, and for a second, she can see herself sitting next to David, too. The vision startles her, and she tries to let it dissolve. But she can absolutely see herself there, and she likes it.

David looks up toward the sky as if he's picturing that scene, too, and she wishes he would see her in it. "I'll try to keep that goal in mind the next time she's telling me I owe her for the cough medicine she sent with the kids to my place." He shakes his head and smiles at Kirsten. "I wish we could get there."

It is foolish and silly, but when he says *we*, she thinks of him and her. She tries to calm herself—tries to focus on the wide stretch of grass, the tall trees, the other buildings off in the distance, the playground at Macarthur Elementary next door. Why haven't her feelings for him changed at all? Her night with Grayson did nothing to extinguish this. David is so sweet. She wants to hug him. She wants to rub his back. She wishes he would kiss her.

Gloria trots back to Kirsten and waits by her feet. There is just something in David's voice she feeds off of, something about the way he looks at her. He is looking at her now, and she doesn't want to go inside.

"You really are too good to be true," he says quietly. "Thanks for listening."

She smiles. She feels herself blush, but maybe it will just look like she's cold. She glances down at Gloria and takes a breath. "Don't mention it," she says.

He keeps staring at her, and she can't look away. Their eyes are locked, and they are breathing together, inhaling and exhaling.

A dog barks inside, and she hears a car pull up in front of the building. She waits for a second before opening the door. He stays where she leaves him. "See you in there," he says quietly.

She walks the halls of Rescue Ranch, Gloria trotting behind her, the lights bright above her, but she has memorized his eyes, and his eyes are all she keeps seeing.

—

At 9:15, she is furiously typing a report that David has to send to the board about grant money allocations when she smells the familiar cologne, the same smell that was on her skin and clothes last night when she got home. "Long time," Grayson says.

She looks up, and he has a wide smile and eager eyes. "Hi, there," she says. He wears a black polo shirt that looks like he ironed it.

He is sometimes late like this, but David doesn't mind because Grayson is taking night classes at Villanova, and David said he'd be flexible. He promised the same to her last year when she was considering veterinary programs, before she stopped considering them.

She looks at Grayson, and her heart drums ten times faster than usual. Being an only child, she always wondered about the idea of a parent loving more than one kid equally, and how was that possible? Didn't the heart assign itself completely, in some way, to one person? But seeing Grayson in front of her, and after talking with David outside, she understands this idea of separate affections.

Her feelings for the two of them don't even intersect or compare. She likes them differently, as though she is living two identities. She likes David's sensitivity and intellect and his want for a better life. She can see herself standing by him while his children ride the Tilt-A-Whirl at Hershey Park. She can see herself older with him, having a house together, the two of them putting out a meal and pouring wine for their guests. She can see a winter Saturday lying with him in a big bed and not wanting to get up. But she likes Grayson's excitement, his easiness, his perpetual grin. She can see this going somewhere, too, but in a whole different direction. She can see living in a city apartment, traveling to France and Belgium for some reason and drinking beer and trying exotic meats and chocolates and just laughing all the time. She imagines they'd be a hip young couple that could have a baby but not become boring. All these scenarios. In one day, she can see a full life with either of them.

She looks at Grayson. Her body feels so awake with him in front of her, and she thinks of how tenderly he kissed her, how she didn't doubt for a moment once it started that she was doing the right thing last night. She wants to do it again—her hands on his strong shoulders, gazing into his eyes. She imagines her smile is wide and lawless.

He drums his fingers on her desk. "Glad you got home safely." That grin again. "I was lonely after you left."

Blushing. She can't help it. Her face is like a hot plate. "You were?"

He nods. "You should've hung out longer. We never even listened to records." Grin.

She looks down at her keyboard. She worries her whole face must look like a cardinal. She takes a breath. "Music would have been nice."

He leans in conspiratorially. "Or we could have just not listened to them some more."

"Don't you have work to do?" She feels a rush of something through her whole body. This damn guy.

"I guess," he says, and raises his eyebrows. "But I was going to say . . ."

She cocks her head. "Yes?"

"That we could order a pizza tonight at my place . . . if you wanted."

Is this really happening? She didn't know what she expected, but she didn't think they'd keep anything going. But he excites her. And his apartment is such a comfortable place—she doesn't know what she pictured before. A lawn chair in an empty living room, a peeling poster on the wall, a den of college friends always there. But it's homey, and she wants to go back. "Oh."

"Pizza and beer."

"And records?"

"Lots of records."

She breathes. She looks around to see if David is anywhere near. She hears the weather guy on the radio talk about scattered flurries tonight. "I'm in," she says. And then he blows her a quick kiss, and she watches him walk away. His walk seems different than usual—as though his feet are gliding, as though she makes him breathless, too.

CHAPTER FIFTEEN

Late that afternoon, Chuck finds the giant bag of games they used to bring to Hilton Head on a shelf in the garage: two packs of cards, Yahtzee, and Boggle, Cat's favorite. He holds it out in front of him.

Who would he even play with? But he brings it inside anyway to put with his things. He heads upstairs, the steps seeming too many, and thinks about how Cat would be amassing paperbacks around this time—mysteries and suspense novels and even an occasional romance from yard sales and library sales.

As he stands there in the upstairs hallway, he feels like he keeps waiting for something that isn't coming.

It was wrong to ask about Cocoa.

As soon as the words came out, he regretted them. The looks on their faces were almost terrified—or at least incredulous. He imagines Marguerite at the hairdresser's saying in a low voice, ". . . and then he wanted to know if our *dog* could go . . . with *him*. All winter!" And he imagines the other ladies sighing and shaking their heads, and now his face burns. Who wouldn't hear that story and be appalled? Sympathy only goes so far, he thinks. He imagines them all thinking he needs help.

Yes, Cocoa would have kept him company, but it was silly to ask. "You failed to consider their side of the deal," Cat would have said, laughing. "They don't want some sad sack taking their dog."

He laughs for a second then, thinking of how she would have

shaken her head and rolled her eyes in a kind way. She probably would have placed her hand on his cheek. "My sweetheart. The world is not ready for you."

"I'm sorry about Natasha," he says out loud now, and his voice sounds strange, and the words are swallowed up by so much silence.

He wants her to answer him. He wants one of her witty retorts. Her laugh. He'd even settle for her irritated voice.

He loved the way she used to make observations about him: the way he winced from ice cream that was too cold; the way his arm flapped when he cut a steak; how she adored him in her own way; how she was never uptight.

She was lighthearted—that's what he misses. That lightheartedness, that laugh shaking her head when she saw something ridiculous. Or the way she'd get flustered before a holiday or a dinner party, and she'd make a buzzing sound with her lips and repeat the Julian of Norwich quote: "All shall be well . . ."

He liked that she was constantly trying on new personas: how she took Pilates and barre workshops and charcoal sketching classes and would introduce them to foods like couscous and pineapple ginger smoothies and hibiscus tea. "I'm not seeing what all the fuss is about," she'd say after tasting the roasted kale chips she made and almost dumping the tray into the garbage.

"Leave them," he said. "I don't mind them."

"You wouldn't," she said, and kissed his head.

She was fearless, inventive. She experimented with paint colors on the walls of their house. She took up knitting and crocheting. She bought African masks at flea markets and studied French and Japanese phrases. She sketched, she journaled, she made pottery. In Hilton Head, they made friends because of how charming and fun she was.

She brought all this texture into their lives, and he never needed to be creative or experiment with new personas. He was like an evergreen next to a tree that transformed itself brilliantly every season—he looked good because she was near him.

And maybe he misses that the most. That no one is daring him to change anymore, that nothing is blooming beside him. If he wants to change, if he wants that excitement, it's up to him now.

He can see her in an orange turtleneck sweater standing in front of their house, taking off her gardening gloves. She'd always want to go pick blueberries or strawberries or peaches. She'd want to buy birdseed or new wind chimes.

The last time they were in Hilton Head, a brochure sat on the kitchen table from the rental company. "We've been expecting you," it said. Last January, he held that brochure in his hands and read those words, and thought about their journey there, their long progression to becoming these people, and he felt as though they'd arrived.

He remembers Leela in college telling him about the pyramid of needs she learned about in psychology—that very few people can get to that perfect state at the top and reach their true potential. When he held that brochure, he felt as if he'd gotten there. *We've been expecting you.* This is what it means to make it, he'd thought.

But now he's at the bottom of the pyramid, and wherever he's hoping to get, no matter where he goes, he will never arrive.

—

For many years, they never even talked about Natasha, and it was just another page in their long history. Of course she forgave him—they had so many good moments since then. They didn't discuss Natasha in Cat's final weeks and days, but now he wishes he could have been more flexible, because he saw how good her intentions were. "I'm sorry, Catty," he says into the stale air of their home.

He gets an idea then and trudges into their office and rummages through the desk drawers.

He finds old calendars and a staple remover and free return address labels they got in the mail once. He reaches to the back of the drawer and pulls out her address book. He flips through the pages and sees names crossed out or addresses rewritten and some annotations by people's listings (their kids' names, if they sent Christmas cards, and other such record keeping), and finally he gets to V, and he searches for Vargas, but Natasha isn't there.

He then goes to N, and he finds her, and it's a local address, one she probably hasn't lived in for years, but he sees "cell number" with a 610 area code, and he wonders if she happened to keep that number all these years.

He writes it on the back of the sketch of Natasha at the café and slips it into his pocket. He imagines what he'll say if he calls her. *Do you remember me? How have you been? Did you hear about Cat? It's my fault what happened. It's all my fault.*

—

Once, when they weren't speaking after the Natasha blowup, he had a vivid dream about Vietnam. He was sleeping in their bed, and Cat was in the guest room, and in his dream he saw the rain soaking everything and the unsure gray sky, the red mud caked to his boots.

He kept looking around, and then he saw his best friend Norman's face, so devastated, so let down, and he thought he opened his eyes and saw Norman standing in the doorway. He hollered so loud and sat up in bed, but everything was still.

He wanted to tell Norman he would have stood in front of him had he been there; he would have rushed out had he heard Norman's screams. He wanted to say he felt for years and years Norman's weight on his shoulders, that he never finished *Old Man and the Sea*, the book he was reading at the time. That when Leela had to read it in tenth grade, he came close to asking her English teacher for an exemption because he didn't want the book in the house.

And he slammed his hand over his heart and breathed like he would never find enough oxygen. When he looked in the doorway again, Cat was standing there with alarm on her face. She just stayed there and watched him, and he could tell she knew what he'd dreamed about.

"You're okay, Chuck," she said, and she went into the bathroom and brought him water in a Dixie cup. She waited for a second as he drank the water and then walked back to the guest room.

"Thanks," he said, but he never knew if she heard him.

—

Chuck drives to Rescue Ranch on Friday, and he doesn't know what he'll do there, but he is game for anything at this point. He notices the clear sky above the brick building, the banner over the entryway that says New Friends Await, and when he closes his car door, he hears dogs barking.

Some people wearing Volunteer shirts walk big dogs up a long trail under bowing pine trees, and as he ambles toward the door, he sees a giant cat house in the front where the kittens sleep in window beds and small hammocks.

"Looking for a friend?" the young woman at the front desk asks. She has a high ponytail and wears eyeliner around her light brown eyes. He feels comforted by her smile, and something about her seems familiar.

He thinks about telling her he lost his only friend, but instead he nods. People will only allow so much of that. "I might be."

"Oh, terrific. Please take a look around." She points her arm like a flight attendant showing the exit doors. "Smaller dogs are straight ahead, older dogs are in the back, and big dogs are to the left. Cats and kittens in those two rooms."

She sips a big iced coffee drink, then squints and cocks her head to the side. Yes, she sees it, too. He smiles self-consciously, waiting for her examination. Her eyebrows knit. "Mr. A.?"

"We know each other, don't we?"

"Mr. A!" She dashes out from behind the desk, and she is hugging him, a hug so forceful, and now he remembers.

Chrissy. Kristen. Something like that. He glances at her name plate. Kirsten. Kirsten Bonato. Cat had her as a student in fourth-grade art the last year teaching before she retired, and Kirsten won first prize in the state youth art competition for an abstract acrylic she did.

She was so young and such a promising kid who seemed like an adult back then. Chuck and Cat joined her and her parents in Harrisburg for an awards ceremony and exhibit. The father, a charming European businessman, and the mother, a science professor at Lehigh, insisted on taking them out to dinner. A few times after that, Leela, who was already in her twenties, babysat for Kirsten, and then Ben filled in a few times once Leela moved away.

Kirsten's father had them over for dinner one night on their beautiful farm—the dinner lasted six hours. He grilled pizza in a brick oven and served meats and cheese from a place he loved in New York. He kept pouring wine and telling them stories. They were such a fun couple—playing off each other as they talked—and Chuck, usually a homebody, didn't want to leave.

When Chuck threw Cat a retirement party, he invited some former students and their parents, and Kirsten and her family arrived first and left last. After that, they kind of fell out of touch. Kirsten got too old to need a babysitter, and he and Cat's retirement years seemed to fly by. He ran into the mother at Rite Aid while he was picking up a prescription for Cat last spring, about a month before she died, and he was distracted and not as friendly as he should have been. "Nice seeing you," he said absently that day. "Give your family my best."

"Ah, Kirsten. What a lovely surprise," he says now. He feels his posture straighten. Some inner worry explodes and breaks into smaller pieces. He has this terrible habit now when he sees people of thinking if they responded to Cat's death properly, and yes, he remembers her parents sent a lovely houseplant with a ribbon on it, one that bloomed with a white flower. He had tried to keep it alive but couldn't.

"It is," she says, and touches his arm.

He feels like he might cry, but then hears a beagle or hound dog barking way too loudly. He crosses his arms and looks at the bulletin board in the lobby. Some news about a pancake breakfast. Pictures of animals that have recently been adopted—dogs with celebratory expressions and cats with nonchalant stares.

"I'm so sorry about Mrs. A.," she says. "I was actually just thinking of her the other day."

"Thanks, dear." He nods, and tries to change the subject. Why is he so emotional? "What's in this room?" he asks, pointing to the door that says Various Buddies.

She smiles. "Take a look," she says.

He walks in, his insides buckling a bit, worried that something will swoop out and grab him. Parakeets chitter in a floor-to-ceiling cage, and there is a huge fuzzy rabbit with hair over its eyes that seems to have free rein of the room. It hops twice and then looks like it's falling asleep in the corner. The whole building, especially this room, is immaculate. There are two ferrets in a rectangular plastic pen, a chinchilla in a metal cage, which gives him the creeps, and then the unmistakable sound of a pig.

"What the?" He peeks over the Dutch door to see a pink, medium-sized pig staring up at him. "Well, hello."

The pig reminds him of *Charlotte's Web*. The kids used to watch that movie with him every Thanksgiving. It would be on at just the right time in the day—early afternoon, when most of the cooking was at a standstill and the house was quiet, and the sun came in and made the wineglasses and gold-rimmed plates on the dining room table sparkle. Leela would say, "Daddy, I think it's Wilbur time," and they'd amble into the TV room, and Chuck would turn off the football game playing in the background, Cat standing in the doorway sometimes and smiling, and one of the kids would snuggle against his side, and the other one would lie across the couch, putting their feet on his lap. The movie would begin with that nostalgic music, and Chuck would feel his kids breathing so close to him, feel Cat nearby as she hummed to herself and frosted the pumpkin spice cake.

His heart always broke when Charlotte died, and sometimes he'd have to wipe a tear from Leela's eyes, and Ben would get that lonely stare when he watched Wilbur's scene at the fair. As the movie wrapped up, he didn't want the kids to leave his side, yet all of a sudden the doorbell would be ringing and there would be relatives holding pies and handing him their coats, and he would be fixing drinks and nodding and saying, "I suppose that's true," to some long story, and now he can't stop looking at this pig.

"What do you think?" Kirsten says with a laugh. She is petite, but her arms are strong, like she does yoga or something. She wears a ring with a ruby that looks like a family heirloom. She glances between the pig and him.

"He's a rescue?"

She nods. "A surrender."

He shakes his head. "Why would anyone give up a pig?"

She sighs. "Well, they sell them on the Internet as tiny teacup pigs, and people buy them, thinking they're going to have this pocket-sized pig forever, but they get big . . . as potbellied pigs tend to *do*." He is amazed how comfortable he is around Kirsten, even though it's been years. But he remembers it was like that with her whole family—they were a trio of good people. She is cheerful, bright-eyed. She opens the pig's door and pets the tufts of hair on top of its head. "Isn't that right, Frederick?"

"Frederick," Chuck says, and he looks down at this animal that could be in commercials because he's the quintessential pig. "That's a shame he's here." He asks if he can pet Frederick, too, and when she nods, he crouches down and the pig nuzzles against his knee. Chuck snickers as Frederick sniffs his hand, and Chuck wonders what it's like to be closed in a room like this all day when you're smart enough to know better.

Some pig, he thinks. He shrugs, and they walk toward the area with the older dogs. "So how are your parents doing?" he asks, and her expression shifts suddenly. He knows this look all too well, unfortunately. He braces himself.

—

That night he dreams about the pig. It lives with him, and he doesn't question it. In his dream, the pig barks when someone's at the door; Chuck pats the bed, and the pig jumps up. He drives his car, and the pig stands on its back legs and looks out the passenger window.

He wakes for a moment and thinks about Kirsten's father. Such a nice guy. What a shame. That man just brightened up a room. Chuck can see him sitting at the head of the table outside, the sun behind him, his life seeming like the exact life he always wanted, he and his wife playfully bantering. When he talked to Chuck, he looked so deeply into his eyes and put his hand on Chuck's arm the way Kirsten did at Rescue Ranch. "Is that a cultural thing?" Chuck asked Cat later. And then Kirsten's face when she told him about her dad. How hadn't Chuck heard? Her kind eyes quickly reduced to the clearest pain.

He turns on his side. Unbearable. He tries to forget about Alberto, and conjures up the pig.

What would Leela say if he told her about Frederick? Would she love him because Wilbur had meant so much to her, or would she think Chuck had started to lose his marbles? Would Ben say, "Good for you. Whatever makes you happy"? Or would he pause on the phone, take a breath, and say, "Um, I think we need to talk"?

Would the rental in Hilton Head allow it, assuming a pig could travel that far, assuming he himself was definitely going to Hilton Head? He is sinking back to sleep and whispers to Cat. "It's crazy, isn't it?" And he thinks he hears her voice, that smile in it, that singsong quality. He thinks she would say, *Yes. Yes. This is that feeling you run toward.*

—

He wakes up later, still the middle of the night, with the pig on his mind. On his iPad he searches "caring for a pet pig" and lies in the dark studying pig facts. He feels an excitement he hasn't felt in months, hope that something is ahead.

Getting a pig is something Cat would have done, and this makes him elated. Now he has to be his own Cat; he has to let her spontaneity and creativity fuel him. Life is short. Look at Alberto Bonato. We must find joy where we can. Maybe the pig will be just the beginning. He can learn tai chi. Go to a music store and buy a ukulele. Try stuffed grape leaves at the Middle Eastern restaurant.

He feels giddy. He feels like he's finding his way. He is leaning toward something, the pig definitely, but there is something bigger, something else that's bringing him joy, and he sifts through his feelings, and finds it. Sun. A bright place. *I'll get there, Catty. I'll get there for both of us.*

He can live for her, he thinks, and it's two in the morning, and he decides to go to Hilton Head.

He will leave Monday. He counts his breaths. He thinks about the pig and the wide-open beach. He smiles as he alternates the images, like the front and back of a dollar bill, and falls back to sleep.

CHAPTER SIXTEEN

At Grayson's apartment Friday evening, Kirsten is wearing his old Eagles T-shirt and resting on his chest. They called in an order of falafel and pilaki from a Turkish place up the street, and it will be ready soon.

They are talking about indie bands, about more snow, about injuries they had as kids (him: a broken nose; her: stitches on her hand), and about work. They talk about their favorite teachers. His was a high school teacher named Mrs. Young. She taught world cultures and European literature. He had her his junior and senior years. He said she encouraged thoughtful discussion and required precision in writing, and he left every class in awe. Kirsten tells him about Mrs. A., how kind she was, how laid back. How they made piñatas out of papier-mâché, how she sat beside Kirsten and expertly explained shading and highlighting to her. She tells him how she felt seeing Mr. A. at Rescue Ranch—how much thinner and older he seemed.

They don't talk about David—she changes the subject if Grayson says his name. Every so often he bends down to kiss her, and the kiss and his now-familiar smell and her body against his feels easy, like floating on a wide raft.

"I like you," he says every time they're together now, and grins.

"I enjoy you," she always replies, and he rolls his eyes playfully and tickles her.

She looks around his bedroom: the pile of books on his dresser, a picture of him and his parents and older sister in the Adirondacks, an old brass clock that was his grandfather's. Already in the few times she's come here, it has all become common to her—even the texture and weight of his sheets feel like an extension of her skin.

What is this, though? She feels like she hopped on a bus she wasn't supposed to be on, and finds herself looking out the window and getting comfortable in her seat. But is this where she wants to be? Is Grayson the right turn, the sign from her dad she needed? She thinks of that pull she feels to David, like when he was sitting out in the cold, and they stared into each other's eyes, and she knew there was so much more there. Would that connection be there if she were falling in love with Grayson? Wouldn't it have started to disintegrate?

Grayson's chest moves slowly up and down, and the old clock ticks. He kisses her again, and she feels herself sink deeper into him. She could sleep this way, her hand on his bridge of ribs, his room washed in such a pale blue that you barely even notice there's color. She would love to stay over and hold one another all night, but she doesn't want her mom to ask too many questions.

"Kiki?" he says now, his voice low.

"Yeah?"

"Do you think we'll keep doing this?"

She looks up at him and notices his long eyelashes, his perfect nose. The shade on the lamp next to his bed is askew, and she sees the photograph of the plane his great uncle flew in the service. "What? Me coming over?"

He nods.

She kisses his hand. "Do you want to?"

"I definitely do," he says. She hears hesitancy in his voice, like he's just about to say another thing but holds back. This surprises her. Does she know him that well already? She is sure there is more. She thinks for a second of her parents, who seemed to communicate without talking, and she always wanted that: that easiness with someone, that knowledge of what someone's eyes or silence or gestures meant.

"What?" she whispers. "What else were you going to say?"

She sits up to look at him. His face gets serious. She hardly ever sees his mouth not in a smile. Something is in the look they share—almost a gratefulness in his eyes that she could tell what he was thinking. "I feel like you're going to end it soon," he says. "And that just seems like a shame."

She doesn't reply for a few seconds. "It *would* be a shame," she finally says.

They lie there for a few minutes more, and she's not sure if they are in a fight or if things will be awkward now. Finally he clears his throat and says he's going to pick up the food.

"Want company?" she asks.

He stands and stretches, his big arms like eagle wings. "Nah, you look comfy." She smiles at him and sits there in his T-shirt as he throws his clothes on and heads out the door, looking back at her one last time as if he's unsure, as if he wants to say more but can't.

While he's gone, she takes two plates out of his small kitchen cupboard and sets his coffee table with napkins and utensils. She walks over to his record player and looks at his albums. She selects Joni Mitchell and watches it spin before she balances the needle on the edge. Joni's voice fills the small apartment, and she heads back to the bedroom and straightens the pillows and pulls the sheets and comforter taut.

She can't explain how at home she feels here, even though some other part of her, the part that couldn't reassure him a moment ago, feels like she's trespassing.

Her foot kicks something under his bed, and she bends down to see a brown leather book with a stretched elastic band around it. She holds it in her hand and wonders if it's a journal. She looks around the room. The whole place is quiet.

She feels the weight of the notebook. Without thinking, she slips off the band and looks inside. It is definitely some type of journal. She sees entries from a few years ago that say Austria, and there are sketches of village shops and notes about how it felt to be so far from home. He wrote about women, about beer, about mountains and castles he saw. She turns the pages and sees more recent entries and can hear his voice so clearly in his writing:

> *Today I learned I'm not good at boxing.*
> *Today I just want to fucking hide.*

She looks out toward the living room again, but only hears Joni and the scratchy sound of the vinyl.

She knows his door makes a loud squeak when it opens, so she'll hear him come home.

She flips through the pages, sees a sketch of ice skaters in New York, and then one of a small cabin in the woods with smoke coming out of the chimney. There are pine trees around it and two rocking chairs on the porch. There is a stack of wood by the side of the house and a dog in the window. In another window is a candle and she rubs her finger across the charcoal sketch and wonders why he drew it. Did he see it somewhere, or is it a house he wished he lived in? She turns the pages until she gets to the end and looks at the last entry.

> *K. is coming over again tonight!! What is it about*
> *her? She just makes me feel lucky and happy. It's*

like I want to spend every moment with her . . .
until she comes to her senses.

Her face burns. She hears a bang at the door then, and her heart races and she slips the band back in place and puts the notebook where it was.

She takes a couple of deep breaths to slow her pulse. When she opens the door, she can feel the cold on him, and from the bag is the heavenly smell of garlic and tomatoes and fried chickpeas.

He must be able to see how nervous and caught she looks, but he holds up the big brown bag and smiles at her. She reaches for him and hugs him like she's convincing him she won't let him go.

—

The next day, she is working her once-a-month Saturday rotation at Rescue Ranch. Kirsten goes through some of the files that are in the room where the vet does her examinations. She comes across Frederick the pig's chart, and sees he is due for a vaccine this week. Someone has made an appointment to visit with him today for a possible adoption, and Kirsten thinks of Mr. A. yesterday who seemed so amazed by Frederick, who seemed to want to find the courage to take him home.

She smiles, imagining her favorite teacher's husband planting tomatoes and parsley with Frederick not leaving his side. She imagines Frederick snoring by Mr. A.'s feet while he does crosswords.

Mr. A. had asked so many thoughtful questions and seemed truly interested, and when they got to the dog room, he seemed disappointed that all the dogs weren't pigs.

She wanted to encourage him to take the leap (she had seen a handful of pigs get adopted during her time at Rescue Ranch, and most were satisfied customers, except for the family with the pig that bit too much and they had to hire a trainer). Once Mr. A. stopped saying how sorry he was about her father, he looked intrigued, like a kid peeking out at an interesting stranger.

She wonders if her dad in his old age would have adopted a pig. She thinks he might have, if he had the impulse. She's actually sure he would have now. He had that gene to take chances. At every party, he found the most exciting conversation; even at his job, he got to travel across the country, out to California sometimes, his tanned arm resting on the window as he drove a rental car. She holds Frederick's file folder and has this image of her father getting to grow older and older like Mr. A., a faithful pig trailing behind him.

She rests her hands on the stainless steel table and smiles.

She wishes she had Mr. A.'s number. She wishes she could call him and say, do it. Go for the pig.

CHAPTER SEVENTEEN

Chuck calls Sal on Sunday and tells him his plans for leaving. He doesn't mention the pig, and since Rescue Ranch is closed today, he has one last day to prepare himself for pig ownership and his big trip, which both seem absurd. Should he really buy a pig and get right on the road? Shouldn't Frederick get used to him first? How do pigs travel?

But somehow he knows it will be okay. Frederick will get used to the road and then Hilton Head. Chuck will pat him and reassure him as they drive. *You did it*, he hears Cat say. *Who knew you had it in you, sweetheart?*

"Good for you," Sal says on the phone.

Chuck pauses. "And tell Marguerite that I'm sorry I asked about Cocoa. I guess I was—"

"Ahhh," Sal says, interrupting him. He clears his throat loudly. "If Marguerite goes before me, they're gonna find me in the nuthouse. I promise you that. So asking to borrow a dog isn't that bad."

"Thanks, Sal." Chuck smiles. "And . . ."

"And we'll look after the place," Sal says. Then Sal starts to list everything he should do before he leaves, as if Chuck's never gone away before.

—

That night, Chuck's legs are restless. He keeps moving them and kicking them in bed.

He dreams over and over that he's on the road, and every time he feels like he's getting there, every time he can almost feel the warm air soaking through the car, he realizes he's still sleeping, and it's all reset again.

He dreams of the kids when they are young, Leela trailing behind him when heading to the hardware store on an errand, or Ben jumping on his back and just hanging there, his tiny hands wrapped around Chuck's neck.

Right before he wakes up, he sees Cat's face for a second. He hears her say something so clearly, so plain as day as if she's right in the room, that he jolts awake. He catches his breath and looks around.

He gets out of bed and puts his glasses on. It is after six o'clock; he has slept later than usual. Cat always said when you have a lot of dreams, you're in a deep sleep.

Her yellow-and-white towel is on the floor, and he stoops to pick it up, putting it around his neck. He wonders if he has it in him to shut down the house today and drive all those hours.

He thinks of the glee he felt the other night, when he thought of the pig, when he decided to go to Hilton Head. He wants to feel that as strongly as before, but something is blocking that—like a sock hanging out of a drawer that won't let you close it.

He wants to be a free spirit—a guy getting a pet pig, a guy making focaccia or joining one of those boot camp classes in Hilton Head. He almost feels like he's ready to take the leap, but what's stopping him?

Natasha maybe.

The fight. All that regret.

He sees Natasha's face from so many years ago, and he wants to leave his worries about her here. He needs to talk to her. He needs to explain himself.

He thinks Cat will come to him more often in dreams if he sets this right. He thinks he'll truly be going forward, to the top of the pyramid again, if he can work this out, buy his pig today, and finally drive to Hilton Head.

He picks up the drawing of her with her number on the back and gets his phone. He dials the last number Cat had written down for Natasha. It rings and rings, and his heart feels like it's falling into his stomach as he wonders if she'll answer.

CHAPTER EIGHTEEN

Ella is late with the papers Monday morning. Her car wouldn't start, just dead and lifeless when she turned the key, and she had to call AAA so they could come and jump the battery.

Cindy had called this morning ("I can't sleep. I knew you'd be up") to check on her. When Ella said she was having car issues, Cindy offered to wake Matt so they could bring their extra car over to her. "I'm happy to help," she said, and even though Ella politely declined, she still had to pause for a moment and take it in. It was odd to reunite with the version of Cindy she knew when she and Kyle first were together, the Cindy who wanted to please her, the Cindy who bought her earrings and hand cream. Ella had stood outside in the freezing cold as AAA got the battery working and had the odd thought that she had lost her daughter but she had found a mother-in-law.

At about half past six she gets to Fillingham Bay Road. The sky is light already, not full sun, but getting there, and the car slips and swerves on small patches of black ice every so often. She fits the papers into the boxes as though they are pegs to a logic problem she's trying to solve. She has to be at TB by eight, and she feels so behind, so out of breath.

When she gets to Mr. Ayers's house, she leaves the car door open and rushes across the driveway to his front walkway. When she gets to the sidewalk, her foot goes out like a character in a cartoon that slips on a banana peel, and in a fast second her whole body jerks, and her tailbone, her shoulders, and then her head hit the concrete.

She closes her eyes and feels awful pain. A blunt ache in her head she's never felt, and she thinks for a second again about cartoons, how the characters would see birds flying around in a circle after they bumped their heads, and that's exactly what it feels like.

She tries to steady herself, to hop up. She is still holding the newspaper like some dedicated employee. Is the paper this important? she thinks. Her head throbs.

The irony of bringing others news when all she wants is to hear news.

She lies there silently and whispers, "Please, *please*." She's not hoping for anyone to save her but hoping for Riley. She's always hoping for Riley. She looks up at the sky and feels pitiful and desperate. *Please get her back to me.*

She wishes she were wearing her down jacket, as she realizes she is just in her sweater and stretch pants. She feels the wind through her thin clothes. Through her knit hat, she feels tenderness in the back of her head. She closes one eye and looks out the other, then switches. She can get up.

"Stay there," she hears the old man call as his front door flies open. He is holding his phone. "I'm sorry. I will have to call you back," he shouts into it, and descends the steps toward her in his pajama pants and baggy cardigan. Even in her pain, she is pleased to see him again.

She has saved his five-dollar bill in her ashtray, and every time she notices it, it makes her smile. She wanted to buy a soft pretzel from Wawa the other day and was out of cash, but she couldn't bring herself to use the bill he gave her. She wants to frame it on a wall if this period of her life is ever behind her to remind her that kindness exists, even when many other things seem awful.

"Sorry," she says to him, and tries to sit up. "I was rushing."

"It's my fault. I should've put some more of that salt down.

Are you okay?" he asks. His hair is combed neatly. He crouches beside her, and she feels like a soldier in a war. He attends to her in a way that seems like he's done this before. His eyes assess the damage. "I was looking from my upstairs window, and I saw it all."

"I was late," she says.

"Can you wiggle your feet?"

She tries. "Yes."

"Okay, don't sit up yet, though. We shouldn't move you until we're sure." He looks around. "Do you know what day it is?"

"Yes. Um, Monday," she says. Another day of the worst year of my life, she thinks. "I'm fine."

"I think you should lie still a little longer." He stands. "Hang on."

In a second, he is back again. He has a wool blanket, plaid, that looks like something from L.L.Bean. When he places it on her, it is warm from his house and smells like her grandparents' place used to: like Sunday dinners and long relaxed days. She can almost hear her grandad's golf game playing in the den. It feels so good on her, and then he slides a rolled-up towel with yellow stripes under her neck. "There we go," he whispers. She can't say how good it feels for someone to care for her, to cover her. To put something soft under her tired head. She wants to get up, to tell him she'll be fine, but she stays where she is.

Her car makes a loud noise in the background, the exhaust rattling, the tin sounds under the hood, and she's embarrassed. He looks up at it and crinkles his nose. "My car sounds like my head feels," she says, and she wonders if that makes sense.

"The back of the head is the best place to bump," he says, and he nods in a gentle way. His eyes are so full of compassion, and she feels embarrassed lying here like an injured animal.

"I really should get up. I have so many places to be," she says.

"Well, not if you're not well." He looks down. "Can you move your fingers?"

She holds them up and trills them as if she's playing the piano or typing. "I'm like an old barn cat. I bounce back."

"I think I should call an ambulance," Mr. Ayers says.

She imagines the bill. She has to stay afloat for Riley. She has to keep everything together. She thinks of not being able to work today, and her questionable health insurance. Last she knew, she was on Kyle's plan, but she hasn't been to any doctors' offices since September, and she has no idea of her status—probably dropped. She aches but feels okay. She can get up and manage. Even though she doesn't want to. Even though a part of her wishes she could just sit in his comfortable living room and be covered with this blanket and watch a daytime talk show, or something like *Let's Make a Deal*.

"No need," she says, and she pushes herself up. Her head really hurts. She slowly moves her neck.

"Now, just hang on," he says, and he crouches beside her. She hears his breathing, and she relaxes. She feels like she and Mr. Ayers are the last two people on a battlefield, and he has stayed behind to help her.

"Your car sounds awful," he says. "Does it need to go into the shop?"

She sighs. "No, this is pretty normal. Sorry about the noise, though."

He stays there, half squatting, looking at her, then glancing at her muddy, rattling car. He waves his hand. "I see you out in this dark and cold every morning. It's admirable. The slipping aside, which was my fault for having an icy walkway, I hope everything's okay with you." Her eyes burn. It feels so good to be seen. Finally,

finally seen. She has felt like she's been invisible these months, aside from the recent check-ins from Cindy. She's realized that the only friends she has seen in the last few years are other parents, and of course they check in on her every so often, but she finds herself not wanting to answer their calls or texts anymore because what is there to say? Mr. Ayers studies her like a healer who can read her mind. "You sure you're okay?" he says.

She nods. He stands slowly, then offers her his warm, rough hand. She imagines all his years of work. He is exactly who she thought he was through the glow of that window every morning— a kind, probably lonely, man. She can spot another lonely person from a mile away, and he has all the same signs: resigned eyes, a half frown, an overall droop. What or who has left him?

She stands now and hands him the blanket. "I've survived worse." Everything hurts—her tailbone, her shoulders, her head. She wants to sit in the car and just cry, calling out for Riley. Riley has never seen her like this—so tired and hurt.

"Hang on then," he says, and starts to walk into the house. "I have to get something for you."

She bends down to pick up the faded towel that was behind her head. Is this the same towel she's seen him wear around his neck some mornings? It is worn and has an unexpected dignity to it. It reminds her of a remnant of a good life, the life she hopes to have when Riley's back.

The back of her skull feels like someone broke a vase across it, but she will take an Advil from her glove compartment. She will take a hot bath later and push through.

She watches him walk into the house, and the wool blanket trails beside him. She is hurt and sad, and even a tad impatient because she has to get to TB, but she can't help but smile at the care he gave her. Why does he seem to understand her so well?

No one else is around—the house just emits a quietness. Where are his *people*?

She wonders why he has gone into the house. She imagines him handing her another five-dollar bill like he did last time, and that makes her glad despite her being so late, despite the aches in her body. She hears the door open and then the squeak of the screen door. He comes out, holding a file folder.

Is he going to show her a photograph? Does he need her to read a document because the print is too small? The morning sun is shy and wholesome.

He is nodding as he walks down the steps as though he has something important to say. She holds his towel, forgets about TB, and prepares to listen. He steps carefully down each step so he doesn't fall, either. He gestures to her with the file folder.

"I want to give you my car," he says. "It's yours if you want it." He takes the key from his pocket, and it almost glows.

CHAPTER NINETEEN

On Monday there is a scheduled surrender, and the woman sounds terrible on the phone. "I'll be here when you come in," Kirsten tells her. "You are doing the right thing, and we'll help you through it."

She hangs up the phone, but the pain in the woman's voice stays with her. She knows they need to hear that they're doing the right thing, so she makes it a point to say that often during the process. She hopes the woman will be okay. Surrenders are usually not easy, but she admires the valiant way some people can put the animal's needs first.

Maybe that is what has kept her here.

She has been orphaned like one of the animals. She lost her dad, whom she dreams of constantly, whom their life seemed to orbit around. And in some ways, she feels as though her mother has surrendered her. Her mother is like one of those overwhelmed people who have nothing left to give.

That's terrible to think, but in some ways, she feels it.

Her mother works more now at the university than she ever did before. She used to take afternoons off occasionally. She used to go in late some days when her dad was home, and they would sip their tea on the faded teak patio chairs. Or they would take one of their long walks, and Kirsten would see them strolling incredibly slowly, just their fingers locked, her father in a baseball hat, her mother in one of her long sweater coats, and Kirsten used to think, *that is love.*

How can she blame her mother then? She has lost so much, hasn't she? She had to surrender everything: the years and years she thought she'd have. No wonder she's hiding at work. And it's not up to her mom to be there for her. Kirsten's an adult now, and it's probably time for her to make her next move, to figure things out.

It's all been easier the last few days. Grayson has made it easier. She thinks of his bed. Of his sketch of that cabin in the woods. The way they sit on the living room floor around his wobbly coffee table and taste each other's food and drink wine and laugh.

Now she smiles thinking of him, can't wait until he pops his head around the corner, and she sits at her desk and organizes some paperwork.

An older couple that donates cat food and litter from Costco each week comes in and waves to her as they leave the few bags by the supply closet. The husband holds the door open for his wife.

Kirsten double-checks her pile of surrender forms. She needs to have everything ready, as giving up an animal can be emotional and draining, so being quick and on top of things is best. She takes a deep breath.

"So just about a week and a half or so, eh?"

Kirsten looks up, and David is standing over her desk, a shy smile, his eyes tired, his elbows on the ledge. He sips from his Sheetz mug.

"Yup, then I'm Italy-bound . . . if I don't chicken out," she says.

"You're going to love it." He shrugs. "I mean, I *think* you will. I've never gone farther east than Bermuda. But in high school I had an Italian friend named Daniele, and we were skaters—skateboarders—and he was the most chill guy."

She pictures younger David on a skateboard ramp going back

and forth, squatting and flipping like Tony Hawk. "My dad was chill, too," she says. "Maybe it's a cultural thing. The *chillness* of the Italian people."

He smirks, and then his face gets serious. She notices he has a small freckle on his earlobe that she never saw before. He cocks his head to the side thoughtfully. "Are you really thinking of chickening out?"

She shrugs. He allows silence the way a good therapist would. "No, I don't think I'll chicken out . . . but a part of me does feel like . . ." She searches for the right way to phrase it. "I kind of feel like, what's the point?"

He nods. "Yeah, that makes sense."

"I mean, it will be spectacular, and I'll love seeing my grandmother and my aunt, and then Switzerland, and the wedding, but . . ." She bites her nail.

"You kind of feel like you're just going through the motions instead of being all aboard the way you would have been had the wedding happened when it should have."

She swallows. "You got it, my friend." She can't say anything else. She feels like she'll crumble. It seems silly to resist time off work, time with family, travel to Europe. But she feels subdued. And so alone. For a second, she imagines Grayson going with her, and this thought soothes her. Then she imagines David, and she can see herself on the plane with him. She can see them exploring historic sights and museums. She can see the two of them dancing together at Bria's wedding. She looks into his eyes and it's as though he imagines the same thing.

He smiles, and she smiles back. His face always comforts her. They stare at each other that way, and his voice gets lower. "You'll be glad you went, Kirsten. You know, I think we need things like that . . . the love of family, the ritual of a wedding, the views of a whole new place." He stares at the wall behind her. "Yeah, I think stuff like that is necessary." He winks at her, and it almost makes her heart stop.

She considers this—this necessity of good things. She hadn't thought of that, and isn't that what has been helping her? The skiing, the laughing at the bar with Grayson, sweet Mr. Ayers who thought about adopting Frederick. "I hope so." She looks at the clipboard and the forms in front of her. She hopes the lady is okay when she brings in the Chihuahua today.

David crosses his arms, leans in. "And thanks for what you did for me the other day. I really needed the pep talk." The music in the background shifts to Prince. David drums his hands on the counter, and she notices that she can still see the line from where his wedding ring used to be. "But anyway, enjoy your trip. I'm a dork who likes lots of pictures, so drown me in them when you come back."

"Then pictures you will get. I'll even set up a slideshow."

He raises one eyebrow. "By the way, have you seen Grayson today?" He holds back a minute, and looks like he might say something else, then grips his side and looks uncomfortable.

"No, not yet," she says. She feels her face get hot. She tries to think of something she would have said back in the pre-sleeping-with-Grayson days. "No wonder it seems so quiet."

He shrugs. "Yeah, I guess he's not much later than usual." He shakes his head, and looks down at her paperwork. "Are the vending contracts ready?"

She nods and finds them on her stack, and when he takes them, her fingers touch his and both of them freeze. He doesn't look like he's breathing, and she's sure she isn't. She stares into his eyes and her brain focuses only on the temperature of his hand. Finally, she pulls away, and he seizes the papers and smiles.

He waves to her, and she watches him walk down the hall toward the offices. The overhead lights shine on David's head. She can still feel the place where his hand touched hers. She watches him, and her heart aches. He grips his left side again, and his back stiffens. She wonders for a second how he and his wife fell out of love. He slouches a little in his blue oxford shirt, and it makes her sad.

Several red glittery heart wreaths hang on a few of the doors around the office. The decorations make her think of being in elementary school when Valentine's Day was a welcome respite in the winter. It is still a month away, but Bryce put up the decorations yesterday.

She feels something flutter inside her for David, but then she also looks around and wonders about Grayson. She checks the clock. It's late, even for him.

She picks up her phone and sends him a text. *Cheesesteak overdose?* She didn't see him last night because she ate with her mom, but he told her he was getting at least two cheesesteaks from Fuzzy's.

She smiles, anticipating a funny reply from him. But a couple of minutes go by and he doesn't write back. She feels something squirm inside her: a brief sense of worry. She imagines a car accident, all the gridlock. She imagines him steering his Saab around the wreckage.

She sits and looks at her phone and feels guilty about his question the other night, when he asked her if she wanted to keep this going.

He's fine. She's sure he's fine.

God, she doesn't trust anything anymore. Her heart feels crooked in her body.

Then her phone rings. Grayson is in her head so much that she assumes it's him, and when she says hello, Bria's voice breaks her daydreaming. "*Buongiorno*, Kirsten. Are you ready? We are so excited for you to be here."

"Bria," she says. She keeps hoping a text alert will buzz in her ear, but it's just Bria's voice, so clear as if she's only a block away. "Can't wait," she says, and she laughs and listens to her father's sister's kind voice, its beautiful cadence, and wonders if she sounds convincing.

—

A half hour later, and still no reply from Grayson. The woman and her Chihuahua will be in soon, and Kirsten will welcome the distraction. It is eleven o'clock now, and she is jittery and can't focus on anything. She keeps feeling like they will get a call soon, and Grayson will be hurt. Or dead even. Probably silly to worry. But she keeps seeing his sketch of the cabin. What was he thinking when he drew that?

She pictures his lovely apartment. The way his face looked the other night as he sipped beer and ate falafel. She noticed she no longer trembles when he touches her—she always does with a new guy. But now his touch is familiar and welcome.

She got up earlier and looked out at the parking lot, as if she could guide him there. The sky was gray with a hint of sun. She closed her eyes and heard his voice, saw his grin. At her desk now she keeps looking at her phone. She checks her email, even, thinking that maybe he has called in sick that way.

"Where are you?" she whispers.

She imagines his reply. *I've been to Mars and back.*

Or, *Nonya. Non ya business.* And then he'd crack up.

And then she sees a figure at the door, bare arms and no coat. She almost leaps from her chair.

"Miss me?" Grayson says as he walks in.

She has to fight the urge to run to him, kiss him. He gives her an extrawide grin. "There you are," she says quietly. "I was . . ."

"Do my teeth look cleaner?" he says. And then she remembers him mentioning a dentist appointment a few days ago, and David joking that their lousy insurance probably only covered a couple of teeth. He shakes his head. "I left my phone at home like an idiot."

It all makes sense now, but her heart won't stop pounding.

She keeps staring at him, and he looks back, squinting at her expression with a puzzled face. She can breathe better now. She takes him in, a trace of frosted ice on the glass behind him. She wants Grayson to stay framed in the doorway, so promising and new, like the missing part of a sketch.

CHAPTER TWENTY

After Chuck gives his Honda away, he stands in the warm house and looks out at the yard, at the woman's old car sitting in his driveway like a scab. He pours himself a glass of milk and can't seem to calm down. He is supposed to be packing up and leaving this afternoon. Outside, some dead leaves blow across the slick lawn.

He thinks of Cat, of Natasha. He thinks of Cat having that key made all those years ago, the key she never put on the key chain. Whatever happened to the key itself? He thinks of that day in November, the bitter rain, when she told him her idea.

Cat was poised, sitting at the kitchen table, and he knew she wanted to run something by him. He thought maybe she wanted them to sign up for that new gym that had just opened off Route 22. Or maybe she wanted to go to Scotland or Ireland, two places on her list. He readied himself for what was coming and felt a tinge of excitement because that's how she was: something fun always up her sleeve. But when she showed him the key in her palm, when she said Natasha would live in the garage apartment, he felt annoyed. Assaulted.

"For how long?" He crossed his arms.

"For as long as she needs." Cat looked down at the key chain on the table. It was as if she was waiting for his final confirmation, and then she would slip the key in place like some ceremonial gesture. She folded her hands together. There was something about how sure she was. Something about that key just waiting for the girl he barely knew.

He imagined Natasha never leaving. He imagined Cat wouldn't want to go to Hilton Head anymore because she wouldn't want to leave Natasha alone for so long. He had *just* retired. They had just finally started that wonderful new chapter of going away for the winter. He imagined Leela and Ben, getting settled as adults, both just out of the house, feeling awkward when they returned home. His heart started pounding, and he wanted to shout at her. He wanted to say, *We waited for this forever! This is it. We're finally here, and you want to toss it all away*.

But instead he just said, "Absolutely not."

Cat's smile disappeared. "What?" she asked.

"You heard me."

"But why?" She covered her mouth. He can still see the pain on her face, like she'd been slapped, and even now, it makes him wince. "She needs us, Chuck. You'll come around."

He had just washed his hands, and he tossed the dish towel onto the counter. "Why do you think you can just do this? This kid is playing you, getting your necklace, hooking you in with all her problems. I never thought you were so . . . so . . ."

"What?" she said. "Say it."

"Gullible."

She shook her head. He saw tears in her eyes. "I thought you liked her."

"I don't even *know* her, Cat. You don't either. We have children. We have a life. Why are you even . . . even *thinking* of this?"

She covered her face. She suddenly looked weak. He isn't sure if his memory is wrong because now he pictures her as she looked in her final days, when the illness had taken everything. She hunched over the table. "I just know we can make her life better," she said quietly.

He wanted to consider her words. He always came around

to what Cat wanted. She could always convince him. But he saw an opening in her silence, in the resignation of her gesture, and he wanted to send a clear signal that he wasn't going to let her ruin their last good years. "I'll *never* change my mind," he said.

She looked up at him, and her eyes. Her terrible, lonely eyes. "Chuck, I thought . . . Can we at least talk about this?"

"No. Not in my house, not in my life." He had never spoken to her this way. Why did he feel it was necessary? He glared at her, and he hated himself in that moment. But he couldn't show any uncertainty.

"You're absolutely horrible," she said, and the chair fell back and cracked when she stood up. She stormed out of the room, and he could see she was crying.

He didn't know why he had acted so forcefully. He was stunned that she hadn't given him any indication of this plan. He felt betrayed, as if she kept secrets from him. Yes, he had thought Natasha was nice enough, but who knew what baggage came with her? What if she found herself with some troublesome boyfriend? What if she was a thief? How were they to know? He imagined them on the news. *Elderly couple duped.*

Also, he felt jealous in an odd way. He had never seen Cat so close, so *familiar* with someone beyond the kids and him—of course she had friends (Marguerite, Linda, Sue), but she never seemed to be so consumed and worried about their happiness the way she was with Natasha. It all was like he knew a flood was coming, and he needed to move their stuff to higher ground.

He stood alone in the kitchen and bent down to fiddle with the broken chair. His bitter tone shocked even him. He and Cat had always had an equal partnership. He clenched his teeth that day and saw himself as cruel. It was as if he was running for his life, for their lives. It was as if all his terrible worries in Vietnam had come back to him and he was saying no. *Hell no.* "Let her manage on her own," he said to himself, alone in the kitchen.

What had happened? How had Cat gotten so far along with these plans, having the key made, maybe even freshening up the small studio apartment over the garage they never used, and she hadn't even asked him? Was he such a pushover, such a passive participant in their home that she assumed it was no big deal? What did she take him for? He was surprised she had even mentioned it at that point. Why not just have Natasha sitting at the dinner table when he got home?

But Cat's face.

He cannot forget it. It was so many years ago, but he sees that hurt face, that face he loved, that body that battled cancer. He cannot separate any of it. He thinks the fight and her illness and dying and their love and the fun they had and her great disappointment are all in one continuous circle, all happening at once. After the argument, he remembers she didn't come home that night. He had fished around, calling both kids that night without mentioning her, but they hadn't let on if they'd spoken to her. Then she came home in the morning and didn't look at him. There were days and days of silence afterward. The hurt they couldn't talk about, eating dinner at separate times, Cat sleeping in the guest room and barely looking at him.

But they'd gotten over it. Little by little, she came around, and he offered her an occasional weak *hey-I'm-sorry* smile. They got over it, and they had thousands of happy days since then, but he can't stop thinking now they only ever had that one fight.

He wonders if, deep down, she ever forgave him. He never apologized properly.

Cat, living breathing Cat, had thought they could change whatever course Natasha was on, give her the love that her family hadn't, that the world hadn't, and he stands here in the kitchen now, their house so still, just the television murmuring in the living room.

He hears the salt truck go by. The winter sun is bright through the open blinds, and he wonders if he's still leaving for Hilton Head today.

Does what Cat wanted seem so unreasonable now? Now Natasha would have been grown up and moved on. Now Natasha, who he thinks he hung up on a few moments ago right when she answered, right when he saw the newspaper lady fall from the window, would be on her own, and why couldn't he have just trusted Cat?

He feels visible, as if Cat can see him. "Now what?" he says to the air.

He thinks of giving the newspaper woman the car. It is clear now how Cat felt. For days afterward, he almost gave in, he almost said, "Okay, just call her," because he hated when they fought, and he wondered if he could get used to the idea.

But he couldn't. They couldn't talk about any of it. She put her hand up in the *halt* sign when he took a breath to say something.

He wondered if the fight would ever be over.

And then one day it was. One day, she was okay, and he went along with it and didn't bother trying to explain himself the way he used to after an argument, and they never referred to Natasha after that.

There were times, lying in bed at night, talking in their low, sleepy voices, that he wanted to roll over, barely making out her face in the dark. He wanted to say, "So what was that all about with Natasha?" but he never did, and the years went by, and they had their winter trips to Hilton Head, and they were themselves. Happy.

Now he feels like a hypocrite. How convenient that he can just give away the car and not have to consult anyone. "I'll fix it somehow," he whispers.

He thinks of the empty space in the garage. He just handed the title and keys over to the woman, told her he would transfer it via a notary later.

She was stunned, standing there holding Cat's yellow-and-white towel, her eyes wide. "You're giving me this?" she said, looking at the little red Honda that sat on the left side of the garage, the small pillow in the passenger seat that Cat used at the end for the pain in her back.

He told her to call her insurance company right away, gave her his cell phone number. If he's in Hilton Head or on his way when she calls, he will call his lawyer's office and tell them to handle the request. He felt like he needed to give her the car today, and he just handed her the title in that folder, handed her the key with the small worn leather key ring. He didn't even take anything out of the car.

"I hope it brings you a lot of luck," he said, and tears ran down her pretty face. He felt terrible that she fell, has thought about her being out in this messy weather every morning, and when she slipped, and when he heard that wreck of a car making such awful noises, the answer was simple. She was his Natasha. Even though he knew her less. Even though he wasn't inviting her to live with him. But still. He basically did what Cat had wanted to do, and he feels rotten now.

"I won't ever, ever forget this," the woman said. She left her old car at the end of the driveway, pulled to the side, promising she'd be back to get rid of it soon.

He took Cat's towel from her and tucked it under his arm. "Drive safe. Especially today while you're still on my insurance."

He smiled. This went against anything the reasonable side of him ever wanted to do.

She looked at the car and back at him. She hesitated, and then limped over to him (he imagined she ached terribly). "Thank you." Tears ran down her face, and her eyes looked like something was released. She put her arms around him, smelling faintly like lilacs, and her hug was fierce.

After she pulled away, he stared at the morning sunlight coming in and highlighting the empty space in the garage. The spare refrigerator hummed. He looked at the shelves of paint cans and terra-cotta pots. God, the hole the car left. He put his chin to his chest and thought about getting on the road. The rental takeover date is tomorrow. No time to lollygag.

The pain of seeing that space in the garage feels necessary—like a wound that needs sunlight.

He imagines the woman, whose full name is on a piece of paper in his pocket with her insurance information. Emma? Ellie? He takes out the slip of paper. Ella. Ella Burke. He sits and thinks of that name. He doesn't know why, but he whispers it out loud.

That last name sounds terribly familiar. Burke. He thinks of the local news, and a story that played continuously for a month. Didn't a Burke man disappear with his child?

He thinks back a few months ago. Summer, early fall? He remembers the picture of the girl and father. The young, kind mother standing next to Sergeant Kinney (whom Leela dated one summer when she was in college). He tries to remember the mother's face. He tries to picture this Ella woman. She seems about the same age, he thinks. Same dark hair.

He remembers the mother on the news had kind eyes—like hers. He remembers he had believed her immediately. He believed her pain, her distress. She had addressed her statement directly to her husband, or ex-husband or whatever. Chuck remembers watching and feeling so sick. "I just want her home safely. I don't care about anything else." Then she had looked more deeply into the camera and said her daughter's name: "Mommy misses you, honey. Please come home."

Yes, he knows it's her. Oh, that poor woman. He can see her lying there after she fell, looking so alone. He never heard an update. Is her daughter still missing? Will they ever find her? His heart sinks. Imagine delivering a paper when your world is gone? Imagine getting up every day in the dark to face it without your child?

It all makes sense. She has been battling this silently. He sees her lying there again. *Ella*. He can see her in the driveway, he can see her face on the news, speaking out and trying to reach her baby. He looks at the empty spot in the garage again, and he is glad the car went to her. It now seems like a small gesture, but maybe it has done something for her.

He imagines that daughter coming back one day, sitting in the back seat of that car he and Cat had barely used. He imagines a stuffed animal beside her, a drink in the cup carrier of the door. He imagines the car getting messy the way their cars used to get when the children were young, and he smiles, as if this vision can change the future. As if he can send it Ella's way, and it will return her girl to her.

—

Later he stands in the bedroom and looks out over the sidewalk, the front yard. He is nervous all over again for Natasha to answer—if that even was Natasha before. Her voice came on, and he saw Ella fall, and he just bolted down the steps, the woman repeating over and over, "Hello? Hello?" Now on the fourth ring, a woman answers. "It's, uh, me again. Sorry about before."

"What? Who's this?"

"Is this Natasha?" he says. "Do I have the correct number?" Looking out the window, he sees Ella's old car in the driveway, and something about it depresses him.

"Yes?" He feels relief. And a new army of fear marches through his body.

"I have a lot to tell you," he says.

"Who *is* this?"

His throat sounds hoarse. He wishes he'd had another cup of coffee. "This is Chuck Ayers."

"Chuck who?"

"I think you knew my wife, Catherine. She used to come to your restaurant when you worked there. With the sketchbook."

"Oh . . . Cat," she says. "*Catty.*" She laughs then. Her voice changes completely, and it calms him.

"The one and only." He taps his fingers on the desk. "I'm sorry to call you so early—"

"S'okay. I'm always up." She waits. "How is she anyway . . . Catty?" Hearing Natasha call her this name makes him realize how hard this will be.

"I'm sorry." He wipes his eyes. "She um, she isn't . . ."

"Oh, no. Oh no."

"Yeah. In the spring. She died on May twenty-third."

"My god."

"Yes." His voice has gotten quiet.

"From what, can I ask?" He hears a beep on her end, as though her coffee is finished brewing or her clothes are done in the dryer.

"Cancer. Lungs, then bone."

"Oh, poor Cat." He hears her sigh. "I wish I'd been able to see her." She exhales, and he feels like she's breathing right into him. "I just pictured her always staying the way she was."

His chest tightens, and he sees Cat in the café with her sketch-book and cardigan. She is sitting at the kitchen table looking right at him with her knowing smile. "Yeah, I'm sorry. It happened quickly." He sees his reflection in the mirror, his hunched-over shoulders in the glass. He realizes he doesn't know what he wanted to tell her. Just this. Over and over. "I should have called you when she was dying, when she died. I'm terribly sorry."

She clears her throat. "Well, you had enough to worry about, sir. We'd fallen out of touch, which was my fault."

"Yes, I guess." He feels a little better. He pauses. "But I'm so sorry I wasn't better about the whole thing."

"What do you mean?"

"I wasn't great about her friendship with you."

"You weren't?"

"I told her you couldn't move in here."

"Wait." He hears her fill a glass with ice, and the unmistak-able sound of a cat. "When was I gonna move in there?"

His heart sinks. Apologizing is one thing, but now he's giving her information she never processed. He assumed they had talked about it. "Um, she was worried about you. She wanted to invite you to stay here. She even had a key made—and bought a fancy key chain, and I told her we shouldn't get involved. I told her to leave you alone."

She sighs. "Oh, Catty." She exhales again, and he is almost shaking. "That was nice of her." He still pictures Natasha as that young, pretty teenager. He hears a little kid talking to her in the background. "Mommy will be off in a minute," she whispers.

"I didn't know how she left it with you after that . . . we had a terrible fight, and we didn't really talk about it for a while." He feels clammy, half sick. "I didn't know you well enough, I guess. I should have tried to understand the whole thing better."

"Mr. Ayers." She clears her throat. "The last time I saw her, she came to the restaurant, and she looked preoccupied or sad or something. She told my boss he was garbage for the way he treated me—he was always swearing at me and slamming pots and pans. She laid him out in front of everyone—it was fantastic. She told me I needed to quit *that day*. She said don't get stuck here. She gave me a handful of money, almost a thousand dollars, and told me to take a bus as far as I could."

"I didn't know any of that."

He hears something in the background, like cereal pouring into a bowl. He tries to imagine what her house looks like. "It was the kindest thing anyone ever did for me. And the best advice I ever got. I left then because she told me to. I believed her."

He thinks of the money for a second, and he feels relieved Cat gave it to Natasha. It doesn't even things out, but it's better than before. Good on you, Cat. "That was how she was."

"I've actually been saving to pay her back—all these years. I should have called. I should have written her. I wanted to have the money, though. It's like when you don't go to the doctor's because you want to lose ten pounds first, and then years go by, and you never end up going. I thought I'd take a trip there one day and we'd have coffee and she'd say, look at what you turned into." She laughs. "Even though I didn't turn into much."

He smiles, as if she can see it. "I'm sure that's not true." He feels a lump in his throat, an unmistakable heavy feeling. This conversation has brought Cat right into the room again, and he misses her worse than ever. "Well, I'm sorry to have called with this news."

"I feel terrible about Catty. She was a gem—my day brightened every time she walked into the café."

"Yeah."

"But can I ask you something?"

He blots the corners of his eyes with his sweater sleeve. He is in no condition to drive to Hilton Head. He is in no condition for any of this. He feels the floor falling out from under him. "Sure."

"What made you not want me there?"

He waits. He looks around the still, quiet bedroom. "I don't really know," he says. "I just thought my wife was getting in over her head." He feels like he's confessing, and he wants her to absolve him. He wants this finally to be over, no matter how wrong he was. "I guess I worried you were some type of con artist."

She gives him a long, long pause. He wonders if she's still on the line. "I was practically a child," she says. Her sigh then is exasperated. "I needed someone so badly."

And with that, she hangs up on him.

CHAPTER TWENTY-ONE

Ella turns the corner in her new car—*did this really just happen?*—and the wheel is tight and aligned. There is no wiggle in it like in her other one. She wonders if the car is even on because it runs so quietly.

It smells new and clean, and she likes the small pillow, which she props against her tailbone that hurts so bad. She stopped at Rite Aid and bought a jumbo bottle of Advil and a big jug of water, and she hopes the pain will go away soon. She has finished up the last of her paper deliveries today, her arm throbbing every time she tossed one.

She has to be at the bridal shop very soon, but after debating, she decides to call in sick. They are actually understanding, and she looks forward to lying down and trying to sleep.

She has felt guilty since Mr. Ayers gave her those keys, and she loves the car, but it's not right to take this from him, is it?

She needs it, but is that who she is? Surely someone else needs it more than she does, and maybe she should just tell him that, tell him thanks, that was so, so sweet, but really I can't accept this. I thought I could, but I can't.

But he had insisted.

And somehow it had all made sense when he'd given her the key—as though she needed the car for something specific. She wishes she could pay him back. If she does end up keeping the car, when things get settled and Riley's back, she will find a way to repay him.

No one has ever been that kind to her, and when she hugged him, she felt something almost break in him, as though it had been a long time since someone had touched him.

He is a good man. She saw it in his eyes. All those months she saw him, she knew. She knew who he was.

She leaves the new car on the street where she usually parks and walks to the steps that lead to her apartment. She will have to ask someone to drive her to Mr. Ayers's house to pick up her car. Maybe her downstairs neighbor, David, when he's home from work.

She is on the first step now, and her phone rings so loudly that it shocks her. The number is a strange one. She stands still and answers, readying herself for disappointment.

She remembers Wendy, a writer friend from college, saying to her the last time she was in town a couple of years ago how she anticipates rejection. "Anytime I get an email from a literary journal, I just say, *I don't want your bullshit anyway*, before I even open it, and sometimes I'm surprised that it's an acceptance."

I don't want your bullshit anyway, Ella thinks, preparing to hear a robot voice that says *Please hold for an important announcement*, but the voice she hears almost knocks her over.

"Mommy!"

She gasps, and thinks this has to be a dream. This day— falling, the car out of nowhere, and this call. The sky seems so bright all of a sudden. Is this real? She has thought about that sound so many times. She has worried she might have forgotten her daughter's voice. She has watched old videos of Riley to hear her, over and over. Her knees feel weak, and her stomach somersaults. "Oh my god. Riley? Riley?"

"Mommy, you're okay!"

She starts sobbing, but she steadies herself. She is so grateful and panicked and in disbelief. Riley's alive. She's *alive*. "Baby, where are you?"

"At the vacation place," Riley says. "Daddy said you were sick. He said Grandma's taking care of you."

Sick? She doesn't have time to react. Her hands are shaking. How can she find Riley? What is the right question to ask? She has practiced so many times for what she should say if this moment comes.

She knew Riley would find a way to her.

She knew that phone number was etched in her, an invisible cord between them. She doesn't want to worry Riley. She decides to play the game. "Oh, I'm feeling so much better."

"I can't wait to tell Daddy you're better."

She panics. "Where is he?" She wishes she had another phone. She wishes her neighbor were home so she could tell him to call Jared Kinney. Could they trace the call like they do on TV? She looks around. Her other neighbor upstairs, Lily, travels for work and is never there. Something tells her to get the details. *Get every last one.*

She hears Riley's calm breathing and casual words, and Ella is so grateful, so relieved, that no matter what, she hasn't been worried. If things have seemed normal to her for these last few months, that is the best scenario. What has that bastard done? She feels fire under her skin. "He went to look for his car keys."

"Baby, maybe don't tell him you talked to me yet." She pauses. "We can surprise him."

"Oh, okay." That's her girl. Riley was always so cooperative.

She wants to scream, or cry. She is so close to her daughter. How can she find her? "Look out the window, Bitsy-Boo. Is he coming back yet?"

She hears her hard breathing as she walks. God, the memory

of her, the ease of talking to her, is instantly familiar. It feels like no time has passed, and she's grateful for that. They are so relaxed with one another. "Nope," she says. "He has all the car doors open and he's looking under the seats."

"Okay." She takes a deep breath. "When you look out the window, what else do you see? Mountains, buildings? I want to see your place perfectly, baby."

Riley laughs. "I spy . . . something blue."

Keep cool, she tells herself. "*I spy!* We'll play that next." She manages a small laugh. "Can you just, as fast as you can, list as many things as you see. Let's race to see how many things you can tell me."

"Okay! A pool, a hill, all cars in their spots." The phone crackles, and her voice is garbled for a minute.

Please, Ella thinks. *Please don't lose the connection.* "Is the pool covered and closed, or can you swim in it now?"

Riley laughs. "It's warm here, Mommy. I just went swimming a few minutes ago." She has an image of her little girl in a bathing suit, goggles on her head, a towel around her shoulders.

"And you're in a hotel or is it like a house?"

"Daddy said he told you this. He said he talks to you every day."

"Oh, I know, but I want to hear what you think of it."

"Well, I like Michelle and her kids. We play a lot. I like Game Zone. Daddy lets me fill my card with ten dollars each time. I won a green alien yesterday."

She tries to jot those items down somewhere. Michelle. Kids. Game Zone. "And how about school? How's school?"

"Mommy, you know I don't go to school anymore." She laughs. Her voice is so filled with sun and pleasantness that it almost knocks Ella over.

"Silly me, that's right." She thinks for a second. "Riley?"

"Yes?"

"Is there a sign out in the parking lot?"

"The Copper Falls sign?" *Where are you? What city? What state?* How does she get that information?

"Honey, this is a tough question, but I want to see what a smarty-pants you are."

"Okay, I'm ready," Riley says, and laughs again.

"How do you spell the state you're in?"

"Oh, let me think. F-L-O-I-R."

"Florida!" Ella almost screams it.

"You know that."

"I do," Ella says, and starts to cry. "Um, where is he now?"

"Oh, he's walking up the steps."

"Hang up, Riley. Hang up, now, and let's keep it a surprise." Ella whispers, knowing how her whispering will make Riley whisper.

"Okeydokey," Riley whispers, and Ella's eyes burn.

"Call me again if you can do it during surprise time. Okay? Okay? I love you. I love you."

"Mommy?"

"Yes?"

"I miss you."

Tears pour down Ella's face. "Soon, baby. Really soon." She pictures Kyle's footsteps. She pictures his hand on the doorknob. She is going to vomit. She is going to faint. Please please please don't let him hear her.

"Love you," Riley whispers, and then there is no one on the line.

Ella holds the phone and stares at it. She has moved down from her step, and she stands in front of her apartment building.

The morning is sunny and chilly, patches of ice on the sidewalk. She no longer feels the ache of where she fell. *She is okay. She is okay. She is okay.* Kyle has lied to her, but Ella is happy for that.

She rakes her fingers through her hair. She feels her legs buckling. She feels the bile rise in her throat, but she takes a deep breath and blows out.

She sits on the step and grips her knees and breathes. *In. Out.* What now? What now? Jared. Can they track the call? What if they mess it up? She knows exactly where her baby is. She can get to Florida. She can Google Copper Falls.

Cindy.

She'll be happy to know Riley's okay. She has to call her. She imagines them hugging each other and jumping up and down. But, but, but . . .

She can't do anything to mess this up. She knows where her daughter is. Exactly.

Ella looks at the new car keys. "I'm coming, Riley," she says to the air, and she rushes toward her gift.

CHAPTER TWENTY-TWO

When his dad was dying, a day after Chuck and Cat had arrived with white lilies and roses and they had talked about the fishpond they used to have, his dad mumbled something about locking the windows. Chuck took his hand, limp but still gripping, Chuck's mother kissed his father's face, and Cat tucked the sheet around his dad's chest and started to cry.

The three of them stood there, an antique clock ticking, and they whispered reassuring words to him: *you can go now, you're safe, we love you*, and Chuck noticed how beautiful the evening sun looked as it came into the dining room where his father's hospital bed was, hitting the wooden bookshelves and corner cupboards, hitting his father's body in a holy way, and Chuck thought, *This is okay*.

When Cat started to die in May, he felt none of that peace.

He felt desperate, pacing around the room as Leela sat with her and wiped her forehead with a cool washcloth, and Ben and Asher held each other in the corner of the bedroom, Ben's hand over his mouth, Asher rubbing his back, and it all felt out of order. Isaac, Leela's husband, had taken Gabby to a new place in Allentown that had bowling and laser tag. "I'll try to keep her mind off it," he'd said, his eyes somber behind tortoiseshell glasses. Gabby was quiet and pale, and she hugged Chuck, who nodded absently. He felt like he was falling off a cliff when Gabby bent over and kissed Cat's cheek before they left.

It was midmorning, a cloudy, gloomy day, and Chuck was

still in his pajamas from last night, his teeth unbrushed, his hair messy.

He hadn't had his coffee yet, and he wanted to yell at someone when Cat started with those long, slow breaths like his father took, like his mother took a few years later, like he remembered his grandparents taking when they were dying.

But he couldn't with Cat. He wanted to send the children from the room, he wanted to say two thousand more things to her.

"I'm sorry, can you just give me a second?" he said to Leela and Ben and Asher. They all looked stunned, Leela lurking for a moment longer, looking back and forth from him to Cat the way she used to do as a child if they were having some small disagreement, and then left the room. He turned to Cat when he heard the door close quietly. "Can you still hear me?" he whispered.

—

Now he's driving his all-packed-and-ready car to Rescue Ranch.

He feels feverish, the adrenaline making him sick and excited inside. He taps his hand on the steering wheel.

He is going to bring home a pig.

He doesn't know if he has to walk a pig on a leash, he doesn't know what his life will be like with a pig, but he knows he will adopt that one he saw the other day. *Frederick.*

He doesn't know if he'll stay in Pennsylvania another day or two, or if he'll just let the pig rest on the front seat and start the trip south. He grins, and he sees his ridiculous, unrecognizable face in the rearview mirror. On the seat next to him is a padded moving blanket. He feels horrified and euphoric at who he is now. This impulsive, pig-buying person. The joy he feels is like a drug, and he is rushing toward it, his foot on the gas. Every second he gets closer to Rescue Ranch feels like it will save him. He should have called Kirsten this morning and told her he was on his way.

Soon he will be petting that pig on the head, and soon he will be FaceTiming Gabby and saying, "Meet Pap's new friend," and it makes him chuckle and feel decadent and crazy. He might as well get a tattoo while he's at it. Cat's name in fancy writing, or Charlotte's spider web with writing on it.

He is getting a pig. A damn pig!

On the same day he handed his car keys to a stranger.

He knows what he would think of someone who did these things. Lost their marbles. Off the deep end. He looks at the mirror again and smiles at himself. He feels like Scrooge at the end of *A Christmas Carol* with his holiday goose and sack of toys. *What day is this? It's Christmas, sir.*

He takes a deep breath. Will Kirsten let him take Frederick home immediately? Is there a process? He wishes he had asked these things.

Oh, Cat. You'd be proud.

When he gets to Rescue Ranch, he half trots to the door like a schoolboy. A big van almost hits him in the parking lot. The notices on the bulletin board flutter as he rushes inside, and Kirsten sits at her desk.

"Hello again, Mr. A.," she says warmly. "Glad to see you back." Her smile is bright and polite, and he notices the hint of gray eyeshadow she wears. He has a hard time looking at her now without seeing the pain on her face behind everything else. But this place is pleasant. He's glad she can be at such a happy place. Maybe it's good medicine.

When he announces he's there to pick up Frederick and where is the little guy, Kirsten frowns.

"Oh, Mr. A., I'm sorry, but Frederick has found a home." Her eyes are compassionate, and she absently touches one of her small hoop earrings when she talks.

"He has?" He feels like he's standing in an empty valley and sees a rush of floodwater heading for him. He gets an out-of-body glimpse of himself. A silly old man with his wallet out, his car keys jingling, a foolish, I'm-ready-for-my-pig expression on his face.

Frederick can't be gone. Chuck has walked himself through this vision so many times: following after Kirsten, the papers he'd sign, the check he'd write, the congratulatory ear rub he'd give Frederick. The way they'd sail off together in the car, the wide sky in front of them and the long, promising road south to Hilton Head.

"Yes, he found a farm." She tilts her head back.

He crosses his arms. "Isn't that what you tell a child when an animal dies?"

"Oh, he's definitely not dead. He's happy. They just came to pick him up a few hours ago." She looks down at her desk and rummages around. She holds up her phone with a picture. "See, look. He's already settling in."

There is Frederick, almost smiling, standing next to a black-and-white pig, in someone's kitchen. They got their pig a friend.

Behind Frederick is a refrigerator with so many magnets and children's artwork. Next to the refrigerator, a boy and girl who must be twins because they are the same height and wear matching polar bear pajamas, smile at the camera.

Chuck's shoulders sag, and he hands the phone back to her. "Well, he couldn't have done better."

"Yes, he's lucky." Regret crosses her face after she says this, as though she wanted him to have Frederick. She gestures meekly to the hallway. "But we have plenty of other animals who would love you in their lives."

He frowns. "I was kind of set on the pig."

She stares into his eyes, and he feels his expression collapse. "I know." She nods. "But please come back if you ever change your mind. I'll help you."

He waves to her, and he heads toward the door. A guy with a crewcut comes through the door and nods to him. He is carrying three coffees from Starbucks.

"Your latte, madam," Chuck hears the guy say, and Kirsten says something sweet in return, and their voices trail off as he opens the door and the bell jingles.

He feels his body weakening. There is no way he can make that long trip now. What just happened? Was he really going to buy a pig? Thank goodness for those other people—the people who now have two kids, two pigs. What a mistake Frederick avoided, and just by a hair.

Outside, the cold wind whips his face, and the sun hides behind gray clouds, and he feels more alone than he has since Cat died. His car looks bleak and salt-stained in the parking lot, and he misses his children.

He misses what he thought he was going to be able to tell them about Frederick. He hasn't been excited in so long, hasn't been able to deliver good news. The pig was an opportunity—to turn over a new leaf, have a whole other chapter ahead of him. If he could buy a pig, he could be the man who saves himself.

He could bring in a hundred other fun things to his life to make Cat proud, and less gone.

He zips his coat, but he has no desire to go back to his car. A small red bench sits near the Rescue Ranch door, and he decides to rest there for a second just to breathe and feel sorry for himself. "Your favorite hobby is feeling sorry for yourself," Cat used to say, laughing.

"I'm very good at it," he'd reply.

The bench is cold against his legs, and he shakes his head, and the lady who almost ran him over in the van is walking toward him.

A Chihuahua strolls a few feet from her, no leash. She scratches her hands and starts crying.

Chuck calls to her. "Are you okay, ma'am?"

She shakes her head. "I'm terrible." She looks down at her dog, which has bulging eyes. "I don't think I can go inside," she says.

—

Kirsten stands up when she sees Chuck walking in the door with the crying woman and the tiny dog. "Hello, ma'am. You must be Mallory. I'm Kirsten."

Chuck notices they use *surrender* as a noun in this place. He thinks life requires surrender now. Today he was trying to surrender his old self, attempting to work toward something better. "Yes, Mallory is here to give up Oliver because she's badly allergic." He realizes after he says it that Kirsten probably already had this information.

Kirsten grasps some papers and comes over to Mallory, and Chuck stands back. "Hi, there, Oliver," Kirsten says to the dog, holding her fist out to him as he shivers in Mallory's arms. Oliver sniffs Kirsten's hand. He lets Kirsten pet him. "Oh, look at you. So sweet."

"He is," Mallory says. "He is." She seems to be calming down as she watches Kirsten interact with Oliver.

Kirsten puts her hands out, and Chuck feels proud of her. *Isn't she something?* Cat would've said. "May I?"

Mallory looks down. "Oh," she says, and sighs. She squeezes Oliver more tightly and kisses him. Chuck stands beside her. He doesn't know if he should walk away now.

His car is outside waiting, but he is pulled into this: the woman, the dog, the Rescue Ranch that handles scenes like this all the time. He thinks of what he can tell Mallory—that her hives will go away, that she will breathe clearly. He thinks of how free she will be, but then he imagines her empty house, the dog bowl in the kitchen, the tiny leash probably sitting in her van. What toys has Oliver left on her bedroom floor? What routines of her daily life did he fossil himself into, and how will she cope without him?

When Cat was dying, it seemed they were glued to doctors' appointments and then radiation and chemo and him trying to figure out insurance paperwork and medical bills and medication. Once, he sat at their kitchen table, she had just fallen asleep upstairs, and he didn't think he could do another day. The thought floated by that if she died, he wouldn't have any of this anymore. He swatted this idea away as quickly as it came, and he hated himself for even having that notion, but now he sees Mallory and the rash on her hands, and he wonders if she'll at least be relieved some things are done with.

—

Later, he walks Mallory back to her car, and he thinks her hands already look less red, less troubled. "It will get better," he tells her, and wonders if he believes this about anything.

When he watches her drive away, he wonders how the heck he found himself on this day in this parking lot, comforting a woman he never met before. Does he feel proud of himself, for getting out of his house, for failing with Frederick, but still standing here?

Hasn't he been more Cat today than Chuck? At her funeral, a friend of hers pointed to his heart and said, "She'll always live in you," and he dismissed this, but now he wonders if having known her so well is pulling him along.

He should be on his way to Hilton Head. He should be listening to their old music with a lump in his throat.

He looks around. It doesn't really get easier. That is the truth. Everyone just tricks themselves. He feels his shoulders sink.

A flock of geese fly overhead. The cars sail by on the highway, and he notices Macarthur Elementary School next door. He wonders if that's where Ella's daughter went before her father took her. He looks at the empty swing set, the sign for the school with a message on it that says something about a January PTA meeting.

The disappointment almost knocks him over. All the hope he felt when he gave Ella the car, when he decided to buy Frederick, has faded. He looks at his shoes.

He thought a pig could save him. He thought he would be leaving this place gleefully, his new life in front of him like a banner in the sky. He keeps feeling worse, as though he came down with something that hit him fast. He is tired. "I'm so sorry," he says to no one.

CHAPTER TWENTY-THREE

Ella cannot for the life of her focus.

She started driving, and knows she shouldn't.

She shakes.

She needs to call Jared Kinney. But something keeps stopping her. Once she calls him, it's out of her hands. The police haven't found Riley. For months, they've been trying.

Her head and heart feel funny. She feels like Cindy is the only one who would understand right now. She should go there. Maybe Cindy will know what to do. But something is preventing that, too, a voice inside her that says, wait. Just wait.

She doesn't think anyone else can save Riley but her, and isn't this car—the car she just got today, this safe, new car on the day her daughter called—a sign that she should go to her daughter? She has everything she needs.

She has found Copper Falls on a map—in Daytona Beach—where they honeymooned of all places. What made him take Riley there? Who the hell is Michelle? Did he think he could hide forever? She doesn't even know this man anymore.

—

She imagines waiting in the parking lot of Copper Falls. Imagines seeing Kyle leave to run an errand, imagines the butterflies and horror she'd feel as she tiptoes up the steps. What's next? Would she bash in the door with a patio chair? Would she knock gently?

Riley, it's Mommy. Open up. And oh, that reunion. How would it feel to see her little face? *I'm here. I'm here like I promised.*

She could be in Florida in about fifteen hours. She wouldn't need to sleep. She could drink jumbo black coffee after jumbo black coffee, this new, well-running car all geared and ready.

Riley is okay. Riley is okay.

She sounds more than okay.

Ella could wear a baseball hat, wait in the parking lot, not blinking, until Kyle or Riley appeared. Oh, how her daughter would run to her.

She had remembered Ella's number. Ella knew she would.

I have so much to tell you, Riley used to say after a playdate.

She has just filled the gas tank, and she's ready. She focuses her energy, visualizes the long drive.

By tomorrow, she will have her daughter. This will be over. She shakes. She feels something sing inside her. It will all be over soon.

But then she imagines Kyle. He had gone to all this trouble—leaving his job, covering his tracks, abandoning his parents—and won't just shrug and say, "Fair is fair, take our child home."

Ella is shaking hard now. She pulls over and takes out her phone. She needs to call Jared.

It is like the day Riley disappeared all over again, but there is a solution here, like a shaft of light in a dark maze. She can barely breathe. She holds the phone, looks out at the highway.

She visualizes her trip south, but the roads seem to vanish in front of her, like everything in a dream dissolving.

She scrolls through her recent calls and presses Jared's number like she's hitting a buzzer for help.

She breathes, in and out, in and out, and waits for him to answer.

—

In five minutes, Jared's cop car pulls up behind her. Another officer is in the passenger seat. She feels frozen.

She can't stand the thought of agents swarming Riley's place. Will Riley cry if they rip her away from Kyle? What will Kyle say or do? Who is this new dangerous Kyle with nothing to lose?

In her rearview mirror, she sees Jared get out of his car and lumber toward her. The other officer moves to the driver's seat. She sees the gun on Jared, his badge gleaming in the late-morning sun.

She thinks of Riley again. That voice. What made her call today? Was it the first time Kyle left his phone out of his sight? She thinks of Riley missing school all this time, and it angers her. What was the point of this? But Ella will help her catch up. Whatever it takes.

Jared seems to take forever. She hears his shoes crunch the gravel. She wonders what Riley and Kyle did for Christmas. She wants to punch Kyle, to grab his shoulders and make him explain. She thinks of the lie of Kyle saying Ella has been sick, and did that worry Riley? God. She was almost close enough to touch, it seemed.

Jared nods at Ella now and opens the driver-side door. People will probably think he pulled her over, but to hell with them. If they had any idea.

On her right is a sidewalk and a wide expanse of grass, dull from the winter. There are trees and a soccer field. Once, she took Riley there, and Riley ran and ran and ran. "Antelope!" Ella shouted, and they giggled together.

Years before that, Kyle and Ella, not married yet, had gone and kicked a soccer ball around. She had gotten a cramp from running so much. He had put his arm around her, the grass-stained soccer ball at his side. They had kissed in the car.

She feels a lump in her throat she can't swallow. She cannot take another minute of this.

She is so close to Riley she could scream. *Please handle this right. Please don't let her be in danger, or even scared.* She thinks of that sweet, unworried voice. It breaks her heart how Riley thought no one was bad—not her father, especially. She wishes she never had to find out.

"Ella," Jared says, and startles her back to the moment. His eyes are patient but serious. She looks up at him helplessly, then clenches the steering wheel. Her hands are shaking.

"Sorry," she says. How did she ever think she could get all the way to Florida?

Jared walks over to her passenger door, opens it and steps inside. Big man in a little car. "We are never supposed to do this," he says, and exhales. "You're lucky your brother covered for me when my mom found weed in my car one time." He looks at the car. "Rental?"

"A gift," she says. "From a man on my paper route." She must look like hell. She tries to smile, but she just trembles. She looks over at him and starts crying.

He has shaved since she last saw him, and his big head and soulful eyes are more pronounced. He looks younger without the beard, too. "We've alerted everyone. It won't be long now," he says.

"Cindy and Matt, too?"

He shakes his head. "We're going to wait on that notification."

"She's his mother."

He raises his eyebrows. "You never know."

"I'm scared." She wipes her eyes. For a second, she wants to call her own mother and hand Jared the phone so he can tell her everything. She wonders if they should be buying plane tickets or how that works. "I want to be there now. I have to get there."

"Let's just wait a little while longer," he says calmly. "They'll call me as soon as we know something, and then we'll get on the next plane." He stares straight ahead, chews his gum. As if reading her mind, he reaches into his pocket, points a pack of blue Extra at her. She reaches for it, slides a foil-wrapped piece out. It tastes cool in her mouth, sweet and refreshing. She folds the empty foil into a tiny square and places it on the dashboard.

"I like this little car." He slides down so his head is no longer pressed against the ceiling. She thinks of Dino on the *Flintstones*, how his head would pop out of the top. She looks over at Jared, and she can picture him in Fred Flintstone's outfit now—the tie, the orange sleeveless shirt, the big bare feet—and out of nowhere, she starts laughing.

"Sorry," she says, and covers her mouth.

She feels delirious. She wants to sing the *Flintstones* theme song. She chuckles and then more tears come. She cannot stop shaking. Riley, oh, Riley.

Please let her get back here safely. She wants to go home and wash Riley's sheets. She wants to tell the police in Florida to grab Mulligan, too. Why can't she just fly there now? She feels useless. She hates waiting.

She wants to bend time forward. Or backward. She wants Kyle to have had a change of heart months ago. Why did he do this? What is left for him after doing this?

Her shoulders start shaking. She chews the minty gum, and the tears fall, and Jared opens the glove compartment, finds a napkin Chuck must have left, and leans over and wipes her eyes.

She doesn't know why, but she reaches for his hand. She squeezes it. It is so big it reminds her of the Hulk. He nods at her, and doesn't pull his hand away.

"It'll be okay," he says. He squeezes her hand one last time and then slowly pulls his away. "Your little girl will be home soon, and she'll be okay."

Then his radio crackles on his shoulder, and he jumps to attention. He scrambles out of the car, and Ella watches his mouth move and wonders what he's saying.

CHAPTER TWENTY-FOUR

It is only 2:00 p.m., and Kirsten feels exhausted. Oliver, the new surrender, sleeps in the bed where Gloria used to sleep, and she keeps reaching down to pet him. She worries about the way he looks at her when she touches him—half mistrustful, half terrified.

Every time she touches Oliver, she warns him ahead of time. "Just me, buddy. Just saying hello." He puts his chin down on the edge of the dog bed and stares blankly. His little body seems to sigh.

She sighs, too.

She thinks of her dad, always in the middle of everything. He'd be singing along with Marvin Gaye on the record player, or Otis Redding, and he'd be baking bread, or he'd have the dining room chairs all on their sides, using an Allen wrench to tighten the legs.

"What would you people do without me?" he'd say.

She loved the chaos he brought, his unpredictability. *Let's go to the Philadelphia Zoo. Let's drive to Point Pleasant for the day.* When she was a teenager, she thought she'd outgrow him one day, but she never seemed to. Even in her early twenties, she still cherished him, still listened to every word, laughed at his jokes. She sat in the back seat as he drove her and her mother somewhere, charming the lady on roller skates at the drive-in hamburger place or telling the employee at the museum that her mother had a painting displayed there. "Honored to meet you," the museum guy said. "Which painting is yours?"

"View of a Slumped-Over Chemistry Scholar," her dad would

say, starting to grin, and her mother would hit his arm and laugh, too.

Kirsten looks down at Oliver now. "You poor thing." She gives him one of the tiny liver treats she keeps there. He gobbles it gratefully, so she leaves another and then another for him. He looks up and wags his tail, waiting for the next one.

Mallory has already called to see how Oliver is adjusting, and Kirsten reassured her he's settling in fine, told her he's right here by her feet. She has a thought for a second of Chuck Ayers, how disappointed he looked. And how good of him to try to comfort Mallory when she needed to feel less alone.

Now her phone rings again, and she's surprised to hear David's voice, the noise of driving in the background. "Did you sneak out?" she asks.

"I'm actually calling it quits today, Kirsten." She looks at the clock. She realizes she never ate lunch with all the craziness this morning. "I'm sorry, but I'm not feeling so hot." She can hear pain in his voice.

"Don't be sorry. You're the boss." She realizes then that she can't remember a day he hasn't been there. Has he never called in sick? Even if he's gotten back from a weekend conference, he has still shown up. "Are you okay?"

"I have this odd prickly feeling in my back. I think I just need to rest. Long days or something." He exhales. "And I have the kids tonight." He laughs. "But there are no sick days in parenting."

She straightens up at her desk chair. "David, is it only on one side, the pins and needles?"

"Yeah, it seems to be."

"Any rash?"

"I don't know. I haven't looked, but my chest itches."

"On the same side that your back hurts?"

"Yeah, actually."

She wipes dust off the stapler with her finger. "Um, you should probably go to a doctor. It might be shingles."

"Shingles?"

She takes a piece of tape off her dispenser and wraps it around her finger a few times and then crumbles it. "My, uh, dad had it last winter, and his started the same way."

When she tells David to keep her posted and hangs up, she thinks of the way he held his side and winced earlier. She thinks about her dad for a second with his shingles, the way he'd hold his rib cage where it hurt, the way he only wanted to wear a light undershirt and lie still on the sofa. The image of him, of course, saddens her, but she finds herself enjoying the diagnosing she just did. It gives her energy she hasn't felt in a long time. *You're good at this*, her dad would've said.

She likes this type of work—logical, systematic. Like a geometry proof you can work through. She is more her mother's daughter than she realized. She wants to learn more.

She felt flashes of this a few weeks back when she noticed Gloria, the bichon, was not herself and had a swollen cheek, thinking it was an abscessed tooth, so she called the vet in for a consult, who confirmed Kirsten's diagnosis. She did the same thing with Fig, the angora rabbit, when he held his paw to the side, and she thought he had a dislocated joint.

She held the pieces like quilt scraps, but didn't realize they added up to anything. The numbness since her dad's death has overridden her desire for a job that could figure out a problem and heal.

But there are countless problems out there that can be fixed. She thinks of Gloria after her surgery, her tooth pulled, her mouth less swollen.

Her dream hasn't left her. It just hibernated for a while.

She is young. She can still go to vet school. She smiles and sits up straighter. When she gets back from Europe, she's going to start applying again. She almost feels giddy.

"That smile," she hears, and she snaps out of it and sees Grayson standing there.

"You," she says. When she looks into his eyes, she feels a similar charge, the sizzle of current through a wire.

He holds up a black laptop cord. "Feel like taking a ride?"

She scrunches her eyebrows. "To where, the HP factory?"

"Our lovely boss just called a second ago. He forgot his charger and needs it to work from home . . . because of course, he can't be home and not work." He raises his eyebrows and shrugs. "He said he'd treat you and me for lunch if we dropped it off for him."

"He said I could go with you?"

He grins. "I asked, and he said it was a good idea because you've been putting in so many extra hours."

Her mind considers the possibility for a second that David knows about her and Grayson, that maybe even Grayson has told him about their relationship, since they work together all day. But David seemed to have a moment with her at her desk earlier, when they touched hands. "Lunch sounds great," she says, and smiles.

"It's a date." He looks at the cord. "Good old forgetful David."

She pictures David getting to his apartment now, a little slumped over, changing into pajama pants and plopping onto the sofa. How lonely it must be to be sick and not have someone take care of you. She wishes for a second she could go by herself. That she could hold a cold washcloth to his head and comfort him. *You're a lifesaver, Kirsten,* he'd say. She imagines bending down and kissing the top of his head. *You'll be over this soon.* And she'd just sit with him.

—

They take her car, and she realizes this is the first time they've driven anywhere together. He keeps his hands on his knees and looks around. She can smell a hint of his cologne. "This is pretty fun," he says, and looks over at her with an unsure expression on his face. They had stopped first at his apartment so he could grab his phone. She watched from the car as he ran in and out like it was a relay.

"It's *very* fun," she says, then reaches over and squeezes his thigh without thinking. She pauses for a second, realizing she didn't have to ask him what he meant—that it's fun that they're in the car together, that it's fun to be leaving work in the middle of the day. Him right here beside her—she imagines they could go on a road trip so easily. An inn in New England, or a cabin in upstate New York like the one he drew. She sinks into her seat and realizes she hasn't once tired of him. With some guys she dated, she looked forward to time alone. Being with Grayson is just natural, and she could relax in the easiness they share and not want to leave. But she still thinks about David. Her stomach twists with excitement when she remembers him touching her hand today.

They decide to eat at North Wind Tavern, a dark, comfortable bar near the university. When she turns off the ignition in the parking lot, he leans in and kisses her. He takes her hand then and places a tiny stone in it.

She smiles. His face is so close to hers. "What's this for?"

He shrugs. "I went for a run this morning, and I just thought it was a perfect pebble. I stopped and picked it up, and the first person I thought of was you, and I wanted you to have it. And then I thought, shit, you must be in trouble, G. You're picking up pebbles."

She looks down at it. White and smooth. She squeezes it in her hand, and she swears she can feel the warmth on it from him. "I love this pebble."

He smiles. "Until I inundate you with them."

She balances it on her palm, memorizing the texture of it. She pauses and looks at him. "Grayson."

"Oh no." The light seems to leave his eyes for a second. He looks down and then looks up at her again. She sees his Adam's apple move as he swallows. "What's up?"

"I think I . . . I might also kind of have feelings . . . for David." She looks at the steering wheel when she says this. When she finally looks over at him, his hazel eyes bore into hers. "I don't know if there's anything there, and I should have told you earlier, but I like this—this you and me—so much, and it keeps getting better and better. And he and I never, uh, did what we do or anything close, of course. But when I'm around him, it still feels like there's something there." Her shoulders sink. She thought she'd feel better saying this, she thought she absolutely needed to say it before things went any further, but now she feels awful. He just gave her a perfect pebble.

He looks over at her, and his face is so serious that she doesn't know what he'll say. "And?"

"And what?"

He shrugs. "I'm not surprised. I kind of sensed that a long time ago . . . I mean, he is adorable, in a teacher kind of way." He gives her half a smile, but his eyes look hurt.

She looks at him. "You knew?"

"Well, you seemed kind of smitten with him, and he seems to really like you. He told me when you two went skiing. And I haven't told him that you and I had . . . I guess I kind of thought I could win you over." He shrugs. "But yeah, David's a good guy—smart, kind, all that. You could do a ton worse."

"But you gave me this."

He looks over at her. "Yeah, he didn't give you a damn pebble."

She holds the small stone and notices there are little flecks that sparkle when she tilts it a certain way.

"So what do you want to do, Kiki?" he says quietly. "He might be interested if you tell him how you feel." His mouth relaxes, and his face is resigned.

She looks at him and nods. "Who knows. And I'm not sure if I want to mess this up." She gestures at the space between them.

"If he is interested, if he feels the same, I can get out of the way."

She doesn't say anything. She hates herself for revealing this, hates herself for hurting him in any way because when she's with him, he is like summer, and she loves the way he makes her feel. She wants to go back and not have told him this. She wants to kiss him again. She wants to find her own pebble to give him. "I'm sorry, Grayson," she hears herself say.

"You're just being honest," he says, and he opens the door and gets out.

—

After a quiet lunch where neither of them speak too much, they are on the way to David's. It couldn't come at a worse time, Kirsten thinks as they see his small apartment with the faded welcome mat and the snow shovel propped beside the door. She imagines David out in the snow with Cooper and Stella, both kids in boots and bright snow gear.

She pulls up to the curb, and Grayson bends down to pick up the charging cord. Kirsten looks at him uncomfortably, and Grayson looks at David's house. "I can, um, wait in the car," she says. "It's probably easier."

"Too late," he says. He points to the door, and David is standing there, a Penn State T-shirt on, waving them both inside.

"Oh," she says, and gets out.

"Awkward," Grayson whispers, and they walk through the dead grass toward him.

"Hey you two," David says weakly.

"Um, shouldn't you be in bed?" Grayson asks. "I figured I'd just put this in your mailbox."

David looks older, and he stands there with his arms crossed. "I heard the car." He holds his side exactly the way Kirsten's dad did when he had shingles, and he has that same wincing face. "You were right, Kirsten. I got a telehealth appointment, and she was certain it was shingles."

"Man," Grayson says. "We'll stay far away then."

"That's terrible," Kirsten says. She and Grayson stand there on the porch, and she keeps feeling embarrassed. Grayson seems to accidentally lean closely to her at one point and then quickly corrects himself and steps to the left.

"So how was lunch?" David looks at Grayson. "You used the company credit card, I hope?"

Grayson puts his hands into his pockets and rocks back on his heels. "We did indeed, boss. Thanks."

"Yeah, thanks." Kirsten looks at a set of wind chimes hanging from the porch, and at that moment, they knock together and produce a solitary note.

"You two deserve it," he says, and winces again. "Okay, then.

202

Thanks for dropping this off. Let me know if there are any issues. I'll try to rest, but I'll keep my phone on."

"Don't worry," Kirsten says reservedly. She realizes she's trying to project a professional and uninvolved attitude toward him for Grayson's sake. She's usually much warmer. "We've got it all covered."

David smiles. He looks at Grayson. "Try not to eat all my granola bars."

Grayson raises his eyebrows. "No promises, boss."

David is about to close the door and gives them a polite wave, but he stops suddenly. "Oh, while I have you here . . . Gray, it's doing that thing again where I can't get on the intranet. Do you remember how we fixed it?"

Grayson looks at Kirsten. "I think so."

"Do you mind?"

"Nah, not at all, as long as I don't end up with your ailment." David laughs; he opens the door and steps back as Grayson steps in. David looks at Kirsten.

"I can just wait in the car," she says.

David makes a puzzled face. "Nonsense," he says, and waves her inside, too.

CHAPTER TWENTY-FIVE

When Chuck was alone with Cat that last day, when she was so near dying and he asked the kids to give them a moment, he heard them mumbling outside in the hallway. He heard Leela crying. He stood over his wife. "Cat, Catty. Can you still hear me?"

He heard the birds, hammers hitting nails a couple of houses down where the Albertsons were putting on an addition. He looked at her expressionless face.

He wanted the gift of her eyes. He wanted to see her one last second—even if she just opened and closed them. "Please, Cat," he said.

She breathed and breathed, and he realized if she woke up how terrible he looked. His tired, unshaven face. His messy hair. The desperate redness in his eyes. Maybe she shouldn't see him like this. Maybe she could remember them in a better way. Maybe she was dreaming of them when they were young and full of promise and hopes and the luxuries of time and building a future. God, how she had quieted his pain, how she had made his life swell with a fullness he had never thought possible.

What happens to her memories? he wondered then. How does all that information, like a complicated computer hard drive, just fade to nothing? "You are extraordinary," he whispered. "Cat."

And then she opened her eyes.

She looked so far away, but she squinted.

"Oh, there you are," he said, and she attempted to smile. He bent down to kiss her. He put his hand to her soft cheek, and she blinked gratefully when he did this.

Why was he still thinking about Natasha then? It was over.

They hadn't talked about her in years. They had small fights over holidays with in-laws and spending money, and he had been grouchy because work made him grouchy, and sometimes they went a whole day without speaking over some trivial matter like disagreeing on new furniture or whether they should go on a camping trip.

But he had never said no to Cat like that, and in all their years, she had never looked so disappointed, and then, as she lay there thin and dying and turning to nothing, he imagined he could have said yes.

He imagined Natasha just eighteen or nineteen eating oatmeal at the kitchen table before classes at the community college. He imagined that they could have helped her with her schoolwork: him looking over calculus problems and Cat expanding on something she learned about in art history.

He imagined the three of them watching *Jeopardy* after dinner, or later, the energy of her as a twentysomething visiting them in Hilton Head and maybe one day bringing a boyfriend who they would be tough on initially but laugh with as they sat out on the porch and played pinochle or Go Fish. He imagined the light on at night in the garage apartment, Natasha entering with her key.

He knew so clearly then that they had had a blessed life, and maybe they were called on in some way to help Natasha, and he had stopped that. It was unforgiveable. "I was wrong," he said, and he meant it, and the tears came.

But her eyes were closed again, and he had no way to say all of that other stuff in time, and goddamn it, he should have said something years ago, he missed the moment, and the bedroom door opened, and Leela wept as she watched them together, and then they were all back in the room again, Asher touching his shoulder and saying he was sorry, and Ben huddled next to Chuck, and Chuck kissed Cat's hand then and slowly backed away.

—

Now he eats a plain hamburger from McDonald's. He wipes his mouth and turns the radio on. He looks at all the items in his car, all the hopes for his trip that feels implausible now, and he wonders how the hell he got himself into this situation. All because of a pig.

Now what beehive have you found? Cat would say, and he almost smiles because her voice rings out so clearly. He looks to the side. He looks out the window and wonders if, in some way, she's watching.

He probably could have been out of two states by now if he hadn't gone to that stupid shelter.

He is already tired. He needs a nap, and he's done nothing so far. Next to the McDonald's is an Ace Hardware store with people going in and out. At the traffic light, cars line up to turn into the Wegmans grocery store across the street. Next to that is a movie theater, a Red Lobster, and a new middle school that sits on the top of a grassy hill. There are patches of snow every so often, even some strips remaining on roofs, and piles left by the plow, but the sun is out and the rest of the roads and sidewalks are dry.

He hates winter. He has loved leaving it all these years.

"I can't do it, Cat," he says, and he crumples up his hamburger wrapper and points his car toward home.

—

When he gets inside, he takes out his handkerchief and wipes his eyes. His nose is running, and he feels like he's getting sick—the flu or something. Ella's car is still at the edge of the driveway where she left it. His car is unlocked outside, all packed. The house inside is bare-bones, shut down, mail-forwarded, refrigerator almost empty, ready for him to go.

His eyes burn. His muscles ache. He needs to leave. He needs to be in Hilton Head tomorrow when the place is ready and the rental begins.

He wanted to get there for her. He wanted to stand at the edge of that wide beach, the packed sand, the people on bicycles riding parallel to the ocean, and he wanted to tell her he was okay.

He can see those dunes as he walked past the beach club up the small embankment, the wide-awake sky, and suddenly, like a magician's trick, the ocean would be there, the generous stretch of beach, the people sitting at the outdoor bar with frozen drinks and card games, and everyone would be so alive.

He wanted to get there tomorrow. Maybe he thought he would find her there.

She had to be there. She was always there. "Isn't it a dream, sweetheart?" she'd say, her hand in his, and they would almost trot toward the sea like they were younger, and maybe these weeks he has believed in the magic of Hilton Head, believed that if he got there, she'd be waiting.

Or if she wasn't waiting, he could find her in himself some way. With the pig. With the right words to say. With the courage she had that he doesn't.

Her dying was unthinkable. When she was diagnosed in early spring, he thought, *well that can't happen*. He didn't have it in him. And yet, she left. And he's been here alone, doing the unthinkable.

He tries to steady himself. He unzips his coat and lets it fall on the floor. The sound of silence buzzes at him, and he plods toward the blue sofa and lets himself fall onto it. "I can't," he says. He wipes his eyes and feels the way he did when he was a child. Like he did that night after Vietnam when he stayed in the hotel by himself. He cries like a lonely old man, and he lies there and knows he will never, ever be able to get up.

CHAPTER TWENTY-SIX

Ella presses her face to the cold window as Jared drives her new car back to her apartment. She sinks lower and lower into the passenger seat and stares at the stoplights in front of them, the businesses one after another: Donnelly's Diner, Skate Away, the garden center. She wipes her face, shakes her head. Jared looks over at her every once in a while.

"He can't get far," he says. "They're close now."

"I just don't know how he knew."

"He probably saw the outgoing call on the phone. Or maybe she said something."

The team had gotten there—agents and officers—and surrounded the place. They had knocked down the door and found no one inside.

They sent over photos of the condo where Kyle and Riley had been staying, and Ella saw the towel Riley must have used in the pool, Snow White on it, and a game of checkers set up on the table. She saw Mulligan lying on the couch. "Tell them to get that moose," she said.

When Jared got that news, Ella had left the keys in the car and started to walk along the highway. The cars rushed by her. Jared had trotted after her.

"Come on. I'm going to drive you home."

She is empty. They were so close. She tries to breathe.

She wants to call her mother, who will say the right thing, but she can't tell the story. It hurts too much. Jared had offered to call

Wyatt, but she made him promise not to. "I want to bring them *good* news," she'd snapped.

The second Riley called, Ella decided the nightmare was over. They would find her, and in a matter of hours, her daughter would be with her again.

She had already resolved to never say no again if Riley asked to sleep in her bed. "Every night if you want to," she'd say. She had decided she would quit the paper route right away. The bridal shop, too. They would always remind her of this time. If she couldn't make ends meet, she and Riley would pack up and move to Massachusetts with her parents for a while. Helping her mom run the café would be a welcome distraction, and Riley could go to a school where no one knew her story.

But now the loss is too much. She can't handle the weight of it. "I want to get to Florida," she says now to Jared. "I think I should go there."

"Please, El. Let's just give it time. We have some good leads—neighbors know the car; the detectives are looking into that Michelle person Riley mentioned."

She clenches her teeth. "I can't be here doing nothing."

His radio bursts with something every so often, but it never seems to be important. "They'll find them. He won't be able to escape."

Her stomach drops further. She imagines sirens behind Kyle's car. What will Kyle do? She imagines him speeding—a terrible crash, a roll into a ditch. Will Riley wear her seat belt? She imagines her still in her bathing suit, barefoot. She imagines her wondering about her mother, upset about leaving Mulligan. Until this moment, Riley had been okay with the odd situation they were in.

Jared parks the car in her usual spot and heaves a sigh as he looks over at her with solemn brown eyes.

He has been good to her, but she feels let down. She worries about a car chase, about her scared daughter. Worries worse that maybe the day will progress and she'll hear nothing, and she'll be back in this same position again but now with Kyle being even more paranoid.

"I'll call as soon as I hear anything," Jared says. He hands her the car keys gently. "Stay tuned."

"Thanks," she says, and her chin sinks down.

He glances back at her once more. "You sure I shouldn't call your family?" She shakes her head.

After the other police officer picks Jared up, she is tempted to get right back into her new car and drive to Florida. Or drive over to Cindy and Matt's house. She knows Cindy would huddle next to her on the love seat, and she imagines her warmth like a heated blanket.

What was the *point* of this? she wonders again. What made Kyle carry out such an idiotic plan? Why did he need to leave Ella so devastated, leave his parents, who always treated him like a crown prince? When will it be over?

She holds her car keys, and her downstairs neighbor's apartment door opens. He steps outside and looks weak. He is with a pretty young woman, sandy hair. Definitely not the ex-wife. Oh, she recognizes her now. From the pet adoption day.

"See, the cold steadies me," David says to her. Ella notices he has a sparkle in his eye when he talks to her. All that tension he had when he fought with his ex seems miles away.

"I don't think that's a prescribed remedy," the girl says. She notices Ella and smiles.

David looks over at Ella. "Oh, hey."

"Hi," she says.

He looks past her. "New ride?"

She turns around and sees the small red car. "Oh, yeah." She flashes a cursory smile. For some reason, he keeps holding his side like he just had surgery. She envies the young woman—something about her brightness, her optimism. Maybe she doesn't have baggage. If she were this woman's age again, would she know not to fall in love with Kyle?

But could she ever wish to undo Kyle, knowing Riley was a result of their time together? Never.

"This is Kirsten," David says. Kirsten radiates something— a certain polished presence. She is the kind of girl Cindy wanted Kyle to bring home. Not someone absentminded and airheaded the way Cindy saw Ella. It only took her son becoming a criminal for Cindy to see Ella's side. She almost laughs.

"Hello, Kirsten." She should introduce herself, but she's too tired. She looks down at her keys again and remembers Mr. Ayers and her old car she left there. She puts her finger up. "Any chance you're going anywhere near the country club?" Of course this feels nervy to ask, but she needs a distraction.

Kirsten looks at David. Relief seems to flood her face. "I think Grayson will be awhile, no?"

David nods. "I thought it was a simple patch, but he's in full IT hell."

"You need to be dropped off at the club?" Kirsten asks.

"No, just at a house near there, on Fillingham Bay Road." She tries to focus on Kirsten's light blue coat. On David's socks with the iguanas on them.

Then in her head she sees a flash of Riley's stunned face in the back seat, looking at the road. She wonders if a cop has spotted the car yet. She wonders if they've set up roadblocks. They'll never find him, will they? *Let the police do their job*, her mother told her over and over last fall after it first happened. She bites her thumbnail, feels her foot tapping. She will not make it through this.

"I can take you there," Kirsten says. She holds her car keys already. She seems eager to go. Ella wonders for a second if there's something going on that Kirsten would like an escape from, but she's probably reading too far into these things. Maybe this girl is just helpful. She smiles constantly when she talks—but not in a fake way. She asks if Ella will need a ride back here, and Ella explains about retrieving her old car.

Ella wonders if she looks as terrible as she feels. She hopes the action of getting the car, of having to be polite to Kirsten, will make her forget about everything else. She checks her pocket to make sure her phone is there, checks to make sure it's on.

"You two drive safely," David says, and he grips the railing. He definitely looks like he's in pain. He waves to them.

"Tell Grayson I'll be right back," Kirsten says.

In Kirsten's car, a Prius with books on the floor and a yoga mat in the back, Ella buckles her seat belt. She takes a deep breath and tries to stop her feet from tapping. "I'm Ella, by the way. Um, you two make a cute couple."

Kirsten blushes as she comes to the stop sign, quickly clicking her seat belt in place. "Oh, actually we're not together. We just, uh, know each other from work."

"Oh." Ella watches the road. "Sorry."

"No, that's fine." She looks over at her and smiles. "I mean, David's nice."

"Yes, he's sweet. A good dad, too." Ella realizes she's still in her paper delivery outfit. The back of her head throbs where she fell this morning. What a damn day. She feels like someone has beat her with a bat and dragged her across a parking lot. She pats her pocket to make sure she has the keys for the other car. She feels like she is lugging around everything—two sets of car keys, her wallet, her phone. "He's not bad looking either," Ella says. She tries to consume herself in this moment. Just two girls having girl talk. *Focus on this,* she thinks. Like meditation.

Kirsten blushes again. "Oh, yeah. I guess." Her smile fades and then she appears deep in thought. The radio murmurs in the background. Kirsten turns it down. "So how did you end up with two cars?"

Ella sinks into the seat. She puts her hand to her head. She feels comfortable with this woman. She doesn't know her, but all of a sudden she is talking about her paper route, and the kind old man.

And then, like ripping paper from a notebook, she shows another layer. She watches the cars passing, and the traffic lights bobbing in the wind, and tells Kirsten about Riley, about Kyle, about Cindy's new kindness. While Kirsten is stopped at a red light, she looks over at Ella and nods, her mouth open, her eyes full of depth and wisdom. She gasps at certain times. She covers her mouth when Ella tells her about this morning, and Ella notices tears rim Kirsten's eyes. "Oh my god," she keeps repeating, and Ella's voice is flat. She is just a detached reporter, delivering all this information that happens to capture the awful state of her life.

"So that's where I'm at." Ella looks out the window as they pass small stone houses and larger brick houses. The farther they drive, the landscape switches from city to country—more fields, more golf courses and farms. Ella is used to this area, but it looks different in the daylight. The land settles her. She wishes she and Riley could live out here. She imagines Riley learning to ride a horse. She imagines long walks with the leaves scattered in fall.

"I don't know you," Kirsten says, "but I am so, so sorry you're dealing with all this." Kirsten surprises her by holding her hand out.

"That's okay," Ella says. She takes her hand. "Thank you."

"I'm sorry you have to do this alone," Kirsten says. "I'm so sorry."

Ella starts trembling then. She half laughs and then blots her face with her sleeve. How did Ella just meet this woman a few minutes ago? Why does she feel like she's always known her? "You're a good listener," she says. Ella points out the turn for Fillingham Bay Road. "The house is right up here." She doesn't want the ride to be over. She doesn't want to be in that terrible other car of hers that only reminds her of loss.

Kirsten turns to her after she parks in the driveway. "Are you okay to drive?"

Ella smiles and nods. The concern feels heavenly. "Yeah, I've been driving while distressed for four months now."

Kirsten purses her lips. "I hope she's back soon." She pauses. "She found you, Ella. Remember that. She *found* you." She takes a small piece of paper from a notebook that's mounted to her dashboard and scribbles something on it. "Anytime you want to talk, or if you need a ride, or anything else . . ."

Ella smiles. "Thanks."

Kirsten looks up at the house. "Wait . . . is the man you talked about Mr. Ayers?" There is a Subaru in the driveway and the driver's door isn't completely closed. The car sits in the shadow of a willow tree.

Ella nods. "That's him!"

"What are the chances," Kirsten says. "I just saw him at Rescue Ranch today. His wife was my favorite teacher."

Ella almost laughs. "Small world." She notices the car is all packed with blankets and bags and golf clubs. She looks up to the house, and the front door is open, just the storm door closed. She feels a flash of panic. Why? Mr. Ayers could just be bringing things back and forth to his car. He could step onto the porch at any second.

She feels her stomach twist, a feeling she had that day, looking at the lake at Freeland Park when she was sipping her coffee and watching the geese—the same day Riley disappeared. She remembers now feeling just for a second that something was wrong—and quickly dismissing the thought. She looks over at Kirsten. "Mind going with me to check on him?"

Kirsten turns off the car. "Not at all."

They walk together down the driveway. Ella steps slowly and warns her new friend about slipping. She wants to reach over and hold her hand again. She doesn't know why. She misses her daughter. She misses her mother. She misses people being kind.

She walks over to Chuck's car and closes the driver's door properly. He probably just ran into the house to grab something, but what if something happened to him? She feels this weird connection between herself and this old man and this young woman, as though their hearts and brains are aligned in a way she can't explain. Like three glowing circuits on the same track.

They walk up the porch steps and Ella calls, "Sir, it's me. Ella. I deliver your . . ." She knocks lightly on the door, but no lights are on inside.

She and Kirsten wait, and nothing. She wonders why he wouldn't close his door, letting the heat escape.

The afternoon sun seems strained as she looks back onto the front yard and driveway. A small birdhouse that's chipped and faded sits beside the outdoor sofa on the porch. Two throw pillows, yellow with blue flowers, are perched on the sofa. A woman's touch. Ella wonders what happened to her. Maybe Kirsten knows. She sees mounting hardware for a porch swing on the ceiling but no swing. Her heart breaks for him, and she knocks again.

"Maybe he's taking a nap," Kirsten says.

"Maybe." But Ella can't explain it, can't shake the feeling of being worried. She thinks of him giving her that car key, that manila folder. It was the nicest thing to happen to her in months.

"What's going on?" a voice behind them says, and they see another old man, dark graying hair, misbuttoned shirt and tight cardigan walking across Chuck's yard. A slightly overweight dog strolls calmly by his side.

His breathing is loud as he climbs the porch steps. The dog comes and nudges Ella, and Ella pets its head.

Kirsten stands straight. "Is Mr. Ayers a friend of yours? We're just checking on him—we saw his car door open."

"I deliver his paper," Ella says.

The old man groans. "He's not even supposed to be here."

He pulls the door open, and the dog pushes in front of them, as though it's her house. The house smells like the blanket he covered Ella with when she fell.

"He should have been gone by now," the man says, stopping to hold the door open for them. He gestures impatiently. "Come on, ladies. You're letting all the heat out."

CHAPTER TWENTY-SEVEN

Chuck thinks this is a dream, because he opens his eyes in his shadowy house and sees Cocoa and Sal, and behind them, he thinks, is that Ella woman he gave the car to and then sweet Kirsten Bonato. They're all looking at him funny, and he's sitting up on the couch, fixing his hair, putting his glasses back on, and Sal is turning on a lamp. "Hey, sleeping beauty, we're worried here."

He looks around, feels the sinking sensation he was feeling before, that pull that led him to this couch. He nods at the two women, and pats the sofa, and Cocoa jumps up beside him. He pets her for a moment and then leans forward and puts his head in his hands.

"Why aren't you talking?" Sal says, and taps his shoulder. "Chuck, can you tell me what year it is?"

"We're sorry to bother you, sir," Ella says. "We just got worried when we saw your car door open. I was just coming to pick up my old car."

Kirsten steps forward. "And I was giving her a ride, not realizing I already knew who lived here, Mr. A."

Chuck hears them, but he can't say anything.

He wants to cover his ears. He wants to point to the door so they leave. He concentrates on breathing because it seems like it's the only thing he can do.

Cocoa rests her head on his lap, and he looks down at her.

He wishes he could tell them how bad his heart hurts over

Cat. He doesn't want to be here anymore, but he is terrified of going to Hilton Head.

It has all become unnavigable. Kirsten now sits on the other side of him.

"Chuck," she says quietly. "It's okay if I call you that?"

He looks over at her and nods. How many scared cats did she have to coax out of a carrier? How many shaking dogs like little Oliver today has she soothed? He imagines himself hiding under the dining room table.

"Can you squeeze my hand?" she says.

He reaches for her, and holds two of her fingers, feeling proud of himself for accomplishing what she asked. He wonders if Frederick the pig was anxious in his new home today. He wonders how long it takes for an out-of-sorts animal to adjust.

Sal is looking back and forth between them.

"Enough of this new age stuff. We gotta call an ambulance." Sal trudges toward the phone, but Chuck puts his hand up in a halt sign.

"He's telling you to stop," Ella says. Sal turns around.

"Do you think you need a doctor?" Kirsten says.

He looks at her, and her eyes are so kind. He feels grateful to have these three people in this room. His heart is so badly broken, and he has been trying to act normal even though he can't sleep, even though he's haunted by what Natasha said, and how he rejected Cat's idea, and this crushed her, and now she's dead.

His wife is dead forever, and that is too much. "I'm fine," he whispers, and his voice sounds like he is trying to speak underwater. He shrugs. "As fine as I can be."

"What can we do for you?" Sal says. "Should I call Marguerite?"

Chuck shakes his head. "I wanted to get on the road," he says, "but I don't think I have it in me."

"Then you'll go tomorrow." Sal shrugs. He looks around the house. "Did you turn the heat off already?"

Chuck lies back on the couch. His clothes feel heavy and loose on him. He feels like his plane just crashed, and they have dragged him from the damaged fuselage. "It's low but not off." He looks up at Ella. "Your daughter. That was you on the news?"

Ella nods, and her eyes say everything. He wants to give her another car. She holds the same plaid blanket he covered her with this morning when she was on the sidewalk and she places it over him. He imagines her covering her little girl that way. He knows she is a good mother. He can just tell. "Should I turn the thermostat up?"

He feels unable to answer questions.

"This is bananas," Sal says. "He's never like this. He usually has all his ducks in a row. He needs a medical professional."

Kirsten is off the couch, standing again. "I think he's just sad." He looks up at her. Poor girl. When she says *sad*, it's like her whole body feels it.

"You don't get sick from being sad. He's been sad since she died."

Chuck looks up at the ceiling. He hears them talking, but he can't respond.

"His wife died?" he hears Ella ask quietly. He sees Kirsten nod.

"She was a good friend of ours," Sal says, and Chuck wants to sit up, wants to yell at Sal for some reason. *You barely knew her*, he thinks, but then he thinks that's a dumb thought. He rests his forearm over his eyes and feels the blanket on him, feels his body sink into the couch. He hears them whisper around him, and his eyelids start to flutter, and he is so grateful to have people in his house, people to watch over things while he sleeps. He hasn't slept well in months, and this sleep that is coming might be the best sleep he will have, and he hears them continue to talk until he is not with them anymore.

He is on a sled as a boy again. "I'm trying to steer," he says, either just in his dream or out loud, and then he is breathing and sailing down the hill. The world is all white, and he keeps sledding.

—

When he wakes, Sal is at the dining room table, shuffling cards and laying them out. He has a mug by him that he sips every so often, and he hums softly to himself. Outside, it is darker, and Chuck can't tell if it's around four or five or later. An old duffel bag sits by Sal's feet. When Chuck sits up, Cocoa trots over to him and sniffs his hand.

"Hey, girl," Chuck whispers. He holds Cocoa's face in his hands, bends down, and kisses the top of her head. He looks around. "Where are Kirsten and Ella?"

Sal examines the card he just placed down and glances over at Chuck. "You look better." He fixes his glasses. "One got a call, and the other had to get back to work or something. They stayed with you when I ran home." He shakes his head and gathers up the whole pile of cards. "I hate solitaire. Want coffee?"

Chuck stands, slowly. He slept so well that his face feels dented. "Yeah, that sounds good."

"And then we'll get going," Sal says.

"You don't have to leave."

"No," Sal says. "I mean you and me." He bangs the cards together in one pile and slides them into their small box. "I'm driving you to Hilton Head." He bends down and holds up his small duffel bag. "Look, I'm all packed."

CHAPTER TWENTY-EIGHT

Back at David's, Kirsten sits at the small kitchen table. She watches Grayson, who sits on the living room floor with David's laptop on his knees. He alternates between talking to someone on the phone from the IT department and typing things into the computer. "Almost there," Grayson says to no one.

David hovers behind him. "I'm sorry, man. I thought it was a two-second deal." He holds his side again.

Grayson shrugs. "No matter. You're either paying me to be at the desk today or paying me to be here, and your kids' Skittles were the bonus." He reaches into a bowl and tosses another handful of candy into his mouth.

Kirsten has barely said a word. She's thinking about all the things that happened today: the talk with Grayson and the silence afterward, the car ride with Ella, the sadness she saw in Chuck as he lay on the couch. She wonders if he woke up, if Sal was able to console him. She feels exhausted from all this, and she stares at David's gray walls, a painting of a sailboat above the sofa. She looks around and sees drawings all over the refrigerator and appointment cards stapled to the calendar. There is a big Fisher-Price castle to the left of the television with a pink dragon peering over the wall, and a shelf with bins that seems to house puppets and toy cars. On the wall by the kitchen table are two whiteboards—one that says *menu* and another that says *January Book Club* in a child's handwriting. She loves seeing how devoted he is to his kids. He must notice her looking around, because he offers her a drink but she shakes her head. "No, thanks."

Grayson's phone rings. "Ah, it's Marty. He's going to help me do the final test to see if we can get in."

Kirsten looks at David again, who slumps against the wall. She gets up and stands by him since Grayson is consumed with the call. "You really need to get to bed," she whispers.

David nods. "I feel like crap."

She puts her hand between his shoulder blades, Grayson's back to them as he talks and types furiously. She guides David to the small hallway. To the left she sees a room with bunk beds, a pirate blanket on the bottom bunk, and a bedspread on top with giraffes. On the other side of the room are two desks, each with a small lamp, and a big shelf with some toys and books. She sees the dark bedroom on the other side, just the foot of his bed visible, and takes her hand off his back. "There you go," she says. "We can let ourselves out."

He turns back to her. "Kirsten, thanks." She has her hand by her side now, but she can still feel his shoulders against her fingers. "And please thank Grayson for me. He's a saint."

"What about medication? Need us to pick up a prescription?"

"Thanks for the offer, but believe it or not, Blair offered to go to CVS for me. I was stunned."

"Oh," she says. "Wow."

"She said she's going to bring me elderflower tea, too." He rolls his eyes, but there is a small smile on his face. "It's a big deal in her family. They all swear by it."

She pauses. "I hope the tea helps," she says, and he looks into her eyes and she looks back, and he waves as he hobbles into his bedroom and disappears into the dark.

When she returns to the living room, Grayson is waiting. "All set?" she says.

"Yup. He should be good to go." He glances back at the hallway where she came from. He closes the laptop.

"He's going to rest. He told me to thank you." She picks up her coat. She looks at him and wants to attempt to explain it all, wants to say mostly how this time with him, even though it's only been about a week, has made her happy again. He has made her pain bearable. She wants to tell him she wants to be a vet again. She wants to tell him his sketch of that cottage made her feel something she can't forget. She is looking at him, no coat, that bright green shirt—green like the promise of spring—and he isn't looking back.

"Yeah, sleep's best," he finally says, his eyes on the floor. He stretches. "It's been a long day."

For a second, she forgets things are awkward between them. She feels like he'll suggest Chinese food at his apartment, and she longs for that night ahead of them, especially of his hands on her, her hands on him. But he is standing at the door now, and he opens it and steps out. He doesn't look back to see if she's following.

—

After she drops Grayson off at Rescue Ranch and checks the notes on her desk from Peggy (a vet to call back, a call from a state agency about a grant application), and after she responds to two email inquiries about Oliver, who David listed on their website before he left, and after she slides Frederick's file into her bottom cabinet with the other animals that are adopted, and after she checks on Oliver in his crate in the small dog room and feeds him and rubs his ears, she heads home.

Her head aches. Her feet hurt. Today was a clusterfuck.

She gets gas so she doesn't have to stop on her way in to work tomorrow, and as she stands there and the gas gurgles into her car, she decides she will pack tonight for her trip to Europe. She has to finalize plans with Bria, look at the weather, exchange money. She was going to buy a dress for the wedding this weekend, but she decides she'll buy one when she gets to Milan. Her mother had said, "If you can't find a dress in Milan, you're hopeless."

She stands at her car now, the wind blowing past her, and takes in the gas station. It looks bright inside, and people are standing in line. She sees someone hold a colorful candy bar. A woman stands with her child, who grips a red slushy. There is a big island of semihealthy snacks: hard-boiled eggs, apples, sliced mangoes. In the back of the store, some employees hand out sandwich orders.

She hasn't been inside a gas station since the end of May.

Her father was almost home.

She closes her eyes and can see him. He was so close. He never felt unsafe. God, he thought no one would ever hurt him.

He had stopped at a minimart outside of Philadelphia. For gas, and maybe for something for her. That was his thing. Whenever he had a business trip, he always brought her something corny: a pair of sunglasses, a cheap silk rose, a bottle of 5-hour Energy, a bag of roasted peanuts. She loved his gas station presents, and she has wondered every day if his stop that night was because he thought she'd be disappointed if he didn't bring her something. He was only an hour from home.

She watches people go in and out. No one is waiting for her gas pump, so she just stands by her car. As she waits, twenty or so people have come and gone. In a night, there must be hundreds. Across the country, there are thousands of gas stations, thousands and thousands of people in and out, and her dad was on his way home. He was on his goddamn way.

He was shot by a guy who was screaming and ordering the

workers to put the money in a bag, witnesses said. Her dad was in line. She imagines him trying to deescalate the situation. Of course he would have. She thought it would make her feel better when the judge finally sentenced the shooter, but nothing.

The gas pump beeps at her to see if she wants a receipt, and it plays an ad over the speaker. She imagines her dad being one of the people who are coming out of the store and heading to their cars. She imagines him seeming victorious in a small way for having lived.

—

She drives toward her house, the busy city of Bethlehem becoming the countryside. She sees the farm where the Clydesdale always is, and imagines him in the stable with a blanket over him. She drives past her neighbors' thick expanse of property, their lights on over barns, the houses looking inviting.

She pulls into her driveway, seeing her mother's old Volvo station wagon. She is glad they had her father's car towed away from the gas station and sold. She would have hated seeing it.

She feels inside out, unsettled. Today was too much, and it's all still swirling around her.

She knows how the heavy oak front door will feel if she goes inside. She knows the dogs will scamper toward her. She knows her mother will have a pot of soup on the stove, a bowl on the counter for Kirsten. She knows her mother will be at her desk, glasses on, grading lab reports, or talking on the phone to one of her grad students who is trying to work out some problem with their research design. Kirsten knows she'll go up to her bedroom and eat her soup and feel alone.

She thinks of Chuck lying hopelessly on his couch today. She thinks of Ella getting the call that there are no leads when they were about to leave Chuck's. The empty look she had on her face as she got into her rattling car. Loss is everywhere. Kirsten looks at her house, so still and sad without her dad, and she reaches into her pocket and pulls out Grayson's pebble.

She holds it in her palm. She looks at her house again and knows she can't spend the evening there.

She knows where she has to go.

She picks up her phone and calls Grayson. It rings and she realizes she has no right to bother him. She essentially told him she wasn't sure, that she had the same feelings for a mere *possibility* that she has for him.

When he picks up on the third ring, she wants to say she's sorry. She wants to tell him only a fool wouldn't recognize how perfect he is, and that she wants to see where her life could go with him. "Hey," she says.

"Hey, Kiki," he replies in a soft voice, and the *Kiki* floods her whole body. "What's up?"

"I actually need a favor. I'm sorry—"

"Kirsten." He exhales. "You can always call me."

She thinks of going from Kiki to Kirsten and what that means. "I have to be somewhere tonight, and I'm sorry to ask you, but I don't think I can go alone."

She waits for him to offer an excuse. She waits for him to say something spiteful like, *Why don't you ask David.* She waits.

"I'll come over now," he says.

—

They are on Route 22, him in a hooded sweatshirt and jeans and her in a baggy sweater and leggings. She didn't tell her mother where she was going, just said she was heading out with Grayson. "Do you think he'd want soup?" her mom said, and filled a thermos.

Her mom looked at her strangely then, as though she could tell something was different about her, as though she had an idea where she was going. "Everything okay?" her mom said, her long hair pulled back. She carefully ladled the chicken orzo soup into the thermos.

Her mom touched her shoulder, and Kirsten looked into her face—tired, sad—and she realized they had both been doing the best they could.

She could smell her mom's soup—each ingredient. The earthy carrots, the onions, the rich chicken stock, and she loved her. She felt such love standing there beside the woman she'd survived this with.

She looked and saw a pot holder on the kitchen counter with a cardinal and a pine branch on the front. She thought of Mrs. A. again, and how once she took a red marker and drew a cardinal freehand that looked so real. Its black eye had such depth, and it had a tuft on its head, and Mrs. A. stood there in her flowing skirt and denim shirt with the sleeves rolled up, a chunky necklace. She had told the story as she always did about cardinals staying around in winter when the other birds leave, and Kirsten never tired of hearing it. "Be someone's cardinal," Mrs. A. said.

Kirsten and her mother stood together in the kitchen until Grayson's headlights lit the driveway.

Her mother looked at the window and then back at her. "He'd love to see you like this. Being young, you know? He was the youngest person I ever knew. He simply refused to be old."

Kirsten nodded. "I know."

Her mom took a breath. "We never once talked about retirement." She laughed, and then shook her head. "I guess we didn't need to." Grayson's car idled outside. "Anyway . . ." She kissed Kirsten's forehead.

Kirsten stepped back and looked at her. "I want you to come with me."

Her mother scrunched her eyebrows, looked down at her pajamas. "Tonight?"

"No. To the wedding. To Europe. Just please think about it." She felt her eyes burn. "He'd want us there—you know him and how he felt about family, and it would mean so much to Bria and Nonnina and all the cousins." Her mother quietly handed the soup to Kirsten. "It would mean a lot to me, too," Kirsten said, and blew her mother a kiss. "It would keep us young."

Now she looks over at Grayson as she drives, and his eyes look tired and serious. "I'm really sorry about today," she finally says. "I don't know what good I thought would come of that, and—"

He cracks his neck. "Let's not worry about it. I just want to, you know, be there for you." He turns to her and gives her a somber smile.

"Thanks," she says. She's about to apologize again, to try to explain some of the David stuff, but she doesn't have the right words.

They take the exit for the Pennsylvania Turnpike, and Kirsten's hands start shaking. He asks her for the second time if she wants him to drive, but she says she'll be okay.

Grayson looks at her. "Kiki?"

"Yes?"

"Don't worry."

She wants to rest her head on his shoulder for a second. "Thanks."

"Also," he says. "Are we going to be experiencing this soup at some point? It smells amazing."

"Let's do it." It starts to rain. Not pouring, but a miserable rain with the wind blowing. She clicks the wipers on.

Grayson pours the soup into a small bowl and is about to hand it to her. "Can you sip it like coffee?" he says, but the bowl is too wide to hold with one hand. "No, wait." He slowly leads a spoon to her mouth. "Here."

She looks over at him, feeding her, his face unsure as he waits to see if she wants more.

He laughs. "I think you're the first person I've ever fed."

"Keep it coming," she says with a smile, and watches the road.

As they pass Quakertown, the rain is battering the car, and they both eat soup. She leans to the right when she wants more, and he steadies the spoon and puts it into her mouth, and for a second, she forgets how nervous she is about where they're going. He expertly holds his hand underneath the spoon in case any drips. It is a simple gesture, and Kirsten is touched by the way some things can happen without anything being said. She feels jittery and scared, but the other cars on the highway sail by, and he keeps feeding her.

"So why tonight?" he asks when the soup is finished.

She taps the steering wheel. "I don't know. I didn't feel like it could wait anymore. I'm impatient to feel better. I've just been wanting a sign from him."

He nods. He stares at the road. "What do you think the sign will tell you?"

She pauses. "Everything, I hope."

CHAPTER TWENTY-NINE

E lla isn't sleeping, of course.

She is slumped on the sofa, flipping through television channels. Anything to distract herself. Will she really get up at the crack of dawn tomorrow and deliver those goddamn papers? She doesn't think she can do it.

She checks her phone.

Nothing. She puts the television on mute. She can hear her downstairs neighbor's music playing. It is loud enough to hear every word. Sometimes he does that. She hopes he might find happiness with that lovely Kirsten. We all deserve peace.

She listens to the music. Leonard Cohen, she thinks. Yes, she recognizes that voice. She looks at the door of Riley's room. She hasn't gone in there in a long time. It is too familiar and unsettling. She looks at the clock on the microwave, the matching time glowing on the coffee maker. Ten o'clock, but then the coffee maker says 10:01, and it is so dark outside, and the rain has let up, but the wind is making the tree branches scrape against her window.

If Riley ever lives here, she will be scared when the branches do that. She will ask to sleep with Ella. *Yes*. The answer will always be yes.

When Leonard Cohen fades out, another song comes on, loud and triumphant, and she immediately recognizes the tune, "Everyone" by Van Morrison. She listens to the lyrics: *We shall walk again*.

The song makes her sit up. She is shaky and panicky, and she can't live another day like this.

She knows she can't.

But the lyrics make her smile for a second.

She wants to run downstairs to David and say, "Turn it up." She stands and her tears are different from the tears she usually cries. The song is an anthem.

The song is definitive.

God, she imagines her daughter, her daughter who knew to call, walking beside her again. She imagines her hair longer, and all her freckles. Ella feels warmth rush through her. When they spoke, it was as if nothing had happened.

There is such uncertainty and darkness now, and she is worried sick about Kyle's next move, but the song stuns her. *Everyone, everyone, everyone.* She thinks of Mr. Ayers. She thinks of the women in the bridal shop looking for the right dresses, and all the houses she passes every morning on the paper route, the paper landing safely on the porches. She thinks of Kirsten who listened to her so patiently today. She thinks of Cindy. Maybe if Riley comes back, things will continue to stay good between her and her mother-in-law. Maybe they will have a new level of appreciation. She hopes so.

She listens to the song, like someone who has hope, and wishes Riley home.

As the music is fading, she waits to see what he will play next, as if he's communicating with her this way.

She goes and stands by the refrigerator and reaches inside and pulls out a small bottle of Orangina. She twists the cap off and sips it.

The music seems to have stopped altogether. She imagines David looking around his quiet apartment. Imagines him holding his side like he did today and curling up with a book to read. She sips her soda and waits.

And then someone is pounding on the door.

—

It's Jared. He's standing at her doorstep, rain on his coat, a blank look on his face.

She keeps her hand on the doorknob, studies his eyes, and tries to concentrate on breathing. "It's not good," she says, "is it."

He reaches up and wipes the rain from his forehead. She hears cars drive by, slicing through the rain-soaked roads. The wind blows the trees behind him.

He seems to hover there on her doorstep, the faded wood railing behind him. His mouth is so straight, and then it curves into a smile. "Feel like flying to Florida?" he says.

CHAPTER THIRTY

The rain is coming down steadily when they arrive at the gas station in Plymouth Meeting, and Kirsten's feet feel numb. Grayson keeps looking over at her, and she tries to steady herself.

She has never been to this gas station. She has imagined it a thousand times. It has six or seven pumps covered by a canopy, which the people getting gas tonight must be grateful for as the rain cascades down.

She looks at the store, On the Go, and imagines her father inside. It is so small, much smaller than she imagined. She pictured high ceilings and bright lights, and this place looks dim, half deserted at eight o'clock at night. She wonders where her dad's car was—maybe in the gas bay with the pump still in it, maybe parked to the side by the ice cooler.

Grayson parks and shuts off the car. The rain puddles on the macadam, and they can see the cashier station inside with tobacco and cigarettes. She wonders if her father was going to buy something for her—a fuzzy pen, a paperweight. She wonders if this place even sells things like that.

She feels like she could vomit in the parking lot, and Grayson reaches over and holds her hand.

"I'll be back," Kirsten whispers, and she slowly opens the car door. Pop music plays over the loudspeaker, and someone at the next pump starts their car. The rain pings the canopy over their heads, and Kirsten looks at Grayson again.

"Want me to come with you?" he says.

She shakes her head. "I'll be okay."

She wants to stall. She wants to throw away their soup bowls or take the windshield squeegee stick from its bucket and wipe it over the already-wet windows, but she walks slowly toward the entrance, leaving him standing by the car, watching her.

She walks through the parking lot, and the rain slicks her hair and soaks her coat. She feels it in her eyelashes. She keeps walking, stomach lurching, as though she's hypnotized by the store's light and can't stop, even if she wanted to.

She came here because she wanted to hear from him. She wanted to say goodbye. She wanted to see how she'd feel. She thinks she can be better if she sees this place and makes peace with it. She can go to Europe next week, and reset everything and have it all make sense.

She wants to stand in this terrible little store now and tell him to rest in peace, to float away. But she wants him to send her a message before he does.

The idea of needing closure has always seemed trite, but maybe she needed to see where her father spent his very last minutes.

The store is brighter when she steps inside. She knows Grayson is still out there waiting for her, and somehow that makes it a little easier. The coolers against the wall in the back make a humming sound, and the TV is on behind the cash register, some movie from the eighties. Kirsten steps out of the way of the customers, some holding a gallon of milk, some filling out the form for lottery tickets, some at the coffee station. There is a slippery floor sign and dirty mop in the corner. Auto part supplies are against one wall. How could this place be the last thing he saw?

She imagines him standing in line. She imagines his hands in his pockets, his eyes scanning the place for something to bring her. She wishes she could go back in time and tell him don't stop. *Just come straight home.*

Her mind races, and she wonders where his body lay until the ambulance came. She wonders where his blood was—if they had to wipe it off the bags of chips, the rack of newspapers. She wonders if anyone comforted him, if they all knew right away he was gone.

She turns in a circle, and knows she has to leave. She feels a rush of hopelessness. Whatever peace she wanted from coming here doesn't exist. She looks at the register area, hoping she'll see something he would have bought her: mugs with Valentine's candies, small T-shirts folded in cubes, even a rack of Zippo lighters. But there's nothing.

She looks at the floor. She looks at all the people coming in and out so indifferently, and she wants to scream.

God, she hopes someone was kind to him. She hopes someone crouched by him and said, "Help is on the way." She hopes he believed he would be saved.

Tears fill her eyes, and she has to get out of there. Her foot bumps the wet floor sign as she rushes away.

She was wrong about coming here tonight. She was so, so wrong.

—

Grayson hurries toward her in the parking lot. A part of her wishes she had come by herself so she could be messy, sob, let it all out. There's so much to let out. But he doesn't hesitate to open his arms for her. "Oh, Kirsten."

"I hate it here," she says, and almost chokes. She feels the tears come more furiously, and he pulls her against him. "It's the worst place to die."

"I know," he says, and he rubs her back as she sobs. "I'm so sorry."

"This was a terrible idea." She shakes her head. "I'm sorry." She steps back from him and wipes her eyes.

"You needed to know," he says.

She thought she'd be embarrassed losing control like this. She has been so strong. She and her mother are restrained, always trying to assure the other they are okay. "I just wanted to see him again." She hears that last sentence and realizes how foolish it sounds. She groans. "I guess I imagined this to be more than it was. I thought I'd figure it all out."

He reaches over and touches her shoulders lightly. "Maybe coming here was important, Kiki. Maybe you just needed to know you could."

She looks at the building. "They're all in there like it didn't matter."

"He mattered. Look how much he mattered."

She wipes her face. They stand there for another minute. Finally, Grayson offers to drive and as he opens her door, they hear two men arguing nearby.

Kirsten takes the napkin Grayson hands her and blots her eyes. "I'm glad you're here with me," she says. She looks at him for a moment, the rain on his shirt, and he looks so solid and pure. She thinks of that sketch of his. She thinks of that cabin, and she could just hold him and not let go.

"I'm glad you called me." Then he looks over at the men who are yelling. "What on earth is going on?"

Kirsten turns around, and she can't believe it. She recognizes the car, those men.

"You need the tools. You don't have the tools, goddamn it," Sal says, standing in front of the car, wet and flustered. What are the chances?

"Grumpy old men," Grayson says, and laughs. "Jesus, that one's ticked."

"I know them," Kirsten says. She wipes her face one last time, takes a deep breath, and without explaining, walks over to Sal and Mr. A., who are fiddling with a wiper that seems to have bent to the side. "Small world," she says, and stands before them. She hopes they can't tell she's been crying.

Sal raises his eyebrows. "You?"

"Kirsten!" Chuck says. "What in the world?"

"You didn't get very far," she says.

"He wanted coffee," Chuck says.

"This car isn't worth a damn." Sal fiddles with the wiper blade, lifts it up, and shakes his head. "We should have taken mine. The wiper blade is crooked and scraping."

"They have new blades inside," Kirsten says. Grayson now stands behind her. "I can replace it." She trots to her car, feeling the cold air blow against her face, and retrieves the small black bag her father gave her at sixteen. How she made fun of the jumper cables, the flare kit, the first aid supplies and flashlight. *I wouldn't be a dad if I didn't give you this,* he said. She thinks of all the practical lessons he went over with her as they stood in the driveway, checking the coolant, checking tire pressure. Wiper blades were an afternoon lesson.

"Impressive," Chuck says.

"I try," Kirsten says, and she goes back into the store, as if it's not *that* store, to buy Mr. Ayers new wipers.

—

Ten minutes later, the rain is letting up. Kirsten checks the wiper blade arm once more. "Give it a try," she says to Sal.

When the wipers slide smoothly over the window, Chuck nods.

"Damn, Kiki," Grayson says.

Sal glares at the wiper and gets closer to examine it. "Not bad."

Cars come and go from the parking lot. Grayson rubs his hands together to warm up.

"Is it too soon for a hotel?" Sal says. He shakes his head. "We're not off to a good start."

"We have to keep going," Chuck says. He tries to nudge a fifty-dollar bill toward Kirsten, but she puts her hand up.

"My treat."

"Nice girlfriend you've got here," Sal says to Grayson, and Grayson just smiles politely and glances at Kirsten. "Well, you done good." Sal stands by his seat, the driver's door opened. "Chuck, say your goodbyes. I turn into a pumpkin soon."

Kirsten smiles as they stand by Chuck's Subaru. She looks at them and thinks of her father. What would he say? *Where'd you find the old men from* The Muppets? Or, *You took that Girl Scout stuff seriously, eh?*

"Nice meeting you both," Grayson says.

"Likewise," Chuck says.

Kirsten stays in the middle of the two cars. She thinks of Mrs. A., her beautiful goodness. How, in so many ways, she made her students see a vision of a kind world. How knowing this world existed has stayed inside Kirsten and countered the cruelty of what happened to her father.

She suddenly feels wide awake. She remembers standing beside her dad in the driveway, listening patiently as he went through the details about the wiper blade, or as he bent down and jacked the tire up and showed her how to loosen the lug nuts.

She can see the spring day, the evening sun on him. She can see his shirtsleeves rolled up, his eyes looking at her.

I just want you to be okay, he said that day.

She looks at Chuck, the bright lights of the canopy highlighting his frail body, and can't look away. His eyes just pull at her. They share this, she thinks. All this pain.

Grayson coughs, and Chuck waves shyly to her, and Sal stretches. "On we go," he says.

I just want you to be okay.

She can see her dad at this gas station, but he's no longer inside.

He's right here next to her. Her dad was smiling as she fixed the wiper, and now she feels him standing beside her.

She ended up here tonight, at the last place her dad had been. She saw Chuck here, stranded and waiting. *Be someone's cardinal.*

"So long," Chuck says, and she feels a zap of something.

She hurries over to Grayson and puts her hand on his arm. She can feel Chuck and Sal watching. "Grayson, there's so much I want to say to you," she whispers, "but I have to say it later."

"Wait. What's going on?"

"I think I found my sign," she says. She feels lighter. She feels like she could fly. She was supposed to be here tonight. She is picking up the baton her dad left for her. She rakes her hand through her wet hair and looks over at Sal and Chuck and then back at Grayson. "Do you think you can take my car home?"

CHAPTER THIRTY-ONE

Chuck sits in the back as two people control his destiny. He can't remember the last time he's sat in the back seat of a car, and it makes him feel younger again, his shoulder against the door, staring out at the dark, at the rushing electric lines and flashes of fast food restaurants and road signs. They are in Maryland now, and soon will be in Virginia.

Everything about this trip has been different from years past: the late start, not getting far at all, the gas station in Pennsylvania, Sal having to take a leak on the side of the road a little later (Kirsten looking away). This car ride is dark, the most miserable weather he can recall. Even though he and Cat had their share of evenings and dark early mornings, what he mostly remembers is sun and shadows and a long, inspiring adventure. This ride is drip, drip, drip.

He tries to stretch his legs, cramped because Sal has his seat back so far, and he looks at the two people in the front and feels like they're all in some story together, like *The Wizard of Oz*. How did he go from being solo to needing Sal and then finding Kirsten along the way?

They drive, and he hears his stuff jangle in the back, his golf clubs he'll probably never use. He wonders how long Sal will stay in Hilton Head, and if Marguerite will enjoy the respite.

He wonders about Kirsten—she doesn't even have a toothbrush. What's the plan? he wants to ask. Why did she join them? She is young and bright and seems to have her act together. How can she stand to be with two old men who don't make good conversation, and now Sal double-checks when she changes lanes, and points when a car is near them. But Kirsten is a saint. Maybe she is going through something, too, with the loss of her dad. Maybe she thinks Cat would want her to do this. He watches her drive and thinks about how Cat believed in angels. He always waved his hand and said, "Baloney."

Kirsten had looked at him and Sal in the gas station parking lot, and she seemed to understand the answer to a question all of a sudden, as though she needed to go with them. He thought she was kidding at first, but then when she was serious, when she hugged the young man she was with, and took the driver's seat, he felt lucky.

He and Sal were barely treading water, and she was like a lighthouse.

But why would she come with them? Maybe Cat was right about angels. Maybe he still has so much to learn. He lies back against the headrest.

He thinks about his children now and wonders what Leela or Ben would say seeing him in this car. He is often amazed these days, and even before Cat died, with how separate their lives have become.

All those years, they were together as one unit. They did everything together—when they traveled, they slept in the same hotel room, and when one of them went to bed on a school night, the rest of them soon followed.

Now he has a hundred thoughts that they don't know anything about, and he makes decisions, like giving the car away, that they will only hear about later. He has no idea how late Leela works some days or what Ben eats for dinner. Each one of them off in their separate orbit, making their own coffee, shoveling their own snow. He thinks of how he read once that orcas stay with their families forever, and he would have loved that. Did they ever, ever think they would scatter this way? He imagines tomorrow or the next day calling Leela, calling Ben, and telling them he got to Hilton Head safely, that he got there with help. He should ask what they are doing and listen. He wants to find ways to unite them more.

The car tires hum against the wet road, and Chuck cracks his knuckles in front of him.

"Where should we stop?" Sal says now. "I doubt our friend here is going to feel like driving another nine hours."

"We could take turns," Chuck says. He just wants to get to Hilton Head.

"I'm good for now," Kirsten says. She gives a slightly uneasy smile, and Chuck watches her eyes in the mirror. Wonders if she is regretting this spur-of-the-moment decision to accompany them. He hopes not.

"I'll drive when she's tired," Chuck says to them, and Sal turns around with a look on his face that makes Chuck want to lean forward and clobber him.

"You?" Sal says. "You're back seat material for this trip." He crosses his arms and sighs. "No offense."

"You're back-drawer material," Chuck says after a few moments, and the three of them laugh.

Kirsten clears her throat. "Let's try to predict what the temperature will be when we get there. Whoever is closest gets an ice cream." She smiles hopefully, but when Chuck looks at her, he can see a flash of something—uncertainty, sadness maybe, in her eyes.

"You'll probably just look on your phone and know it before we do," Sal says.

"What a dumb thing to accuse her of," Chuck says.

"I won't look." She moves a piece of hair from her eye and focuses on the road. "I think it will be seventy-three degrees."

"Well, it depends if it's morning or night, doesn't it?"

"Oh, shut up, will you?" Chuck says. "The poor kid is trying to be pleasant." He remembers lying on his couch and looking up at her and Ella's kind faces. Thank goodness they found him today. He feels like he would have disappeared if they hadn't. Though he doesn't feel perfect now, he feels settled on the trip. The house in Pennsylvania seems galaxies away, like a place he might never go back to. He hopes it stays safe. "I think it will be sixty-eight degrees."

Sal moves his head back and forth like he's thinking. Chuck thinks he will do one of those moves like on *Price Is Right* where they only add a dollar to what the last person says. Jackasses. Chuck hates when they do that—it feels slimy. "I say fifty-two degrees." He gestures to a car on her left and Kirsten nods that she sees it. "But I'm going to keep thinking about it before I say it's final."

—

When they are near DC, Chuck notices Sal has dozed off for a few minutes. Kirsten looks over at him and slowly reaches for the radio. Soft jazz music comes on, and Sal stirs. "I'm awake."

"You looked wide awake," she says, winking at Chuck in the rearview mirror. She glances at her phone for a second to see what the navigator is telling her.

Sal sits up straighter. "So, if I may ask, what made you take this on out of the blue? And what the heck were you doing at that gas station?"

"That's none of our business." Chuck leans forward. "Sorry, the more tired he gets, the less manners he has."

"It's okay."

Sal shrugs. "What? I'm curious."

Kirsten looks over at him for a second and gives him a polite smile. Chuck waits to see if she'll say something. "I, um, just wanted to help."

"Very nice of you," Chuck says. He knows Sal is furrowing his eyebrows.

"But *why*?" Sal shakes his head. "On this rainy night, a whole long road trip. I'd rather just go home with that rugby player or whoever that guy is."

She laughs. "I thought I could pitch in with the driving, and I was . . . I was looking for something." Her voice gets lower. "I had a tough day."

Sal crosses his arms. "Right place, right time, I guess."

"Certainly." Chuck wishes he could steer the conversation to something easier before Sal pries anymore.

"My dad was murdered at that gas station. It was the first time I'd been there."

Chuck breathes in and doesn't exhale. He had no idea that was where it happened. Of all the places for him and Sal to end up. Oh, that poor, poor kid.

He sees Sal turn and look at her. "Is that so?" He purses his lips. "Well, I'm awfully sorry to hear that."

She seems to grip the wheel harder, and Chuck sees pain in her eyes. Damn Sal. "How terrible for you," he says.

She nods. "Thank you." She stays silent. The jazz music is continuous, and the rain seems to be letting up.

"I won't ask you more about it," Sal finally says. He waits for a few seconds. "But you've got two old dads in this car, and we're really impressed by you." She looks at him and doesn't say anything, and out of nowhere Sal starts clapping. Chuck wants to shush him, but Kirsten is smiling. Sal's clapping like he's on the bleachers and his grandkid just hit a home run. Clapping like a solo went well at a school concert.

Kirsten seems to be okay with the applause.

—

At almost one in the morning, they find a Hampton Inn in Richmond, Virginia. Chuck buys Kirsten her own room and another for him and Sal. When the woman is typing in their information, Chuck thinks about Sal in a bed right next to him, or in the same bed, depending on the room, and he immediately regrets the idea. "Actually, do you have a third room?" he asks, sliding his credit card toward her again.

"I can check," the woman says. Her shirt is untucked. She stares at the screen, her lips pursed.

"Why?" Sal says, looking up from the brochures section.

"So we can all have our space."

Sal scrunches his eyebrows. "We'll only be in bed a few hours. Don't waste your money." He stands right next to Chuck, and Chuck feels Sal's belly nudge him. "Don't worry about it, ma'am."

She looks up at Chuck, and Chuck tries not to sigh. "Okay, just the two rooms then."

The woman at the desk gives Kirsten a package with a toothbrush and razor and a small deodorant and lotion in it. "Thank you so much," Kirsten says, and Chuck wonders how comfortable she'll be in her clothes, but then he thinks how lucky she is that she doesn't have to sleep near Sal.

"Don't worry, buddy," Sal says as the three of them walk toward the elevator. "I won't bite. But I may snore."

—

Sal comes out of the bathroom wearing a large blue T-shirt and a pair of faded pajama pants. "The hot water comes on fast," he says. "Be careful."

"Thanks." Chuck holds his leather toiletry bag and folded pajamas against his chest. When he closes the bathroom door, he sees Sal's blue toothbrush and baking soda toothpaste in the plastic hotel cup. He looks at his face, and he looks so haggard. Is this all that's left of me? he wonders. He is shrinking, and his hair is more gray. His hearing is worse. He feels like dust some days.

He brushes his teeth and closes his eyes while he does this because he's sick of looking at himself. When he returns to the room, Sal is under his covers.

Chuck switches on the small light that swivels from his headboard, and then he trudges over to turn off the floor lamp. He looks around the room. It is pleasant with its dark gray carpet and the grass cloth wallpaper, something like Cat wanted to put in the downstairs bathroom. He reaches over and touches it.

"Make sure the chain's on the door," Sal says, and turns over.

Chuck flips the brass lock into place. He turns the bolt by the doorknob, and for whatever reason, he peers out the peephole before heading back to bed. "Well, we're getting there," he says as he shakes the covers and slides into them.

"Tomorrow, you'll be there," Sal says from his bed.

Chuck switches off the light. "Yeah."

Neither of them talk for a few minutes, and Chuck tries to

breathe. He folds his hands on his chest, turns over, and flips his pillow to the cool side.

This is his first night away from home since Cat died. He lies there and feels his muscles settle. He thinks of his dark house, the heat turned low, the dreadful quiet. He stays still and imagines the refrigerator humming, a solitary spider creeping across the ceiling. He is not sure how much time goes by, but he lies there for a while and counts his breaths and looks at the glow of the clock without his glasses.

"Sleep well, Chuck." Sal's voice startles him in the dark.

"You, too."

Then it's quiet again and Chuck turns the other way. He can almost see the outline of Sal in bed.

"Hey, Chuck," Sal says.

"Yeah?"

"You won't feel this bad forever."

—

The next morning, he is awake before six, his usual time, and he gets dressed quietly. Sal is snoring in his bed, and Chuck slips the room key into his pocket and closes the door. He takes the elevator down to the lobby, and outside it's still dark. He thinks of Ella delivering her papers, every day, up so early, and he wonders where her girl is and if she'll ever get to see her again and have some version of her life back.

In the breakfast area, a television plays the news on CNN, and a woman is stocking the cups and napkins and making sure the juice machine is working. "First customer," she says when she sees him.

"Sorry if I'm early."

"I'm ready for you." She gives him a big smile. "Coffee's over there." She points to a long counter where all the newspapers are stacked.

He pours his coffee and finds a seat, and looks out the window.

So here we are in Virginia, he thinks, and he hopes Sal and Kirsten won't sleep too late so they can get moving. They have another six or seven hours, and he thinks he will ask to drive first. Maybe between the three of them, and a stop for lunch, they can get to Hilton Head by the afternoon. The lease agreement begins today.

A maintenance guy with a box of garbage bags says good morning to the lady who is now touching the waffle maker quickly to make sure it's on. She makes a *ta-da* pose, and he thinks of Natasha in the café that day, a teen with her life fully ahead of her. Her purple nails. Shiny hair. Her determination to make a go of things.

The woman scoops balls of cantaloupe, and then she disappears into a back room. Chuck thinks he hears *kidnapping case* on the news, and he perks up, but the woman is back, and she's changed the channel to a sports talk show. Chuck sighs and thinks of Ella. He knows he has her number somewhere. He will have to check in with her. He silently wishes her well. Wouldn't it be nice if she were, at this moment, finding out good news? He would love to know they were reunited.

He looks around then. "Well, Cat. Getting closer," he whispers.

Closer to what? Closer to finding out there's no escape, he thinks.

He sips his coffee and crosses his arms. He hears a commercial for dryer sheets and he yawns and sinks back into his seat.

—

He opens his eyes a few minutes later, and Kirsten is sitting across from him, sipping tea and cutting a banana nut muffin in half. "Hey," he says, and he fixes his glasses and wipes his face. He is a full-fledged old man now, falling asleep in the middle of a place like this. He never used to do things like that.

"Morning," she says, and she bites into the muffin and smiles at him.

"They should advertise this lounge as very relaxing."

She laughs. "I guess so."

"It's nice of you to help us out." He looks at his coffee cup, and there is just a little left in the bottom. He swishes it and drinks it, tastes grounds. "If you've had enough, though, I can rent a car for you or take you to the airport and get you a flight. You've done plenty."

She shakes her head. "No, I want to see you get there. What else would I be doing anyway?"

He smiles, holds out his hands. "I don't know. Working. Going on dates. Playing online games . . . finding another pig for me." He laughs.

"Oh, I wanted you to have Frederick so badly."

"Wasn't in the cards." He refills his coffee, and when he sits back down, he looks at her. "So you told Sal about your dad last night. He was such a presence, your dad, and I can still see him laughing and delighting people with his stories. I would want my kids to remember those things."

Her face reminds him of a sky, the clouds passing over it. He can see her really thinking. "His favorite American food was ketchup," she says. "He loved dipping hoagies in ketchup, eggs in ketchup, even pizza. I think of him every time I use it, and I think I use it more now because he can't."

Chuck smiles. "That's one of a kind."

"He loved cough drops, too. They were like his breath mints, but cherry or licorice. We found them everywhere after he died— always a solitary one. In a drawer, in the bottom of a backpack. And he had beautiful skin. My mom used to say she had a five-step regimen, and all he did was take a bar of Dial to his face." She sits back in her chair, and he sees her eyes fill with light. "And his laugh. It sounded like a cartoon character. It was exaggerated and wheezing and echoing." Yes, yes. Chuck remembers that. She rests her chin in her hand and stays still. "I never wanted to outgrow him." She shrugs. "I guess that's how much I loved him."

He takes it all in, and it almost makes him cry. He also feels an odd pang of jealousy. He hopes he made such difference in his kids' lives. He wonders if they never wanted to outgrow him.

Her face looks calmer as she speaks, and he thinks sometimes you just need to say all the things that are inside you, hurting your heart. Has he done that enough? He thinks about her and Ella— how his problems are so much more regular than what either of them have experienced. He lost his wife when he was in his early seventies, and that is something that is inevitable, happening all the time.

But how many people's fathers get shot? How many parents have their child taken? All things considered, his life has been lucky.

He looks out the front doors of the lobby, sees the pink-orange glow of the sun stretching its rays onto the trees. The day looks promising. She tells him about Italy and Switzerland next week.

"You have a lot ahead of you," Chuck says. "You shouldn't waste your time with us."

"I'm glad you let me come along," she says, wiping her eyes. She pauses. "I thought maybe my dad sent you to me, or sent me to you."

He sits back and nods. Now it makes sense. He hopes this is worthwhile for her. He's not sure how he feels about looking so needy, but he likes her presence on this trip.

"We're both getting over some stuff, Kirsten," he says, and he can't help it. He pats her hand the way he would do with Leela or Ben. She doesn't pull away.

"Yeah."

"You more than me, of course. I'm just a sad old guy. You're a brave young person. It was remarkably courageous of you to go to that gas station."

He sees the gratitude in her eyes, her half smile.

"You faced that fear, and then you had room in you to do this."

She shrugs. "I also thought about your wife and what she said once about cardinals."

He can hear Cat's voice then. He can imagine her saying it so perfectly. "Be someone's cardinal," he whispers.

A young couple with two kids comes down and chooses a table close to the food. Their little boy runs to the juice dispenser.

"So is Hilton Head your gas station?" Kirsten says now, looking into his eyes like she's ready to help him.

He grips his coffee cup and looks at her. "I think I've been living at the gas station."

She starts to clear her stuff away. "That's no place to live."

He taps his hands on the table, and his heart flickers. "I think there's someone I should see today, Kirsten, and I'm wondering if you'll help me find her."

CHAPTER THIRTY-TWO

Palm Beach International Airport is cheerful and welcoming, but Ella storms past the closed-down shops and Oceanfront News, past the Starbucks and pro golf shop, Jared Kinney struggling to keep up. She has never been on a flight that felt so endless, and her whole body is shaking now, very early morning on Tuesday, as she pulls her small suitcase and Jared clomps behind her.

She follows the sign to the ground transportation. She looks around this airport as she rushes and she mentally takes note, for a later time, how calm and easy it is here, how uplifting it feels, but her hands are trembling. She can't even tell if she has to pee, if she's hungry.

On the plane, she went into the bathroom and took a look at herself. She wished that she had taken time to shower or find a nicer outfit. She wants Riley to see her looking happy and put together. She tried to fix her hair, straighten her navy blue blouse. She didn't look horrible—she looked tired and overwhelmed, her normal look. She wishes now she had gotten a haircut at some point, or brought some makeup, but she doesn't even know what she packed. Two outfits for Riley. A favorite book of Riley's. A doll, Anna Leaf, that she's had since she was a baby, a new toothbrush, a bottle of lavender lotion that Riley used to love.

"Are we getting a rental car or a cab or what?" she says to Jared, and doesn't even turn around as she asks. He comes up alongside her, and she can hear him huffing.

"Man, thanks for the workout." She looks to the side, and

his face is red. His jaw and neck are stubbled, and he's wearing an Adidas pullover. He looks around for a second and points outside. "There. They sent a patrol car for us."

"Good," she says, and darts through the automatic doors, the sky starting to turn light, over to where the police SUV sits. Jared trots alongside her, and she sees his backpack bobbing as he runs. They were lucky to get a flight late that evening—right out of Lehigh Valley Airport, with a stop in Charlotte, where they stayed on the plane. She prayed for no delays, no engine trouble, just to get here. If there hadn't been a flight then, she would have gotten in her car and driven.

She thinks of Chuck's tiny red car at home in her usual parking space, and her old car parked right behind it, like a butterfly with its battered cocoon in the background. She imagined she would use that car to find Riley, but now here she is shaking hands with the young West Palm Beach officer, climbing into the back of his car.

"Thanks," Jared says to the officer before he gets in. Then he talks in a lower voice, and she sees the officer nodding, but she can't hear what they're saying.

"Can we go?" she mouths. He nods, and the officer gets behind the wheel.

"A couple of things to go over," Jared says as he slides beside her in the back seat.

She looks at him. She doesn't want obstacles. She just wants Riley. She wants to hold her daughter. She wants to erase all the pain her poor girl has felt, all the confusion about her terrible dad. She wants to take them on a vacation somewhere—to Disney, to Myrtle Beach, even though she can't afford it. She doesn't want any red tape. "Yes?" she says.

"I imagine he'll have a lawyer already. Don't say anything to the lawyer if they talk to you. You and I will talk to the police and do everything on the up and up." He looks at her. "If you happen to see, um, your husband, you are not to say a word. Understand?"

Panic rushes through her. She doesn't want to see Kyle. Ever again. She feels afraid. She doesn't even know this person who took Riley. She also wants to rush at him, to scratch his face for doing this to their girl, for making her sick with worry these four months. "Oh god," she mumbles.

"I don't think you'll see him. I don't. He'll probably be away."

Away. She tries to process what this means but can't. She imagines Kyle, fresh-faced when they first met. Then imagines him sitting in a medieval-style jail cell. She pushes the thought aside. "Okay."

Oh, miserable, horrible Kyle. *Why?*

She had gotten the story from Jared on the plane. It was almost too much to process. Jared had been briefed by the detective while they waited to board, and he had nodded and listened, his face expressionless. Apparently, one day last summer while she and Riley were away visiting her parents in Massachusetts, Kyle had signed up for a dating app. He had met a woman named Michelle, a pharmaceutical rep from Florida who was in Pennsylvania on business for a few days.

The affair was passionate and all-consuming, and they had met up repeatedly. They had gone hiking and kayaking. He had even taken her to the house one day, Jared said Kyle told the detective in Florida.

Jared tried to hold back on those details, but Ella sat upright in her plane seat, and said, "Keep going. It doesn't matter."

She listened to the story like she didn't know the people involved.

Kyle was smitten with Michelle, calling in sick to work, texting her on a burner phone whenever he had a free moment. He was so enamored that once he even drove all night to Georgia to meet Michelle over Labor Day weekend when Ella and Riley were in Massachusetts again. Michelle had her own kids, and during that visit, she encouraged him to move to Florida.

Kyle told the detective he was ready to leave everything in early September—he was going to write a long note to Riley. He was going to tell Ella they would file for divorce. He was going to tell his parents. But he had looked in on Riley one night while she slept at his parents' house. He watched his daughter and started to cry. He couldn't leave her, but he couldn't not be with Michelle, who was putting pressure on him to either move down there or forget about their future.

He told the detective he thought he was having a breakdown, and he called Michelle and told her he wouldn't be able to leave. She comforted him and they brainstormed a plan over the next couple of days. He didn't mention a thing about his plan to anyone else. He left almost everything behind. Jared said the detective in Florida said the Pennsylvania authorities did a "shit job" on their end with discovery, and if they had dug deeper into his Internet activity, this wouldn't have taken so long. Michelle had let Kyle keep his car in her garage, had let him use her car for everything.

"What did they think would happen?" Ella asked. Kyle had to think that he was smarter than the police and smarter than Ella. He had to think Riley was better off without Ella, and that's what angered her the most.

Ella decided at that moment that Kyle's actions were beyond censure, beyond the ability to be understood. He and this Michelle had decided in a brief conversation that Ella was disposable, and this was impossible for her to process. Any parent who could cause that level of hurt, knowingly, to another parent—it wasn't to be rationalized or forgiven.

She thought of Cindy for a second. She felt grateful she didn't know about any of Kyle's actions, and it felt odd to be on the same team as her, both of them left behind by Kyle. She thought of Cindy's worried face and wondered how happy she would be to welcome Riley home. *I know we've had our differences*, Ella imagined saying. She imagined Cindy pulling her and Riley into a big embrace, and that image felt like a relief, as though they could keep one good part of the old Kyle.

The whole thing overwhelmed her. What would Kyle have done after the money he took from his and Ella's savings had run out? Did he and Michelle not realize they'd never get beyond this?

Jared had shaken his head. "It was unstable. These kinds of crimes are usually like that." He had reached up and adjusted his air vent. "I mean, if he were rational, wouldn't it have been better to take her on a day when you wouldn't be getting her off the bus?" He rolled his eyes.

Now in the car with the Florida officer, Jared reaches into his pocket and pulls out his phone. He dials and clears his throat. She watches his eyes, a deep blue, as they move back and forth and the phone rings. "Sergeant Kinney for Detective Winter, please."

Ella drums her fingers on the door handle. *Winter.* The name sounds like something Riley would have made up in one of their games where they invented a town out of big boxes and blankets. They'd interact with imaginary Mrs. Summer and Mr. Fire. Mr. Winter could own an ice-skating rink. God, she wants to get back to that. She wants to help Riley forget these long four months where she lived in a strange place with no contact from her old world.

She realizes now she should have called her parents and

brother. She quickly sends a group text. The worst way to do something like this, but she will tell them more when she knows more. She will have Riley speak to them when the time comes. Will that time come? She worries about being tricked again. She feels like it's her destiny to be in that lonely apartment by herself forever.

The officer waits at a light, and Jared hangs up with Detective Winter. "We're all set," he says. "She's waiting for you."

And with that Ella starts to cry. It reminds her of when she went into labor, taking an ambulance to the hospital, and in the rush of everything, her brain never realized she was going to take a baby home afterward. Now the early sun is coming up, and it looks propitious and pink, and there are palm trees and blooming mandevilla as they drive, and she will be coming home with her daughter—hopefully. These last few months have made her doubt everything, though, and she tries to be ready for someone to say Riley is gone again.

She's waiting for you.

She can't fathom that.

Jared is looking at her, but she can't swim to the surface to speak. She feels like a hundred different mattresses are piled on top of her body. *Waiting for you.* She looks down at her hands and they are shaking. "She's waiting?" she says quietly.

Jared grins. "At the station." He looks at her, and his smile is bright and generous, his eyes lifting slightly, his mouth so wide that she wants to cry at the beauty of this day.

Yesterday at this time, she was driving along the cold roads of Pennsylvania, her daughter lost and gone. She was slipping on Chuck's sidewalk. Yesterday was a thousand years long. Her body still hurts, but even the hurt feels far away. She can't feel anything except the anticipation of her daughter. She roots through her purse and finds an old tube of lipstick. She practices smiling for Riley, not caring if Jared sees or not. Lord, she hasn't smiled in over a hundred days, has she? Her muscles barely remember.

"How much farther?" she says to the officer, whose haircut is barbershop fresh and neat, and he tells her just a couple of minutes. She takes a deep breath and slaps the sides of her legs, watching her chest rise and fall as she breathes in and out. Jared keeps looking over at her. "You're making me nervous," he says, and laughs.

"Did they say if she was upset or if she's okay or what?"

"They told her you would be there soon, and she's been great ever since."

Ella's fingers touch Jared's, and she squeezes his pointer and middle finger as tightly as she can. She looks at him as if to ask permission, and he smiles.

When the officer pulls up in front of the police station, she grabs her purse, leaving her luggage, and darts inside. Of course, the young officer would have led them, but she's tired of waiting. She's tired of being polite.

The automatic doors glide open, and she is out of breath, asking for Detective Winter. The guy at the desk points her down the hall, buzzes her in, and the door opens slowly. She turns around and sees Jared trailing behind with his backpack and her suitcase.

She remembers taking Riley to Disney once, and she was so tiny, trying to find their hotel room. She kept running down the hall, and Ella said, "keep going, keep going," and she tells herself the same thing now as she passes desks of officers and a conference room and doors of different important people, the whole place seeming more like a hotel than the bleak police stations in Pennsylvania.

Finally, a man in a suit with white hair says, "Mrs. Burke," and he is Detective Winter, and she nods and looks around frantically.

"That's me." She clutches her purse. "Do you need identification?" she says.

He shakes his head, his lips in a calm smile. "Right this way," he says.

He leads her past a vending machine, through a room with more desks, and they stop in front of a door with a glass window. Ella can't see inside for a second, and she squints as she stands there.

"Mommy!" she hears, and the sound thrashes her insides.

She feels everything, all that stress and tension, fall to shreds, and she is stripped down to nothing as she opens the door, and Riley, *Riley*, jumps out of her seat, knocking it over, and runs to her, colliding with her, and Ella gasps.

"My baby," she says, and when she touches her head, when she puts her hands around her shoulders, she hasn't grown too much, she hasn't really changed. Her freckles are still in the same places. Her wavy hair is longer but pulled back and clean, and she is crying, and almost clawing at her, and Ella is crying, too.

"Oh, Bitsy-Boo," she says, trying to hold back the sobs. "My beautiful, beautiful girl. I've missed you so much."

"Mommy, Mommy," Riley says, crying in a way Ella's never heard her cry, and she squeezes her as tightly as she can, feeling hot tears soak into her blouse. Ella kisses her head, and it feels like every journey she will ever take is over, every decision she ever has to make has been made.

She is in the place she always, always wants to be, holding her daughter, her daughter whispering in her ear. "Mommy, I missed you," she says through her tears.

Ella hears Jared sniffle behind her. She hears Detective Winter mumble a few things to him. She hears phones ring and people typing and talking outside this door. She leans back for a minute and holds Riley in front of her like a portrait.

And then Ella holds her again, holds her and says, "I'm here."

CHAPTER THIRTY-THREE

Sal is driving, ten miles from Norfolk, when Chuck gets a text from Ella and relays the news to the other two. Kirsten cannot contain herself; she shrieks. She wonders how Ella's face has changed since she saw her yesterday, now that she has her life back. She imagines the loneliness washed away, the struggle gone. "That is the best thing I've ever heard."

"What a day," Chuck says from the back. "Good for her."

"Who's that now?" Sal says, and Kirsten glances back at Chuck, who rolls his eyes.

"The lady who lost her daughter. Who was at my house yesterday."

"Ah," Sal says, pressing his foot against the gas. "Terrific . . . I tell you what they should do with the husband: electrocute him." Kirsten and Chuck stay silent as Sal watches the road. "Unless we're not getting the whole story."

Chuck makes an exasperated noise. His hand is up for a second as though he might bop Sal on the head, but he puts it back on his lap.

Sal puts one arm out, gesturing while he talks. "There's always two sides. Maybe she had a drug problem. Maybe she wasn't fair to him, you know?"

Kirsten shakes her head. "Maybe she doesn't need us speculating," she says.

Sal chuckles. "You're getting quite comfortable with us, aren't you?"

"Unfortunately," she says, and the three of them laugh.

Chuck reports that Ella's mother and brother are flying to Florida to meet them. Kirsten tries to picture how good that reunion must feel. She wonders then if she'll ever have children. She always assumed she would. She thinks of David in the park with his children, him walking with them on either side holding hands, but she's stunned to picture Grayson for a second with a baby against his chest, holding it and looking down on it. She imagines that cabin he sketched, and him and her and a baby inside.

She checks her phone and then looks up. "It says it's about three miles from here." She reads Sal the directions, and glances back at Chuck, whose expression is frozen. He has the yellow rental agreement in his hand, the rental agreement he has been holding all morning for some reason. His right hand shakes.

Poor man. She knows he feels this stop is necessary, but she worries it might upset him more. Her phone is ringing then, on silent, and it's David. She stares at it as his name keeps flashing, but she doesn't answer. Half because she doesn't want to talk in front of Chuck and Sal, and half because she doesn't know how she'll explain her decision to drive to Hilton Head when he's out sick and she left Grayson to take care of Rescue Ranch on his own. She had tried to explain everything in a text to him this morning, but he never responded. She figures he'll understand, though, and Grayson can handle the place.

After she talked to her mom last night from her hotel room and told her about the gas station, she called Grayson. He seemed glad to hear from her. "The car ride was pretty lonesome. I felt like there were still a million things to say."

"Me, too," she said.

"I'm glad those scamps didn't hurt you."

She smiled. "I'll keep you posted," she had said.

She directs Sal to make a right-hand turn now, and he hits the brakes dramatically hard. "You gotta warn me earlier, kiddo," he says. She worries about Chuck's distracted face. She just wants him to have peace.

She looks at the gorgeous harbor to her right, the sun everywhere, and the tall buildings. She sees a handful of impressive naval ships. So far, she thinks, Norfolk reminds her of Boston, where her old boyfriend Evan had lived—the harbor looks almost identical. Just sunnier here, it seems. She bites her lip.

"Then you're going to go two more blocks and turn right after the stop sign," she says now to Sal.

"See, that's better notice." He looks over at her. "I have to get a phone that can do that. Navigate."

"It's pretty handy," she says. Out of the corner of her eye, she sees Chuck sitting up straighter, and she gets butterflies for him.

"And you're sure this is the right address?" Sal asks.

"It's the best my Googling could find. It seems like she's been here for quite some time."

Chuck looks down at his shirt and fiddles with a button. He crosses his legs and then uncrosses them. He licks his hand and pats down his hair. "Do you think you can come with me, Kirsten?" Chuck says now.

"Oh, absolutely," she says. She isn't sure what she should say, but she thinks of her dad who would tell her, "Why not? No dog in this fight," and shrug.

"And Sal," Chuck says. He leans forward and pats his shoulder. Sal's eyes look to the rearview mirror. "Can you stay in the car?"

There is silence for a second, but then Sal shakes his head. "I figured, you old crow." He grumbles to himself. "I don't even understand why you think you need to be here, but let the record show I'm a good sport."

"You're a very good sport," Kirsten says, and she points to the building. "It's here."

It's a calm day as Kirsten and Chuck step from the car, and Sal leans back and stretches. "A little beauty sleep for me then," he says through the open window, and Chuck ignores him.

Chuck glances every so often to make sure Kirsten is by his side, like a kid walking with his mother. Kirsten wonders if she looks like a nurse with a patient, or a young woman with her grandfather, his glasses sliding to the edge of his nose. But he walks well. His clothes are nice, too: sporty and timeless—a button-up shirt and cargo pants, a loose sweater that hangs from his thin frame.

Kirsten is still in her same outfit from yesterday, and she looks around and realizes how far from home she is. She hopes David's feeling better. Did she disappoint him by abandoning work? She imagines Grayson from the car ride, and the way he held the soup spoon to her lips. She looks around now—at the sailboats on the sparkling water, and in the distance the clusters of restaurants and places to shop.

The building they're visiting is called Harbor Breeze, and there is a fishing boat outside and some houseboats off a long dock. One of the white boats is so polished and immaculate, and the man cleaning it looks a little like her father. She stops to watch him, but as they get closer, she sees he is shorter. He waves at them, and she and Chuck wave back, and she sees the name on the boat. *Pelican's Flight*.

Chuck's hand is trembling, the yellow paper bouncing in his grip, and she stands closer to him. "There's nothing to be afraid of," she says, and he nods, and for some reason she takes the rental agreement from his hand and he looks relieved that she's holding it for him.

"I'll be glad I did this, right?" He looks stiff, preoccupied.

"Yes, I think so."

"Here," she says, and they stand at the directory at the front entrance. She scans the names. "Is this it?"

"N. Vargas," he says. "That's her." He looks around. "What do we do?" She loves how he says *we*. It feels nice to be a part of this with him. She doesn't know if he's worried this woman will yell at him or how she'll take him showing up here, but he breathes heavily.

"It's going to be fine," she says, and he nods. She looks at her watch. It's almost nine. A bit early, but he needs to get this over with. "We press her numbers here on the keypad, and then the star," she says.

He presses two buttons and then the star, and waits. Nothing. They look at each other. "Maybe she's in the shower," Kirsten offers, but then the door swings open and a beautiful woman with rich, curly hair is coming out. She wears a hooded jacket and long yellow-green pants. Hoop earrings twist as she walks. With her is a boy, around six or seven, who squints in the sunlight and holds a drone or spaceship with a remote. Kirsten can smell her perfume— something with jasmine. The woman doesn't seem to notice them, her shoes making a steady noise, but Chuck's mouth is open and he holds his hand up.

"Natasha," he says, his voice quiet and his mouth sounding dry, and the woman stops. She turns, and raises her eyebrows. The boy stands behind her and looks at his toy.

"Mr. Ayers?"

Chuck fidgets with his hands. He looks so sad and hunched over. Kirsten hopes she doesn't yell at him. How could she? "Yes, it's me," he says. He gestures to Kirsten. "And this is a friend of mine." He gestures toward the parking lot. "And I have another friend in the car."

"You look the same," she says quietly. She glances back and forth between the two of them, her eyes pleasant toward Kirsten, but puzzled.

"I think he wants to talk to you," Kirsten says gently.

"That's a far trip."

"He's on his way to South Carolina," Kirsten says. Is she talking too much? She might be overstepping her boundaries here, but she wants Natasha to see the pain he's in, the forgiveness he needs. "It'll be his first time there without his wife," she says, her hands folded in front of her.

"I'm sure you're busy, and I won't keep you," Chuck says. His voice sounds so weak.

She looks at the boy. "I have the morning off, so we're flying his spaceship thingy." She smiles briefly, and the boy looks impatient. "Just a sec," she says.

"Well," Chuck says, "a voice keeps telling me to come see you, to check on you, to say I'm sorry again, to try to make things right." Kirsten watches Natasha's eyes to see how she's processing this, but she keeps a poker face, her thick eyelashes bobbing up and down every so often as she blinks.

After a few seconds, Natasha nods. "Thanks for thinking of me. I mean, there's nothing to say, really, right? It's water under the bridge." She looks at the boy and takes the spaceship from him and holds it against her chest. She points toward Chuck. "I'm sorry I hung up on you." Her face seems to relax. "I just had a rough few years, and when you said Catty wanted me to move in there, I just thought, oh that would have been . . . different."

Chuck looks down. "I was wrong, and I'd undo it if I could. I think we would have benefitted by having you even more than you would have benefitted by being there." He moves his sneaker to kick at an acorn. "Our loss."

She nods. "Mr. Ayers, I've made mistakes, too. I know what good people you are." She tucks the toy under her arm and reaches out and touches his shoulder. "How were you supposed to know, right?"

He stands straighter. "But still."

"And thank you for your apology. I think things play out, and you get your ending because of the way they played out." She sighs. "I'm doing okay." Natasha tilts her head toward the boy. "I have a beautiful son." She gestures at the water. "I live here and love it. What else is there, right?"

"What else is there?" he repeats, but he doesn't look satisfied. His shoulders sink.

She smiles. "You didn't have to come here. Really, what did you owe me?"

His face has a hangdog expression. Kirsten wants to pat his back.

"Is there anything else I can do?" He looks down at the boy as if he's seeing him for the first time.

"It's done, you know? Your wife was so original. No one ever made me feel like I was . . ." She looks up at the sky. Someone comes out on their balcony above them, stretches, and goes back in. "Like I was, I don't know, worthwhile." *Yes*, Kirsten thinks. That was exactly who Mrs. A. was. She made you feel worthwhile, a person whose light beckoned everyone.

Natasha swallows. "She listened to me. I never understood how other kids felt with a parent or grandparent, but when I met her, I had all those feelings. I looked up to her. I couldn't wait to tell her about a test score or a poem I'd written because I knew she'd be proud. I saved details of my life for her because she liked hearing that stuff. When I got on the bus, when I got out of there, she was the only thing I missed about Pennsylvania."

Chuck nods as he listens. His face remains still, and Kirsten thinks he's seeing his wife again through her description. His eyes look red, but he smiles. He looks at Natasha, and then at her son. "You've done good here. She would've been proud."

Natasha takes a deep breath and smiles. "I know you felt bad about me, but I don't feel bad, and if I might speculate, I don't think Catty felt bad. Maybe she felt better knowing I was heading to a new place. I wish I had called her. I should have checked in. So we all have regrets—that's just what you have when someone dies. Lots of regrets."

"Yeah," Chuck says, and Kirsten thinks of her father. She'd give anything to call him up right now and tell him about this encounter. She regrets not hugging him enough, not fully appreciating those gas station gifts.

Natasha's son comes over and hands her a small feather. "The main thing I don't like is how much this weighs on you, Chuck, so I hope our talk helps it start to go away." She squeezes Chuck's arm for a second. "So maybe it hasn't been about me. Maybe you miss having disagreements and making up. Maybe her dying has felt like a big disagreement without any making up." She shakes her head. "It was only that one thing, and maybe she never told you that you had some good points, too. It's not always yes or no."

Chuck breathes. "Well, that's a lot to unpack." He stares at the water and nods. He finally looks at the boy. "What's your name, sir?"

"Quinn." The boy looks at his remote and flicks the small steering wheel.

Chuck nods. "Quinn, it's a pleasure to meet you." In a move that surprises Kirsten, Chuck puts out his fist, and Quinn bumps it. "My granddaughter taught me fist bumping. I'm sorry we've kept your mom from your flying adventure."

"It's okay," Quinn says. He looks at Natasha. "You two can watch me fly it before you go if you want."

Chuck looks expectantly at Kirsten, and she feels refreshed. Is seeing all this peace the reason her dad sent her here? He loved people so much. He loved family. *Wait until we're in Italy*, he kept saying all through winter last year. She thinks of the hope he always had, and she is greedy for it.

Natasha looks at Quinn with pride, and she winks at him. "He loves an audience."

"Count us in," Chuck says.

The sun is up high above them. A boat glides through the water in the harbor, and another boat's horn sounds as it takes off. Three bright white seagulls let out a call in the sky and swoop away. Quinn takes the spaceship from Natasha and carefully flicks it in the air. Kirsten thinks it's going to go in the water and Chuck looks worried, too, but Quinn expertly takes the control and presses some buttons and the spaceship lights up and rockets upward.

"Look at it go," Kirsten says, and it climbs higher and higher.

"How about that," Chuck says.

Natasha watches her son, her eyes delighted. "He's quite the pilot, isn't he?"

Quinn stands there holding the control steady, a smile on his face, and Chuck smiles the same way. They are mesmerized by the movements of the spaceship. Every so often, it beeps out a new sound effect. To Kirsten, it feels for a second like there is nothing else besides the boards of the dock and the startling blank sky and the flashing drone.

"How about that," Chuck says again.

—

When they are leaving, Chuck shakes Quinn's hand, and then he holds Natasha's hand for a second.

"Thanks for letting us come by," he says.

"Yes," Kirsten says. "Good flying, Quinn."

"Take care of yourself, Chuck." Natasha waves to them from the front steps of her building, and Quinn holds his toy and beams.

"Oh," Chuck says as they start to walk away. "I forgot." He reaches into his back pocket and pulls out a piece of folded sketch paper. "I've been carrying this around for a while. Maybe you'd like to have it," he says to Natasha.

Kirsten studies the picture the same time Natasha does, and she can see right away it's a drawing of Natasha. Kirsten looks back and forth between the image and the woman, and she can't get over how right it is. Her eyebrows, her hair, her smile: it's all there.

Natasha looks deeply into the picture. "She was something," she says, and squints down at her own face and waves to them as they walk back to the car.

—

Later that day, in Hilton Head, Chuck is wandering around the townhouse. The place he rented is in a community called Ocean Dunes that has beach access and its own golf course and tall pine trees and inlets of water. Groups of live oaks hang with Spanish moss. Kirsten sees alligators sunning themselves on the bank and people on bikes, on golf carts, people walking with tennis rackets, with beach chairs on their backs.

She has never been somewhere so energetic. No wonder he and Mrs. A. liked coming here. In Pennsylvania, people basically hibernate in winter. Here they are out everywhere, like ladybugs.

None of them won the temperature bet because it was seventy degrees when they arrived, right between Chuck's guess and hers. Sal just rolled his eyes. "Feels colder," he said.

The townhouse has worn carpets, and instructions for tenants about how to use the washer and dryer, how to work the thermostat, and how to check out. It has a pleasant musty smell that most rentals do, and there are framed pictures of sea turtles and beach landscapes on the wall. There are sliding glass doors straight through the living room that lead to a porch that looks out on a canal, and from one of the bedrooms, you can see a wide expanse of green with men and women twisting their bodies and hitting golf balls.

She loves all the trees, palm trees and palmettos, and the pine needles scattered on the ground. She loves how aligned the businesses were on the main road, all the same colors—tan, olive green. When they first turned into the condo community, they passed a giant farm with horses and a nature preserve, and all Kirsten wanted was to hop on a horse and stroll leisurely along the canal, the sun coming through the awnings of branches.

"All that driving to get here," Sal whispered to her in passing. "Maybe I'm nuts, but is it any different from the Jersey Shore?"

"A little bit," she replied.

After the bags are in the kitchen and his golf clubs are standing in the corner and his suitcase is in his closet, Sal puts some groceries in the cupboards, and they all stand there and look around. The sunset is gorgeous, the sky pink and encouraging beyond the water and pines. Kirsten sees a woman walking a dog in the distance and a little girl throwing bread at ducks.

Now what? she wonders. She has to think about when and how she'll get home. In about a week, she heads to Europe. She feels tired all of a sudden.

"How about we go to dinner?" Sal asks. "I could use a nap, but if I lie down, you ain't going to see me until morning."

"Good idea," Chuck says. "I'm treating."

"You better believe you are," Sal says, and pokes Chuck in the side.

Chuck gets a text and shows it to Kirsten.

She clicks on the picture, and Ella's caption says, "Look what I found in Florida." Kirsten smiles and shakes her head.

There is Ella, barely recognizable, her face next to a beautiful girl who looks so much like her—the same color hair but a slight curl to it, bright eyes, random freckles. The photo is so alive, so bursting with joy, that she can barely handle it.

"My word," Chuck says.

Kirsten's shoulders tremble. Ella has gotten her girl. They were all in Chuck's house in Pennsylvania twenty-four hours ago, and as if that house were a portal, now Kirsten and these guys are in South Carolina and Ella is in Florida. So much has happened. She shakes her head and looks at the picture again. "Life is crazy," she finally says.

She thinks about finding the person you've missed more than anything.

So many times she has imagined their front door opening and her father stepping in, holding some gas station prize. So often, she imagines how she would sob against his chest, how she would hug him tightly.

She feels happy for Ella, and envious, too. She hopes Ella and Riley will have a hundred good years together. She looks at the love on both of their faces, Ella's like a veil has been raised, her eyes smiling, too, her whole face lifted while she holds this beautiful person next to her.

Kirsten looks at the phone again. She can never have her dad back, but there is still love. Love everywhere. The love between her mother and her. The love for the animals at Rescue Ranch, for her renewed desire to go back to school. For the family she will see in Europe, the friends who have constantly checked on her. She loves that she was able to help Chuck in this small way, too. And life has this possibility of deeper love, always around the corner.

She hands Chuck his phone, and she wants to feel the way Ella looks in that picture.

"Well, let's get ready," Sal says.

She nods.

Something has jolted her awake. She scampers up the stairs to the room she'll stay in, the two twin beds with wicker headboards. She pulls her phone from her purse, and she hits the FaceTime button.

When he comes on, she recognizes his bedroom in the background. His eyes are lit by the lights behind him, and he grins in that way that could destroy her forever. "Well, well," he says.

"There's no choice, Grayson," she blurts out. She pulls his pebble from her pocket and holds it up so he can see it, like something she was directed to find on a quest.

"What's that?" He tilts his head. He looks so sweet in his apartment. He wears his gray Eagles T-shirt she liked sleeping in.

She feels tears come to her eyes. "I'm so sorry, Grayson. I'm sorry I made you feel like I'm torn or that you're second best. The first night I went home with you, I didn't want to be anywhere else. It was clear." She is so out of breath. "I just kept giving weight to those leftover feelings, to something that was more like a crush. I care about David. He's a really good guy. But when I was in his apartment, I didn't feel like I was *home* the way I do with you. Because it's you. It's you, Grayson. Am I too late to say it's you?"

"Me?" he says, and points to himself with a shy expression that kills her.

"If you still want me." She holds the phone in front of her and looks down at the pebble. She feels grateful she's in a house with two old men who don't hear well. She looks out from the bedroom's sliding doors, and she can see the sun almost gone, the golf course backlit with streaks of yellow across the green.

He is watching her, but doesn't say anything. "I did something I shouldn't have, Grayson. I looked at your journal, and that was horrible of me, but I want to live in that cabin you sketched. I saw it, and it was just a place I wanted to be. The feeling. It just had such *contentment* . . . such hope. I haven't been able to stop thinking about that place, and you drew it."

He shakes his head. "This is a lot of confessing, Kiki."

"Yeah." She wipes her face, and feels like she could sleep for two years. "That kind of day."

He reaches down and takes something off the table by his bed. He flips through it and holds the picture up to her. "I drew this when I was in a night class for grad school. It was one of those days where I felt like nothing made sense. I felt lonely or something, homesick maybe, driving to Villanova, trying to take notes in a research methods class I didn't understand. And I asked myself, what makes sense to me? And I drew this." He raises his eyebrows. "So the fact that you snooped is one thing, but the fact that you landed on my favorite sketch is quite another. God, Kirsten, I'm so glad you called."

"I miss you," she says, smiling. "I think I love you. Actually, I know I do."

"You should read my latest journal entry," he says, and grins. "Um, should I come and get you?"

She shakes her head. "I can get home. It's a hell of a drive." She looks at her watch. "Can I call you later tonight?"

"The scamps are waiting?"

"They are. Dinnertime."

"Jesus. Early bird special." He watches her. His smile is growing. "Kiki, did you really just call and say all this stuff? I'm not imagining it, right?"

She shakes her head. "No, you aren't."

"And you won't change your mind?"

She smiles. "I promise."

"Well, good," he says. He blows her a kiss. "Because it's you, too, Kiki. It's you and me . . . and maybe someday that cabin."

God, the smile that brings to her face. She can feel it. "I hope so," she says. She stares out at the barely lit sky. "Hey, before I go?"

"Yeah? Are you going to tell me you looked at my bank account online? If so, sorry in advance."

She smirks. "No. I was going to see if you like fondue."

His eyes narrow. "I do enjoy the occasional fondue."

"Interesting. I'm going to a wedding in Switzerland that will have an amazing fondue station. I believe it would be worth the trip."

He gets a crease in his forehead. "You're? No . . ."

"Think about it," she says, and blows him a kiss. "You might have to dance with my grandmother and sit next to my mom on the plane, if she comes, but everyone will want to meet you."

She hangs up and sees the stretches of grass, and an occasional golf cart, the ocean in the distance. She will call David tomorrow, and it won't feel the same. Their futures are different paths. She won't tell him any of this, of course, but he probably already knows. In her head, she will wish him well. When he spoke yesterday about his ex, she heard peace in his voice for the first time, and she realizes that's what she was drawn to in him: the way he was lost and needed peace, too.

Now she hears Sal and Chuck shuffling downstairs, and then the sound of the front door opening. She looks out again at the black hills, at the dots of light off in the distance. Her heart feels like something with new wires and parts. She stays there for a moment, just a woman who has learned to see in the dark.

CHAPTER THIRTY-FOUR

There is a lull on this warm Saturday in March as Chuck sits back on the camp chair he bought for the front porch, hands on knees, tumbler of iced tea beside him, and looks out at Ocean Dunes. It is that perfect hour of quiet after last week's tenants have checked out, after the cleaning people have come to the vacated units and run the vacuums and hauled out the linens in clear garbage bags, that hour or so of stillness he enjoys every week before the next batch of tenants arrives.

Soon there will be the sound of car doors opening and closing, the sounds of parents calling out to their children not to go in empty-handed, the lovely chaos of ice being poured into coolers, and people pedaling off on bikes to explore what they'll do this week.

"Here we go again," his friend Seymour from 209 calls to him as he sprays his beach chairs off at the bottom of their porch steps.

"Don't I know it." Chuck holds his iced tea up and nods.

Seymour squints up at Chuck. "Closing's next week?"

"The Ides of March." Chuck screws up his face. "We'll see."

Seymour nods and starts to walk away without saying goodbye, the way old men do. "Well, good luck. I think you'll be glad you did it. Enjoy your company, too."

Chuck nods and watches a lizard dart across the parking lot. Today should be interesting. His guests will be here soon, and he's eager to see them. He straightened up the townhouse where he's been for the last two months, and he bought a variety box of cereal at Piggly Wiggly and chips and pretzels and a tub of that pimiento cheese he's been eating way too much of lately. He bought wine and bottles of water and pink lemonade. He hopes they like it here, even if it's only for a few nights.

When Kirsten flew home, and then Sal a couple of days after her, he felt a loss he couldn't imagine. He even started packing up his things afterward, imagining the only solution was to get back to his home up north.

But he held Cat's towel and he stared out the window at the golf greens that looked like velvet, and he said, give it one more day.

And he did. And then Seymour and Cece, whom he and Cat had known for years, asked him to play cards, and then two sisters Cat did beach yoga with persuaded him to join their pickleball group, and all of a sudden, a week had gone by.

One day he went to the bike rental place, and he rode on the packed sand of the wide beach, the wind behind his back, pedaling and pedaling parallel to the ocean.

"You got here," Kirsten said to him that first day. And when he pedaled, he kept thinking that. He got here.

He left that loop of being in the cold, being by himself, visits from Sal and up-early days in that house. There are some moments where he can bring Cat back so clearly here that he thinks she's right around the corner, and some days where he misses her terribly, and some moments, once in a while, where he catches himself not missing her for a second—and those are the times that startle him.

He thinks about Kirsten and how she was instrumental in getting him here, and how getting here has made the difference. Maybe it's the activities: the bingo at the community center, the origami class he took where he tried to fold a paper crane and it ended up looking like a snake about to strike. What he likes about being here is the promise of the next day, the anything's-possible vibe. A month ago, in mid-February, he, Seymour, and Cece, went to a wine tasting at the bar on the beach. When they walked home, he felt so tipsy that he couldn't stop laughing, and Seymour started to sing "Too-Ra-Loo-Ra-Loo-Ral" as they crept home on the path. He smiled when he put the key in his door and thought, this isn't bad.

The next morning, he called his Realtor and asked if the owners of his place had any interest in selling the condo. He'd forgotten about the call after a week when the Realtor phoned him and said, "They're open to your idea. Let's make them a fair offer." And he didn't tell his kids until they visited over President's Day weekend. Ben looked at him and said, "Wow, Dad. You did that?"

Chuck nodded. "I close in March."

Leela was putting sunscreen on her nose and forehead. Concern crept across her face. She had paused her sunblock application. "But what about the Pennsylvania house? You're not selling it?"

Chuck shook his head. "No, I'm not ready for that yet." Her worry soothed him. To think he had pegged her as someone who wanted to clear out his house and put it on the market. He stared at his family—Isaac and Gabby playing Old Maid, and Asher and Ben cutting up papaya in the kitchen. "Plus, if I don't spend some time up there, that means Sal will keep coming down here."

Leela looked around. "Well, I think this is a really good idea," she said, and then she made a list the next day of improvements he should make once he takes possession of the place.

"I wish we bought it when your mom was alive," he said.

Ben nodded. Leela placed her head on his shoulder. "You can't do that to yourself. She loved that you both came here, and she loved being in Pennsylvania. Being with *you* was what she wanted."

Now as he waits, he finishes the last of his iced tea, and his phone buzzes. It's Kirsten. A picture of the Matterhorn, she says, and it stuns him for a second that she's there right in front of this majestic mountain, gray and purple, covered with snow. She and that boyfriend, Grayson, decided to stay in Europe for a while at her aunt's urging, and Kirsten told Chuck a week or two ago she might study veterinary medicine at a university there.

"I'm still just taking it all in," she had said.

"That's the right thing to do when you're young," he wrote back.

The next picture she sends is her and Grayson, their heads pressed together, the background of sky and mountain behind them like a movie. Chuck smiles at the scene and thinks how necessary love is. How much love changed his direction, renewed him after Vietnam, gave him hope to come home to someone every day who understood him. "Good for you!" he writes.

He takes a breath and reaches into his pocket and pulls out the Monet key chain. All these years, the beautiful key chain never had a key on it. He has held it so often that he has memorized its weight, and the scene—the swirls and lily pads and blue water—is like something he has lived inside.

He runs his finger along the gold of the key chain, and with his nail, he lifts the ring for a second, the opening where he could slide any key. The circle is empty inside, and he thinks of the hole Cat has left.

Maybe that is love. Maybe loving someone so deeply means accepting the fact that they occupy a specific, clear place in you. You accept that there will be a hole if you lose them—the same way a painting or photograph will leave its shadow on the wall after it's gone, the way a tree will leave a crater where the roots and stump were.

He thinks of all this—this is the price he has paid for loving so much, and it doesn't feel better, but it makes sense. It seems reasonable. "I'm not sorry anymore, Cat," he whispers.

He regrets that big fight, and all those small fights they had over the years. He regrets the times he wasn't fun enough, he didn't jump at her ideas and say, "I'll grab my coat." He should have sat on the front porch swing with her more, he should have flown that darn kite with her. But he's not sorry.

They were fortunate to have love—to have the love they felt so strongly for each other, and another version of that love work its way to other people: their children, their friends like Sal and Marguerite, Natasha, even Ella and Kirsten.

He looks out at the bright early afternoon light, the shadows the trees make over this lovely place, and he holds the key chain and decides when the closing goes through next week, he'll slip the key to this condo on the Monet key ring, and he will feel her with him every time he enters this place, whether it sits empty in summer and fall, or whether he's here longer and longer because he doesn't want to leave.

Once the house is his—*theirs*—he'll buy a new kite and put it in the hall closet, so anyone who's here can fly it.

Today he used her towel for the first time. He has been carrying it around, sleeping with it occasionally, but he never used it the way she did. But he had stepped out of the shower after getting the groceries, and the white rental towels he had been using were small and thin, and Cat's perfect towel sat folded on his bed. Before he knew it, he shook it out and was patting his arms and chest. It felt worn and absorbent, and the warmth of his body released the smell of her pink soap again.

He wasn't sure if it was wrong or okay, but he used it, and he let it hang on the back of the door afterward as if it were any other towel, and maybe it's better to keep using it than to hide it away the way he planned to.

Now he sees a flash of color, and a car creeps toward him. He recognizes it like it's a piece of his world that left him and returned, and he stands up and waves.

The car gets closer, and he holds the railing and walks down the step. He directs them into the reserved space for his unit, and as the car pulls in, he can see the familiar face from the inside, and another face that watches him.

The window rolls down and he crouches beside it. "No newspaper?"

Ella shakes her head. "My newspaper days are over, sir."

He winks at her, and then he looks past her to her little girl in the back seat, a pillow and some stuffed animal beside her, a sandwich bag of animal crackers on her lap. "Well hello there," he says.

"Hi," she says.

Ella gets out of the car and stretches. "That is quite the drive," she says.

He nods. Her hair is shorter and maybe a lighter color. The sun hits her, and she wears capri pants and a light blouse and looks like a whole other person from the woman he used to see in those dark, cold early hours, covered in a long coat. Riley's door opens slowly, and she looks up at the trees and points to a bird on one of the branches.

He looks around and holds his arms out. "So what do you think?"

"I can see why you needed to get here," Ella says. Absently, Riley's hand reaches for hers, and Chuck watches as Ella takes her girl's small hand and doesn't let it go.

He offers to get their bags, but Ella says there's no rush. He watches them climb the stairs, and he turns around to look at the small red car, parked alongside his again. He thinks of the car's former life, and all those months it sat and waited on the left side of the garage. Once, the lightbulb over it had burned out, and for a few days, before he could get the step stool, it sat there in the dark like part of a heart not working. He is glad Ella and Riley are using it now. He's glad it got them here safely, and they wanted to come down for Riley's spring break.

He thinks about how lost he was all that time, thinks about Riley being found. He looks at the car, and a few stray pine needles fall on it. He turns, and he sees that Riley and Ella are waiting for him, and the day feels cloudless and new. He imagines Hilton Head should have a motto under its welcome sign: Your Other Life Awaits.

The porch step creaks as he steps on it, and Riley has let go of Ella's hand and stands in front of him. She looks up into his eyes. "Are there really alligators here?"

He wonders if she's afraid of them at first, but her expression is eager, and he notices her two missing teeth in the front and how resilient her face seems. He wants to pat her head. He wants to say, welcome. *Welcome.*

"You bet there are," he says, and he holds the door wide open as the three of them step inside. "I have a whole sketchbook I can show you."

ACKNOWLEDGMENTS

I started this book because one morning I heard a man on the boardwalk say he was making his first trip to Florida without his wife who had died, and I couldn't stop thinking about him. To that man and his brave journey.

To the novel workshop in the Rehoboth Beach Writers' Guild (Judy, Paul, Ellen, Kathleen, Chris, and Deb), who saw early chapters of this and gave me some valuable feedback. To my good friend Maribeth Fischer, who tirelessly looked at the first complete draft of this and cared enough to tell me I could do more. The book is better because of you.

To Madeleine Milburn, world's greatest agent, who cheered this book on from the beginning and helped make it stronger; who one winter's day told me it was ready. I am so lucky to know you and have you represent me. To Georgia McVeigh for her insightful editorial suggestions. To Valentina Paulmichl for her assistance with Kirsten's father's Italian expressions. To everyone at the MM agency, especially Rachel Yeoh and Liv Maidment, who are always a dream to work with.

To the Scribner team, who all feel like family. Kara Watson, editor and checkmark supplier: there aren't words. Thank you for taking a chance on this when you didn't even know how the first book would be received. It feels like yesterday that you left your Mother's Day lunch to pass the edited manuscript to me in the parking lot. Nan Graham: I will never not be starstruck, but you are as humble and kind as someone who isn't a legend. Sabrina

Pyun: you're so caring, and you always know just what a book needs. An absolute honor to work with Mia O'Neill, Ashley Gilliam Rose, and Stu Smith. Also, Wendy Sheanin and Tim Hepp. To Jaya Miceli and Elizabeth Yaffe for yet another exquisite, unforgettable cover.

To the Lehigh Valley, a wonderful place to grow up, especially my hometown of Pen Argyl, which gave more love to *A Little Hope* than I could ever have imagined. To Hilton Head, the happiest place to escape.

To Gail and Joe Comorat, just because.

To Susan Kehoe and all the staff at Browseabout Books in Rehoboth Beach. There aren't enough chocolate cupcakes to properly say how grateful I am. Seven-year-old Ethan who stood in the kids' section would never believe this.

To all my Joella-Gallagher-Racciato-Romano family: much love.

To Gia, my fellow writer and co-Mandalorian. To Frankie, the best reader and Hallmark movie companion. You two are the center of everything I do and feel.

And most of all, to Rebecca, who I couldn't make any trip without.

ABOUT THE AUTHOR

Ethan Joella teaches English and psychology at the University of Delaware and specializes in community writing workshops. He is also the author of *A Little Hope*, which was a Read with Jenna Bonus Pick. He lives in Rehoboth Beach, Delaware, with his wife and two daughters.

A
QUIET
LIFE

ETHAN JOELLA

This reading group guide for A QUIET LIFE *includes an introduction, discussion questions, and ideas for enhancing your book club. The suggested questions are intended to help your reading group find new and interesting angles and topics for your discussion. We hope that these ideas will enrich your conversation and increase your enjoyment of the book.*

INTRODUCTION

Chuck Ayers can't decide if he should make the annual trip to Hilton Head without his late wife, Cat. Ella Burke works two jobs to make ends meet and fill the hours while she waits for news about her missing daughter. Kirsten Bonato put her aspirations for veterinary school aside after her father's sudden death and finds comfort working at an animal shelter.

These three individuals' stories intersect in surprising and heartwarming ways as each person discovers how to move forward with their lives. *A Quiet Life* is a tender, emotionally powerful novel that explores how grief can push us toward unexpected new experiences and connections.

TOPICS & QUESTIONS FOR DISCUSSION

1. While replaying through his long relationship with his late wife, Cat, Chuck feels "as if he's in a supermarket of guilt, and his cart's overflowing" (chapter one). Several other characters also express similar remorse over lost loved ones. How does guilt function throughout the novel?

2. In her daughter Riley's absence, Ella can't help picturing her everywhere she goes. "She imagines going to the market and making a French picnic for Riley" (chapter two). What is it about someone's absence that makes their presence loom larger? Who else experiences this in the book?

3. Natasha and Cat's friendship made Chuck nervous and even jealous at times. What was it about their connection that sparked his reaction? Compare this to Grayson's lack of jealousy when Kirsten opens up to him. Discuss why these characters react so differently in their respective situations.

4. Kirsten essentially put her life on hold after her father's sudden death and "feels like she's waiting for a sign" to restart it (chapter four). How often do people rely on "signs" to make life decisions? Why might that be? Do you find yourself waiting for signals in your own life?

5. Both Kirsten and Ella had traumatic experiences losing family members, and Chuck experienced trauma as a soldier in Vietnam. How does trauma present itself throughout the novel?

6. Kirsten has chemistry with both David and Grayson. She can even imagine what a future would look like with each of them. What did you make of this love triangle? Were you rooting for one outcome over another?

7. Ella's husband betrays her trust. Chuck feared that Natasha might swindle him and Cat if they let her stay with them. How do people respond to betrayal throughout the novel?

8. *A Quiet Life* is about both small and huge acts of kindness. When was the last act of kindness you performed, witnessed, or experienced?

9. David's struggle with his ex-wife over their kids mirrors Ella's custody tensions with her husband, Kyle. What do we gain as readers by juxtaposing these dynamics?

10. Kirsten and David open up to each other about their personal experiences with loss, which is a cathartic conversation for both of them. How can sharing feelings of grief improve one's mental health and relationships?

11. While Kirsten and Chuck are both dealing with permanent losses, Ella's missing daughter has the potential to come back into her life. What effect does this comparison have on the overall story that's being told?

12. Kirsten and Chuck both try to gain closure by searching out emblems of the past, but neither situation goes exactly as expected. Talk about closure and why the characters feel the need for it.

13. Discuss the shift from Kirsten's thought that "loss is everywhere" in chapter twenty-eight to "love [is] everywhere. . . . And life has this possibility of deeper love, always around the corner" in chapter thirty-three. How does the novel build to this uplifting conclusion? How might we adopt this into our own lives?

ENHANCE YOUR BOOK CLUB

1. Visit your local animal shelter! If you're interested, ask if it's possible to volunteer.

2. Purchase a sketchbook and carry it with you, sketching when inspiration strikes, like Cat.

3. Read Ethan Joella's first novel, *A Little Hope*, and discuss the ongoing themes and also how the two books differ.